M000303228

TOXIC EFFECTS

BOOKS BY JOEL SHULKIN, MD

THE MEMORY THIEVES
Adverse Effects
Toxic Effects

JOEL SHULKIN, MD

TOXIC
EFFECTS

**BLACK
STONE**
PUBLISHING

Copyright © 2022 by Joel Shulkin, MD
Published in 2022 by Blackstone Publishing
Cover and book design by Alenka Vdovič Linaschke

The characters and events in this book are fictitious.
Any similarity to real persons, living or dead, is coincidental
and not intended by the author.

Printed in the United States of America

First edition: 2022
ISBN 978-1-0940-2288-8
Fiction / Thrillers / Medical

Version 1

CIP data for this book is available
from the Library of Congress

Blackstone Publishing
31 Mistletoe Rd.
Ashland, OR 97520

www.BlackstonePublishing.com

To Isabella and Valentina: may you never forget who you are and who loves you.

CHAPTER ONE

Chilled September rain bounced off DB's black balaclava and drizzled down her cheeks as she skulked in a grove of oak trees. From her vantage point in the darkness, she could see Meridian Hill Park's illuminated statue of Saint Joan astride her horse, sword raised overhead. DB's shoulders stiffened, chin lifted. She and Joan were kindred spirits. Both trained as warriors. Neither could rest until they finished what had to be done.

And both were plagued by visions that drove them mad.

She forced away those thoughts and donned leather gloves, focusing on the matter at hand. She had a job to do.

Before long, a big man stumbled past the statue wearing a gray hoodie, torn jeans, and white high-top sneakers. A ratty backpack slung over his shoulder. He twice glanced behind him with the jerky movement of a fearful man, granting her a brief look at his face. She recognized him from the photo her handler had sent as Mateo Gonzalez. Several days' growth of stubble clung to his cheeks and chin. His eyes darted everywhere, as if Death itself were hot on his tail.

It wasn't far from the truth. He'd been reported dead six months ago.

She gave him a thirty-second lead before following. The smell of musk lingered in the air behind him. Raindrops bounced off her skin, pale as the moon rising over the treetops.

Mateo blundered down the stone steps, kicking up mud and gravel as he went, before turning north onto the path running parallel to the street. He stopped and leaned forward, hands on his knees, panting and looking back in her direction.

DB slipped into the shadows.

His gaze narrowed.

She didn't move.

Mateo let out a few more ragged breaths, then he straightened and started jogging down the path, his white sneakers flashing in the moonlight.

Creeping down the stairs, she followed.

His footfalls echoed on the wet pavement. *Thud. Thud. Thud.*

DB stayed on the grass, careful not to snap a stray twig or trip on a branch.

His head jerked to the right. He listed that way, headed for the park's east entrance.

He was going to chicken out of the meeting, as she'd feared. If he disappeared again, it could take months to relocate him, and her employers would hold her responsible. As much as she wanted to find out who he was meeting, she couldn't let Mateo Gonzalez escape or she herself would be in trouble with her bosses at Zero Dark. She slipped her hand under the back of her black T-shirt, feeling for the cold metal strapped there, picking up her pace.

As if suddenly realizing where he was, Mateo veered to the left.

She removed her hand. He was back on track. *Good.* She held back and waited under an oak tree. The rain lightened to a sprinkle.

Mateo followed the path to the next intersection, then turned right, heading north again. His head rotated side to side as he ran, like a child's toy robot.

A child's toy robot . . .

An image formed in her mind. A playroom in a New England colonial house. There was a chalkboard on an easel and a bookcase lined with picture books and stuffed animals. She sat crisscross applesauce on a Minnie Mouse carpet, playing with the robot and laughing. A man sat on a white couch with his back to her, watching a soccer match. He turned, but she couldn't see his face. He called her by a different name, but she couldn't make it out.

DB jolted back to the present. The glitches, as she'd nicknamed them, had recently become more frequent. Memories, hallucinations—she didn't know what they were, but she couldn't deal with them now, not with her prey slipping away. If this mission fell to shit, there'd be hell to pay.

She cut across the grass, chiding herself for getting sidetracked. Her employer promised to eliminate the glitches for good, but only if DB obeyed. She clenched her fist. One day, she'd be done following orders. One day—but not today.

The abstract white lump that was the Serenity sculpture loomed atop the hill ahead. As DB approached, her breathing hitched. She couldn't see her target. Had he already made the drop? Had he fled, after all? Or did he know she was tailing him and was now hiding in the bushes, waiting for her to get close enough to ambush?

Her hand returned to her back, muscles tensing as she crested the hill.

She relaxed. There he was, next to the statue like a good little soldier.

Keeping to the trees, she crept closer. She stopped behind the bushes, where she could make out the worn marble of the statue, the missing hand, the cracks at its base. The seated figure's face had all but worn away, leaving only two vacant holes for eyes that seemed to be observing from afar. It looked anything but serene. A fitting place for this rendezvous.

Mateo paced next to the sculpture, fumbling with the strap on his backpack, eyes wild. He mumbled under his breath.

DB inched closer.

His head snapped in her direction.

She froze. Still as the sculpture.

He squinted, staring straight at her.

She held her breath.

A twig cracked off to the side.

Mateo whirled around.

"Easy," said another man, this one in a business suit—Armani,

DB guessed. He held a briefcase in one hand, the other extended palm-forward to show it was empty. "It's me."

"Were you followed?"

"Were you?"

Mateo wheezed, eyes bouncing around like rubber balls. He spoke with a Mexican accent, his voice rough, almost a growl. "I feel like I'm being followed all the time. You told me they wouldn't find me."

"How about a thank-you? Do you know how much red tape I had to go through to pronounce you dead on arrival and transfer you to a secure location to patch you up?"

Mateo glowered at Armani. "Thank you."

Straightening his back, Armani said, "You're welcome. If you hadn't bolted afterward, you could've been under safety watch for the past six months instead of hiding in dumpsters and tunnels. At least you were smart enough to call me. I promise your identity will be safe."

"Did you make that same promise to Kitty and the others?" Mateo bit off each word as if it were dripping with wormwood. "Is that why they're all dead?"

As she listened, DB reached under the back of her shirt once more, removing a slim Kahr CM9 pocket pistol from a holster taped to her spine. She checked the magazine. Satisfied, she threaded a suppressor onto the barrel.

"That's why I asked you to meet me alone," Armani said. "We had a breach, but it's been handled. You need to—"

A silver gun appeared in Mateo's hand, glittering in the moonlight. "I need to stop listening to people like you."

DB paused. This man was braver than she'd thought.

Armani raised his hands again. "Take it easy, Mateo. We'll figure this out. We'll move you into full witness protection and—"

"Protection?" Mateo barked out a sharp laugh. "You can't protect me from them. They are the *Nagual*. Shapeshifters. They steal your mind and make you one of them. Friends, lovers, employers—none of them can be trusted." He aimed at Armani's forehead. "You could be one of them and you would never know until it's too late."

The guy sounded like a raving lunatic, yet his words resonated in DB's ears. *They steal your mind . . .*

"I promise I'm not one of them," Armani said. "We'll get you out of the country, under twenty-four-hour security. I'll guard you myself."

Mateo's grip on the gun slackened. "I'm finding it very difficult to trust you or anyone else."

"I have the papers right here, in my briefcase." Armani set the satchel on the ground. "Everything you need to create a new identity. You can take it and run. Or you can come with me, and I'll make sure you're safe."

For another tense moment, Mateo kept the gun trained on Armani's face, his hand wavering a bit. At last, he lowered it. "All right."

"Thank goodness you've come to your senses." Armani buttoned his jacket. "But first, don't you have something to tell me? You said on the phone someone else was involved in the ReMind affair—someone not dead. So who would that be?"

DB raised the CM9 and adjusted the night sight, aiming at Mateo's forehead until a ring appeared on the scope. As soon as he handed over the information, she could eliminate them both, collect what she needed to satisfy her employers, and head home.

Mateo stared at the ground, his chest rising and falling. He looked up at Armani and said, in a voice so low she almost couldn't hear, "You promise my wife and daughter will be safe?"

She froze.

Daughter? They didn't say anything about a daughter.

Armani tilted his head. "You have my word. They'll be under the best of care. They already think you're dead. They'll never know they were in danger."

Blood coursed through the arteries in her temples. *He has a daughter. Daughter.*

Another vision erupted in DB's mind. This time, she was driving. Rain pelted the windshield. A stately dark-haired woman with refined features rode next to her. A man's gruff voice came from the rear seat. Her heart swelled with something she couldn't describe, not at first, but as she homed in on it, she understood what it was: love.

Hot, white light flooded her field of vision. The sound of metal crunching against metal filled her ears. The woman screamed.

DB jerked back to the moment at hand. Her heart raced. She forced her breathing rate to slow.

Stay in control, she ordered herself. *You have a mission.*

Clenching her jaw, she raised the gun again, telling herself not to think about Mateo's family. His wife. His daughter.

Damn it.

She could do this. It was what Zero Dark had trained her to do. If she failed, she would be next.

But DB would not fail. She never failed.

Mateo was holding something out to Armani. It looked like a print-out from the internet.

"Everything crashed down when she showed up," he was saying. "If you want to know what happened that day, find her. She's the reason for all of it."

Armani grinned as if possessed by a demon. "I knew you'd come through."

His hand slipped inside his jacket.

DB shifted her sights and fired.

A hole appeared in the center of Armani's forehead, filling with blood. His mouth contorted and puckered. He crumpled to the ground.

Mateo whirled, raising his pistol. He moved into a fighter's stance.

She leaped from the bushes.

As she expected, he took a step backward, off guard.

Before he could recover, she dropped to the ground, rolled, and kicked out his legs.

He tumbled and dropped his gun.

She lunged like an anaconda. Her arm constricted around his throat. She pressed the gun barrel against his temple.

"Please," he said, voice cracking with tears. "I don't know anything. I was only a security guard."

"I won't tell Zero Dark about your family," she whispered. "They'll be safe."

His body stiffened. Then he nodded.

He understood. That made it easier.

She pulled the trigger.

His body sagged.

Her stomach heaved. DB closed her eyes and counted to twenty. The nausea passed. She laid him on the ground and searched him, removing his wallet, and stuffing it into her pocket. She took his gun and replaced it with hers—unregistered, serial number wiped clean. Covering his fingers with hers, she fired into the ground, allowing residue to coat Mateo's hand.

She crossed over to Armani, slid a hand into his jacket, and removed the Sig Sauer P226 with attached suppressor he'd been seeking. She stuck it in her waistband next to Mateo's and searched the rest of his pockets. Empty. No ID.

She unfurled Armani's fingers and withdrew the paper Mateo had given him. Her mind started racing as she read, the moonlight on her pale skin giving her a ghostly appearance befitting her name: *Dama Branca*. The White Lady.

Her phone vibrated.

When she picked up, the caller asked in a distorted voice, "Is it done?"

"Affirmative. But why send me? Your mole seemed to have it covered."

There was a pause. "Mole?"

"The one the target was meeting. He was one of ours, wasn't he?"

Another pause. "You eliminated both?"

Her chest tightened. "You told me to leave no witnesses. Why'd you order me to kill one of our own?"

"That's not your concern."

"But I think—"

"You're not paid to think. Now, any loose ends?"

DB glanced at Mateo's body, imagining his wife driving their daughter to school, blissfully unaware of what had happened to her husband, moments before a truck rammed into their car and killed them both. She wrinkled her nose. This operation stunk. There was more her handler wasn't telling her.

"I said, any loose ends?"

She set her jaw. It would do DB no good to lie. Her bosses would find Mateo's family anyway. The only thing that would happen would be she'd be next on Zero Dark's hit list.

Unless she gave them something else to worry about.

"Who is Cristina Silva?" she asked, trying to sound indifferent.

No response.

"Why does that name sound familiar?" asked DB.

"Never mind." She could hear the hitch in the caller's voice over the distortion. Anger? Aggravation? "She's not your mission. Proceed to the next target."

"Copy. I'll call when I've arrived in Salt Lake."

The caller disconnected without a response.

"Dick."

She stuck the phone back in her pocket and studied the news article again. The *Boston Herald* headline read, "Psychiatrist Cristina Silva to join Longwood Memory Center."

DB outlined the photo with her fingertip, memorizing the contours of the woman's face, the shape of her eyes, the line of her nose.

"But first," she whispered, her voice like a stranger's to her ears, "I need to make a side trip to Boston."

CHAPTER TWO

Dr. Cristina Silva sat in her Mini Cooper, gripping the steering wheel and summoning every bit of courage she had. A few minutes ago, she'd convinced herself she was ready to get back to work, that a fresh start was her best way to move on with her life. Now, as she stared at the Longwood Memory Center building from the parking lot, her resolve slipped away.

You can do this, the voice of her alter ego, Sabrina, murmured in the back of her mind. *This is our life now. New identity, new challenges. And, hopefully, some answers.*

Cristina closed her eyes and willed herself to relax. Six months ago, she'd discovered that every memory she'd recovered after suffering global amnesia in a car crash had been a lie, fabricated by the experimental memory drug Recognate. Her new identity had been stolen from a woman the manipulative criminal mastermind known as Quinn had killed. Quinn had made her believe she was Cristina Silva in order to keep her hidden away until he could access the secrets locked away in her brain.

But the drug they'd used on her was flawed, and memories of her true past seeped back. She learned she was actually a researcher from Rio de Janeiro named Sabrina Carvalho, her mother was dead, and she had no idea who her father was. The thoughts and personality of Sabrina had become an incessant voice in her head. It was only by accepting her dual identities that she was able to avoid sinking into total madness.

After weaning off Recognate, she'd tried to integrate her two identities and become Sabrina Carvalho again, using an approach similar to that used for people with dissociative identity disorder, once called multiple personality disorder. It had worked at first, and Cristina was able to sustain a fulfilling romantic relationship with Detective Gary Wilson, the only one who'd believed her as her world was being torn apart by Quinn. For two months, she'd thought of herself only as Sabrina.

But Cristina Silva's memories, real and fabricated, remained in her head. Despite being built on a foundation of lies, Cristina somehow remained dominant, with Sabrina only gaining control in times of duress.

As Cristina once again felt a loosening hold on reality, she mistrusted her ability to treat her patients in her psychiatric practice. She broke up with Wilson and sold the practice. For weeks she floundered, trying to come to grips with being two people in one body, until she at last concluded there was a good reason why her efforts had failed.

Unlike dissociative identity disorder, her dual identity was the result of Recognate-induced changes to her neuroanatomy. Her memories and thoughts as Cristina Silva were structural, not psychological. She had experienced something unprecedented, which meant she had to deal with it differently. The best way to understand what had happened to her was a return to research.

Cristina squeezed the steering wheel so tightly her median nerve went numb as she studied the gleaming glass-and-metal building before her. Dr. Winston Campbell, the Memory Center's director, had tried to recruit Cristina a year earlier and she'd declined, thinking she had all the support she needed from ReMind, the pharmaceutical company manufacturing Recognate. Once ReMind's fraud had been exposed and it was revealed that Recognate created memories instead of restoring them, she had started looking into other approaches to the study of memory. Dr. Campbell's work on delusions in dementia seemed right up her alley. After all, Cristina Silva's entire identity was one big delusion.

You're being too hard on yourself. I don't think of you as a delusion, even if you once considered me a hallucination.

Despite her tension, Cristina allowed a smile to creep across her face. She and her Sabrina persona had seemed more at odds with each other lately than in agreement, but when she really needed a boost Sabrina was there for her. Hopefully this research job would help them find a way to create one main identity, but for now, they had to learn to live with each other.

"Maybe we would've been better off moving somewhere else," she said aloud as she exited the car. She'd never felt comfortable conversing with Sabrina in her mind, even though her one-sided conversations tended to elicit stares. "You're the biotech researcher. You should be the one in charge of the work."

All our ID is under your name. It would take forever to establish Sabrina Carvalho's reputation here. Don't worry. If you screw up, I'll be here to pull you out of the fire.

Cristina grimaced at the image—and the implication. Swallowing her anxiety, she approached the building and recited the mantra that once kept her sane . . . before the real madness occurred. "You can do this. Yesterday was bad, but today will be better. Every day's another step forward."

After checking in with the front desk and taking the elevator to the third floor, she found her way to a small office tucked away at the end of a long hall. White lettering on the door read: Cristina Silva, MD. Neuropsychiatrist. She stared at the letters, willing the name to ground her, make her feel more solid. Instead, she felt disconnected, as if any moment she might fade away.

The sound of someone clearing their throat disrupted her thoughts. She turned around to find Dr. Winston Campbell, wearing a white lab coat over a cream-colored shirt and a vibrant yellow bowtie. His dark eyes radiated warmth.

"Good morning, Dr. Silva." Cheeriness laced his already rich voice, accentuating his Jamaican accent. He indicated the lettering. "It's nice to see your name up there."

"It is, thank you." Cristina smiled back, hoping her anxiety didn't show. "And thank you again for giving me this opportunity."

"Nonsense. You're doing me the honor of joining our team. I needed a psychiatrist for this study and to have someone with your vast experience is more than I could've asked."

"Well, I'm glad it worked out for both of us."

"I find the whole concept of confabulation fascinating. Korsakoff syndrome, Alzheimer's, schizophrenia." He snapped his fingers, startling her. "Capgras syndrome. That's a particularly bizarre one. Can you imagine believing that an impostor has replaced someone you love?"

A chill ran down Cristina's back. Was that comment directed at her? But how could he possibly know the truth?

She searched his face for signs of malintent, but he looked as cheerful as ever. The more she thought about it, the more she realized it was nothing more than an innocent observation, one she'd taken personally because she was on edge. Forcing her shoulders to relax, she nodded. "The research being done here has the potential to help so many people who suffer from false memories and delusions. I'm really excited to be a part of it."

"Splendid." He clapped his hands and rubbed them together. "Let's get started then, shall we? After you get settled in, I'd like you to come down to the EEG lab to get oriented with your first case of the day."

"Oh! I'm going to be hands-on already today?"

His brow furrowed. "Is this a problem for you?"

"No, not at all." The idea of jumping right into a neuroscientific study was daunting, but she could use the distraction. She smiled more easily. "I'm excited to get working."

His grin returned. "Wonderful. I'll see you soon."

As he trotted away down the hall, Cristina drew in a deep breath and entered her new office. Mixed feelings stirred in her belly. It was smaller than her old office, with barely enough room for an oak desk and a couple of leather chairs. At least it had a window. She crossed over to it and peered out. The view of the dumpsters in the back alley was less than spectacular, but if she crouched and titled her head, she could make out the tip of the Prudential Tower peeking out over the Brigham Hospital.

Cristina sank into the plush office chair behind the desk and scanned the walls. Maintenance had hung her diplomas and certificates for her. Well, Cristina Silva's diplomas and certificates, anyway. What would the real Cristina Silva have thought of her, living the life that had once been hers until Quinn cut it short? A thought flittered through her mind, a fantasy of fleeing somewhere no one knew her, creating an altogether new identity that was neither Sabrina Carvalho nor Cristina Silva.

We'd still be two minds in one body, Sabrina said. *It's confusing enough without trying to remember a third name.*

Cristina sighed. It had just been an idea. Her gaze fell on the photograph of Jorge and Claudia Silva, neatly framed but somewhat askew on a corner of her desk. Despite knowing they weren't her real parents, she kept the portrait out of habit. When her Recognate-fueled memories emerged, studying that photo and imagining them watching her with pride and love had given her the strength to keep searching for her past. Now, knowing those memories were lies, she felt judged and unworthy of their love.

That's ridiculous. You're keeping the memory of their daughter alive. You have no idea how they would feel about you if they met you now.

"Maybe that's the problem." Cristina adjusted the position of the picture frame and traced her finger over the outline of Jorge, and then Claudia. "Although I remember our mother now, I still have no idea who our real father is. There are still so many holes in your memory, and they keep shifting and merging with mine, making it impossible for us to integrate. And I don't know which of my memories are based on truth and which are pure fabrication—confabulation, to use Dr. Campbell's terminology. Maybe we need to try the opposite approach: learn as much as we can about the real Cristina Silva and her life, so we can sort out fact from fiction."

And then?

Withdrawing her hand and squeezing it into a fist, Cristina said, "And then, once we fill in the remaining gaps in our memory, we can sort out who we are."

Cristina's phone rang, disrupting her line of thought. The caller ID was blocked, but she recognized the number.

"Special Agent Jefferson, what a surprise," Cristina said upon answering. "I was planning to call you later this week. Have you tracked down more Recognate subjects?"

"Not since the last one." Milton Jefferson's rich baritone resonated over the phone. He'd taken over the FBI investigation of ReMind's wicked memory experiments after a previous agent, Charles Forrester, was killed by Quinn. In a matter of two months, Jefferson managed to locate over sixty of the nearly one hundred subjects on ReMind's list and got them the treatment Cristina devised to help them safely withdraw from the drug. And he'd kept his promise to safeguard Cristina's identity from other agencies and the public. "The rest may be dead or don't want to be found."

Cristina bit her lip. "I don't want to accept that."

"You may not have a choice." Jefferson cleared his throat. "I called for another reason. Do you know a Mateo Gonzalez?"

"Should I?"

"He was Chief of Security at ReMind."

An image of the brusque giant popped into Cristina's head. "What about him?"

"He's dead."

Cristina barely knew the security officer, but she felt a pang of sympathy over a life cut short. "How?"

"Gunshot wound to the head. DC Metro PD found him and one of our field agents in Meridian Hill Park last week. They think Mateo shot our agent and then himself."

"Your tone of voice suggests you don't believe that."

"Our agent's firearm was missing, and the shots were too clean. We believe this was a professional hit."

"Working in security, Mateo wouldn't have had access to the most sensitive information at ReMind."

"No, he wouldn't, and it looked like he'd been living on the streets for some time." Jefferson cleared his throat again. "But there's something else. Over the past two months, eighteen former ReMind employees in the southeastern United States have been murdered."

The blood drained from Cristina's face. "Oh, my God. That's horrible."

"It is, and my fear is that this is only the beginning."

"What do you mean?"

"Someone is systematically eliminating anyone who worked with ReMind," said Jefferson. "And the reason for my call? Your life may be in danger."

CHAPTER THREE

The sunlight was filtered through a dense canopy of oak trees, casting an eerie glow over the clearing. Flies buzzed around Detective Gary Wilson's head as he crouched over the body next to the gurgling creek. He used one gloved finger to push aside the tarp for a closer inspection. Male, late teens, sandy blond hair, and a mask of fear frozen on his face. The head was twisted to the side, arms splayed. Wilson panned up to the crumbling stone bridge ten feet overhead. The fall was far enough to have snapped the teen's neck.

A cold breeze bit into Wilson's skin. He shivered as he recalled the first time he'd seen a dead body. No, make that two dead bodies. He'd been a kid, younger than this one, when he'd had to identify his mom and dad. It didn't get easier, seeing death like this, but when he managed to find answers to ease the suffering of a dead person's loved ones—answers Wilson never got for himself—it gave him the strength to keep going.

Wilson replaced the tarp, removed his gloves, and stood. Judging by the skin pallor, he guessed the teen had died three days earlier, but they'd have to wait for the medical examiner report to be sure. He tossed the gloves into a plastic bag and nodded to the crime scene investigators, who returned to snapping photographs. Wilson glanced over at the young couple huddled a few yards away, looking frightened as they answered Detective Rick Hawkins's questions. The old bridge, a fifteen minute walk from Somerville Preparatory Academy, was a poorly kept secret make-out spot for students. These two, who'd skipped an afternoon class, had gotten a far different intense experience than expected today.

"Almost done." Hawkins turned to face Wilson as he approached. The older detective's white hair stood out against the autumn colors. "I have a few more questions for these two."

Wilson studied the pale-faced teens. The girl looked about to vomit.

An ache started in the back of Wilson's throat as he remembered the cold, almost robotic way the police officers had informed him his parents were dead. He turned back to Hawkins. While his partner had more experience overall, Hawkins's military training made him distant. These kids needed a more sympathetic ear.

"I'll take it from here." In a low voice, Wilson said to Hawkins, "Call the coroner and see what's taking them so long. I want this kid tucked in before any reporters show up."

Annoyance flashed in Hawkins's eyes, but it quickly passed. Despite being the elder, Hawkins almost always deferred to Wilson's track record for solving cases. He handed Wilson his notepad and pulled out his phone as he ambled over to the crime scene investigators.

Wilson skimmed the notes before turning to the teens, whom Hawkins had identified as Penny and Stephen, and asked softly, "You two doing okay? This is scary stuff."

Penny's lip trembled, but she nodded and leaned closer to Stephen, who put his arm around her. He sucked on his lower lip and asked, "Can we go home?"

"We'll take you to your parents soon. Don't worry," he said when their eyes widened. "You're not in trouble. But I need your help understanding what happened here. Stephen, you identified the deceased as Danny Trevino?"

"Yeah." Stephen rubbed his eyes. "He's a senior at Somerville Prep. Well, he *was*. *Shit*."

Wilson's lips pressed tight as he jotted his notes. Accepting death was never easy. Memories crept into his brain of traveling to the morgue that first time. His skin crawled and he shook off the vision.

"Any idea what Danny was doing out here by himself?" Wilson asked.

The teens exchanged looks. Penny wiped her nose and said, "We didn't talk much to him. At least, not anymore. He used to be popular: captain of the debate team, star forward on the soccer team. But when school started this fall, he seemed different. He spent all his time in the library and wouldn't talk to anyone."

"Did he seem depressed?"

"Not really." Penny touched her chin. "But three days ago, Danny got pissed during US History, screaming at the teacher that he was getting all the facts wrong."

"Yeah, and then it got even weirder." Stephen sat up straighter. "He spewed dates and names and yelled we were all going to die."

Wilson stopped writing notes and looked up. "Did the school report that?"

"I dunno." Stephen scrunched up his shoulders. "Danny didn't say he was going to kill us or nothing. He said it more as a warning, like he knew something was going to happen."

"Anyway, Mr. Pierce talked to him," Penny said. "Danny seemed calmer afterward."

"Who's Mr. Pierce?"

"The school security officer. He's a real cool guy. Good at talking to people."

Wilson tapped his pen against the notepad. If the kid calmed down, it made less sense that he would run off and kill himself, unless there was more going on. "What happened after Mr. Pierce spoke to Danny?"

"School ended and everyone went home." Penny shook her head. "But Danny didn't show up for school yesterday or today. That was strange because we had a US Government test yesterday, and Danny never missed tests." She sniffled and gazed at the riverbed, where a diener had arrived and was preparing a body bag. "Now we know why. Dad said that old bridge was dangerous and should've been torn down years ago. I guess he was right."

Wilson started to say it was no accident and stopped himself. The skin behind his ear itched, like it did when things didn't add up. He scanned his notes. "Do you know if anything traumatic happened to Danny over the summer? Did his parents get divorced, or did his girlfriend break up with him, maybe?"

"Not anything we heard about," Stephen said. "Like I said, he didn't seem depressed or anything, just different. Danny was always a good student, but for the past few weeks he'd been getting perfect scores on every test. I guess the studying paid off. Who knew?"

"His grades improved?"

"Yeah."

Puzzle pieces clicked together in Wilson's mind, but there remained a gaping hole in the middle. Danny's erratic behavior suggested he was depressed or using drugs, but a sudden drive to excel academically didn't fit either picture. After clearing his throat, he said, "I need a list of all of Danny's friends and anyone who might've wanted to harm him."

Penny shrugged. "That's easy. He only hung out with one guy, Reggie Horne."

"He and Reggie weren't friends," Stephen said. "They were more like . . . I dunno. Rivals. They competed with each other to get better grades."

"How did Reggie handle it when Danny started to ace all his exams?" Wilson asked as he wrote down Reggie's name.

"He seemed fine." Stephen scratched his cheek. "Maybe jealous, but he didn't seem mad or nothing."

"Can we go home?" Penny hugged herself and shivered. "My parents are going to be wicked pissed that I was even out here."

Wilson glanced at the bridge and then gave them a reassuring smile. "We'll take you back to the station where your parents can pick you up. If you think of anything else later that might help us understand what happened to Danny, call us, okay?"

The teens nodded.

When Wilson returned to the creek, Hawkins was standing watch as the diener zipped up the body bag. Wilson tapped the diener on the shoulder. "Tell the medical examiner we want a full medicolegal autopsy."

"We do?" Hawkins narrowed his gaze. "The kid slipped and fell. Unless he was drunk or high, there's nothing criminal here."

"No?" Wilson pointed at the bruise on Danny's forehead. "If he fell backward off the bridge, as the position of his body suggests, how would he have hit his forehead?"

"Maybe he hit face-first, then rolled."

"No injuries on his chest."

"Okay, so he bounced off the side of the bridge on the way down."

"If he jumped, he would've cleared the bridge. And there were no skid marks up top to indicate he'd slipped and fallen."

Hawkins frowned. "What are you saying?"

"From what those two told me, Danny might've made himself a few enemies. These injuries are not accidental. More like someone wanted it to look like a suicide." He looked up, mentally picturing Danny falling from the bridge to the creek below. "He was pushed."

CHAPTER FOUR

For most of the morning, Cristina found it nearly impossible to concentrate on anything but the idea that someone was killing former ReMind employees. Special Agent Jefferson had assured her he had his best field agents on the case, but the Bureau's lack of any suspects failed to fill her with confidence. Jefferson had offered to assign an agent to watch over Cristina, but she declined. Jefferson may have earned her respect, but knowing how easily Quinn had infiltrated the FBI, she wasn't sure she could trust them to keep her or the remaining ReMind employees safe.

Minutes after hanging up with Jefferson, Cristina questioned her decision. Yes, she'd kept her reflexes and fighting skills honed by going to the gym four times a week, but would that be enough if a professional assassin wanted to kill her?

We don't know for sure they're after us. You weren't a ReMind employee.

"No, but I worked with them," Cristina whispered as she absently rearranged items on her desk, trying unsuccessfully to distract herself from her fears. "If they're tying up loose ends, they may go after me next."

We don't even know who they are. ReMind's CEO made a lot of enemies. And Agent Jefferson said all the other murders occurred in the southeastern US.

Cristina stopped shuffling items. Maybe she wasn't a target. But it would be foolish to lower her guard. Out of habit, she reached for her phone to call Gary Wilson, then stopped herself. He wasn't likely to help her, not after the way she'd dumped him. They'd dated for a few months, but when things started to get serious, she cracked under the pressure and cut him off. She pressed her palm against her forehead. Who breaks up with someone over the phone? A coward, that's who.

A soft chime came from her desktop computer. She logged in and found a pop-up reminder to go to the EEG lab, first sublevel. Cristina wrinkled her nose. Apparently, Dr. Campbell didn't trust her to remember on her own.

Minutes later, Cristina stepped off the elevator into a brightly lit hallway. It took a moment for her eyes to adjust. The fluorescent lights reflected off bare white walls as they stretched into the distance, making her feel like she was entering an MRI machine. Her heels clicked on tile as she walked, the sharp noise reverberating around her.

At last, she reached a double door at the end of the hall. Swiping her ID badge across a sensor, the doors swung open. A room stuffed with machinery and digital monitors greeted her. Wires gnarled everywhere like a tangled spiderweb. On the opposite side of the room stretched a wide observation window. Cristina could barely make out what appeared to be an operating room inside.

"It's really something isn't it?" a soft female voice said behind her.

Cristina jumped and spun around to find a woman close to her height standing there, holding a clipboard. Blond hair poked out in short spikes from her scalp. Her brown eyes peered through circular lenses, amber flecks complementing the yellow blouse she wore under her white lab coat.

The woman gave a nervous laugh and said in a husky voice, "Sorry to startle you. My mum used to say I was like a tawny owl, always sneaking up on her."

Cristina managed to smile, her nerves soothed by the woman's carefree British lilt. "It's okay. I'm a little on edge. It's my first day."

"Oh, I understand that. I started last week." The woman held out her hand. "Victoria Weiss."

"Cristina Silva." Cristina shook Victoria's hand, impressed by her firm grip.

Victoria's eyes widened. "*Dr.* Silva? Oh, this is brilliant. I'm your research assistant."

"I didn't know I had an assistant."

"Yes, I'm here to help you gather and enter data, organize your schedule, and anything else you need to do your job here at the Memory Center."

"That sounds wonderful." Cristina studied Victoria's demeanor. She seemed pleasant enough, if not overly zealous. "But you did say you've only been here for a week?"

Victoria's cheeks reddened. "Yes, I finished neuroscience coursework at Birkbeck a few months ago. I came here on a work visa but the company where I was supposed to work shut down. Out of desperation, I made random calls. I was so chuffed when Dr. Campbell said he had an opening here."

"I'm glad he did since I've never seen any of this equipment before. Have you?"

"Those are geodesic sensor nets." Victoria pointed to a pile of wire webs dotted with white sticky pads. "It helps detect voltages over the entire brain surface and obtain detailed EEG readings and even an estimate of the neural geometry. Plus, it's faster than a traditional EEG."

"Wow," Cristina said. "You do know your stuff."

"It's all quite fascinating. The brain is simply remarkable." Victoria covered her mouth with her hand. "I'm rambling, aren't I? Please forgive me."

"No, it's all right. I like the enthusiasm." Cristina surveyed the complicated equipment. "But I wish I had a little more clarification on my role here."

"I thought that would be obvious." Dr. Campbell's voice echoed through the room. Cristina and Victoria turned to find the neurologist standing in the doorway, holding one of the sensor nets. He smiled thinly. "I'm going to study your brain."

CHAPTER FIVE

The Somerville Police Department was bustling as usual when Detectives Wilson and Hawkins arrived. They chuckled as they overheard a female detective complaining about her latest case: a man claiming a sex worker had stolen his wallet. Recent calls to the station had been mundane or ridiculous. Approaching his desk, Wilson groaned at the stack of case files he needed to finish writing up.

"All right," Hawkins said after they'd each poured a cup of coffee and settled into their desks. "Explain to me again why you think Danny Trevino's death wasn't an accident."

"The parapet on that bridge was waist-high," Wilson said and took a sip of coffee. "He'd have to have been running to fall over it, and there's no gravel or dirt to slip on."

"So he jumped. His classmates made it sound like he was on something."

"The body position only makes sense if he was pushed. And some things don't fit. Yeah, a teen using drugs might withdraw from his friends, but not to spend all his time studying."

The corners of Hawkins's mouth slipped downward. He unlocked his computer and started typing.

"What are you—?"

Hawkins cut him off by holding up his palm. Wilson waited while Hawkins searched through the police file database. He typed a key and the screen filled with a report. The photo of a teen male, dark hair and eyes, occupied the upper left corner.

"That's what I thought," Hawkins said a moment after scanning the report. "Eduardo Sanchez, senior at Somerville High, age seventeen. Died three weeks ago falling onto the Red Line tracks. You know the case, right?"

Wilson couldn't recall the details. Cautiously, he said, "Oh yeah, I remember something about it. Who was assigned to it?"

"Malone. He classified it a suicide." Hawkins scrolled down the report, then pointed at the screen. "The medical examiner found a bruise on Sanchez's arm that looked like he'd been grabbed, but it may have been from the Good Samaritan who fled the scene. She ended up supporting suicide as cause of death."

Scratching his chin, Wilson asked, "Think they're connected?"

"Not sure, but it's curious. I'll see if I can get more information."

Wilson stood and buttoned his jacket. "You do that while I interview Trevino's parents."

"Deal. Hey, you wanna grab a beer and a pizza tonight? They're showing the Bertolli fight at O'Hara's."

"Can't." Wilson took a sip of coffee. "I've got plans."

"Oh, I should've known." Hawkins grinned. "I better watch out or one day you're gonna walk in here with a ring on your finger."

Wilson winced. While he hadn't gone ring shopping, he'd thought he had a future with Cristina Silva until out of the blue she'd ended their relationship. She'd given him an excuse about finding a new job and needing space, but he could feel she wasn't telling him everything. She'd ignored his calls and texts since, but despite all that he couldn't stop thinking about her. It had taken him weeks to gather up enough needed energy to arrange a date with someone else.

"All right, enough already." Hawkins was the closest he had to a best friend, but he felt uncomfortable discussing relationships at work. "I don't want to have to transfer back to Boston to get away from your nosiness." Wilson sniffed the coffee and wrinkled his nose. "Why does this taste like shit?"

"It's a pumpkin spice decaf someone brought in. They ran out of regular."

"No wonder I'm feeling edgy." Wilson dumped the coffee in his trash can and dropped the cup on his desk. "I'll stop at Dunks on the way back from the Trevino's. You want anything?"

"How about a decent pension?"

"Keep dreaming."

CHAPTER SIX

A cold knife cut deep into Cristina's bones as she stared at the EEG net in Dr. Campbell's hands. Had he found out the truth about her, that she had two distinct personalities and sets of memories? Was that why he'd hired her?

"I don't understand," she said, choosing her words carefully. "You want to study *my* brain?"

Dr. Campbell pursed his lips, glanced at the cables, and then looked back up at Cristina. "Well, no, not really. I merely want to test the sensor net on you, so you gain a better understanding of how it works before you start your own work with our subjects. I didn't mean to startle you."

"She's a bit jumpy, is all," Victoria said, playfully elbowing Cristina. "First day jitters."

"I'm fine," Cristina said as embarrassment washed away her paranoia. She couldn't let her reaction to Special Agent Jefferson's news about the deaths of ReMind employees affect her job performance. Not only did she need the income, she needed to understand her condition. "I didn't realize I'd be directly involved in diagnostic procedures. I thought you wanted my input from a mental health perspective."

"Yes, of course, I do," Campbell said, sucking through his teeth. "But everyone here is transdisciplinary. That means I expect you to be flexible with requests and perform tasks that may be outside your comfort zone. I apologize if that wasn't clear."

Realizing how ungrateful she sounded, Cristina injected levity into her voice. "I must have misunderstood, but it's no problem at all. I'm always eager to learn."

His face brightened. "Splendid. And I see you've already met Victoria, so we can skip the formalities and get started. Please, follow me and I'll show you how everything works."

Dr. Campbell explained how they used the sensor nets to assess the electrical activity in frontal and temporal cortical regions, areas associated with decreased metabolism in both patients with delusions and with Alzheimer's. He elaborated that paranoid delusions could also be seen in conditions such as temporal lobe epilepsy, and therefore their working hypothesis was that at least some delusions and confabulation could be related to atypical brainwave activity.

"A recent study at Boston Children's Hospital identified unusual brainwaves that could be detected as early as three months of age," he said as he attached the sensors to Cristina's scalp after she lay down on an examination table. "Those brainwaves had a near one-hundred-percent positive predictive value for autism by eighteen months."

"That's incredible," Cristina said, trying to hold still and refrain from wincing at the cold squish of the sensors being applied to her skin. "So, you're hoping to find similar brainwaves to identify delusions?"

"It could be a useful way to differentiate someone who is truly confabulating from someone who is malingering." He finished attaching the last sensor and nodded to Victoria. "Please turn on that monitor."

Victoria complied. The screen lit up, displaying an array of squiggly lines.

"Each sensor will collect data," Dr. Campbell continued, "and then compile it to create a topographical map. Typically, we'll have subjects perform a series of exercises. We'll show them pictures of both family members and random faces, ask them questions about their lives, and perform other tasks designed to elicit delusions, as well as more formal neurobehavioral and dementia rating scales. Differences in the evoked response potentials will provide insight into how the brain responds to these various stimuli."

"What if they know they're having delusions?" Victoria asked. "If they have memories that they know aren't real, would that show up as different brainwaves?"

Cristina was surprised by Victoria's question, as she'd been thinking the same thing. Her assistant really was a deep thinker.

"Yes, it's possible they might." Campbell tapped his chin with his forefinger. "But False Memory Syndrome is very rare. Some argue it doesn't exist at all. I'd love to enroll some subjects in the study but I'm afraid they'd be hard to come by."

Maybe not as hard as he thinks.

Cristina clenched her jaw, thankful the sensor net wasn't capable of reading her thoughts—or those of her alter ego.

Dr. Campbell typed on the computer keyboard. The screen shifted and a 3D image of a head filled the screen, displaying top-down and frontal views. Most of the image was green, with yellow and red concentric circles making it look like a photo of Jupiter's red spot.

"This is what the image will typically look like," he said, pointing out various areas. "We'll be looking for variations in the . . ."

He trailed off and leaned closer to the monitor, tilting his head this way and that.

"Is something wrong?" Cristina asked.

"*Hmm?*" Dr. Campbell stood up straight and rubbed at his eyebrow. "No, no. Nothing's wrong. Just a blip. It happens sometimes. Do you have any questions?"

Cristina looked to Victoria for reassurance, but her assistant simply shrugged. Had Dr. Campbell noticed something unusual in her brainwave activity, perhaps when Sabrina had chimed in? Suddenly she couldn't wait to remove the sensor net.

"No, I'm good," Cristina said. "But will we be solely doing EEG studies?"

"Oh, no, this is part of a much larger project that includes neuroimaging and lab studies. We even have a neurosurgeon on staff for intraoperative monitoring." Dr. Campbell tilted his head and studied Cristina as if admiring a priceless portrait. "But your perspective will be quite helpful. If you think about it, the human brain is the most secure data storage device ever created. Even if you wipe the hard drive, the memories aren't truly erased. They're still there. The problem is accessing them."

A feeling of spider legs crawling along her skin came over Cristina. Accessing memories was exactly why she was there.

"Sometimes, it's a hardware problem," he continued, turning now to Victoria, who leaned forward on her toes, eyes wide with interest. "Alzheimer's, brain injury, MDMA encephalitis, or toxins. That's what we're studying here. In those cases, we can find a way to physically go in and rewire the brain. But if it's a software problem . . ."

"We have to work with the code." Cristina nodded. "Post-traumatic memory suppression, delusional disorders, and so on."

"Precisely. And that's why you're here, Cristina. Your insight into the mental health side of memory access will help us bridge the gap between neurology and psychiatry." He turned to Victoria and jerked his thumb in Cristina's direction. "I think you'll learn quite a bit from her."

"Oh, I'm sure I will." Victoria smiled at Cristina. "I can't wait to get started."

CHAPTER SEVEN

The Trevino residence smelled of lavender and Pine-Sol, as if it had been recently and thoroughly cleaned. The bookshelves were organized by title. Seashell coasters formed a neat diamond pattern on the coffee table. Framed photos of Danny and his parents sat on the mantel over the brick fireplace. The dead kid had the same dark hair and upturned nose as his mother. Mrs. Trevino hunched over on a tufted sofa, sobbing, and blowing her nose with a tissue. She'd been like that for the past five minutes since Detective Wilson arrived.

Sitting on an ottoman and trying not to squirm, Wilson waited for her to calm down. Informing families of the deaths of loved ones was his least favorite responsibility of the job, even worse than visiting the morgue. Breaking the news was hard for most cops, but Wilson found it excruciating. It had taken him ten minutes preparation before the visit to set aside his feelings of being on the receiving end of bad news, but now, with Mrs. Trevino blubbering in front of him, he realized he'd wasted ten minutes.

"Mrs. Trevino," he said at last when her tears showed no sign of abating, "I'm so sorry for your loss, but I have some questions about Danny that I hope you could answer."

Her head jerked up and she stared, bleary-eyed at him, as if rediscovering he was there. She dabbed her eyes with the tissue and nodded. "Yes, yes, of course. I understand."

"What kind of kid was Danny?"

"Oh, he was such a good boy." She turned to stare wistfully at the photos. "When my husband died, Danny was thirteen, but he stepped up as the man of the house. He took on summer jobs until I was able to return to work at the hospital, all while studying hard and playing sports."

Making mental notes, Wilson said, "That's a lot of weight on an adolescent's shoulders. Did he ever seem resentful?"

"Never." Her eyes flashed defensively. "He wanted to help. I didn't ask him to do all that."

She felt guilty, Wilson knew, despite her words to the contrary. It was common when a child died for a parent to assume it was their fault. Did they push too hard? Did they fail to push hard enough? Was there some sign they missed? Wilson would have to tread carefully to keep that guilt from getting in the way of finding the truth.

"Ma'am, did you know that Danny had a violent outburst in class three days ago?"

Mrs. Trevino's head jerked backward. "No. What happened?"

"Apparently, he went off on the teacher and told the rest they were all going to die."

"Oh, my word." She clapped her hand over her mouth. "Why didn't anyone from the school call me?"

"According to classmates, the school security officer talked him down," Wilson said. "He didn't say anything to you when he got home that day?"

"I didn't talk to him. I work evening shifts during the week, so we almost never see each other. When I get home in the morning, he's already off to school."

"So, you didn't realize he hadn't shown up to school for the past two days?"

Her face paled. "No."

"You had no idea he'd been missing for that long?"

"The dinners I prepared for him were untouched, but I think he sometimes ate out."

"What about his bedroom?"

"He always made his bed and put fresh towels near the shower every morning." She bit her lip. "He knows I like everything in its place."

Wilson glanced again at the pristine living room and scratched behind his ear. For someone who obsessed over organization, she had been oddly unconcerned about her teenage son's whereabouts. "When did you last talk to Danny?"

"On Sunday, we went to church together, and then we watched a movie about the American Revolution." She sniffled and wiped her nose. "He loved it. He's always been a history buff."

"So he seemed happy?"

"Yes, very. He'd been studying extra hard this semester, and I know why. I found applications for Yale, Princeton, and Dartmouth under his bed. He was trying to surprise me, and now he . . . he . . ." She broke into sobs.

The hairs on Wilson's arms prickled as he studied the photos of Danny Trevino. He looked like a happy kid. Nothing his mother said pointed to suicide. But there was another possibility, one he may have been too quick to discount.

"Mrs. Trevino, this is a difficult question, but do you have any reason to suspect Danny was using drugs?"

"Why would you ask me that?"

"It sounds like his behavior changed dramatically over the past few weeks. If he was high when he went walking by Willis Creek, his judgment could've been clouded. He might've tried doing stunts on the bridge parapet and fell."

"My baby didn't do drugs." Her face darkened. "He was too smart for that. And he didn't do reckless things, not ever since we treated his ADHD."

"He was taking medication?"

"Yes, he's been on dextroamphetamine for the past three years."

Gears began turning in Wilson's head. Dextroamphetamine was a powerful stimulant with high street value. If Danny had been sharing or selling his personal supply, or if he abruptly stopped taking it, that could've explained his erratic behavior. "Did he ever forget to take it?"

"No."

"Could you please get the pill bottle?"

She did as he asked. The bottle was empty. He copied the doctor's name and phone number into his notepad. "May I see his room?"

"Of course." As she escorted him, she stopped halfway up the stairs and turned to him. "Detective, please tell me the truth. Do you think my son's death was an accident?"

Wilson hesitated, afraid of misleading this grieving mother. "Any death of a minor warrants proper investigation. I promise to notify you once we have more facts. But do you know of anyone who would want to harm your child?"

"No, Danny was friends with everyone."

The conversation with the high school students who found Danny's body replayed in Wilson's head. Apparently, Mrs. Trevino didn't know how withdrawn the teen had become. "What about Reggie Horne? I understand they were rivals."

That made Mrs. Trevino pause. She wrinkled her nose. "Reggie's a good boy, very dedicated to his mother ever since his father left. Maybe that's why he and Danny understood each other so well. Yes, they've been in competition ever since seventh grade, but there was never any animosity between them. A few weeks ago, on one of my nights off, Reggie had dinner with us."

"Did anything happen that night?"

"After dinner, they studied together, watched a movie in Danny's room, and then Reggie went home." She touched her chin. "But that night, Danny had a nightmare. I heard him screaming that the Sack Man was going to get him."

"Who's the Sack Man?"

"I don't know. When he woke up, he said he didn't remember anything. I figured it had to do with the movie they'd watched. Danny loved horror films almost as much as history."

"Do you remember the name of the movie?"

She scrunched up her face, then shook her head. "Sorry."

The boy's bedroom and bathroom provided Wilson some insight into the boy's life: a few horror movie posters on the wall, bookshelves filled with books on American history, a video game console, and clothes folded away in drawers. But nothing suggested Danny had been suicidal or afraid for his life, and no posters or books about Sack Man.

After they went back downstairs, Wilson handed Mrs. Trevino a business card. "If you remember anything else, please give me a call. And, again, I'm sorry for your loss."

As Wilson walked back to his car, he studied the card with the number for Danny's doctor, then tucked his phone in his pocket. So far all he had was a hunch that the teen's death was more than an accident. But when things didn't add up, his hunches were rarely wrong.

CHAPTER EIGHT

At fifteen minutes to noon, Cristina locked her computer screen and grabbed her purse. They'd spent the rest of the morning reviewing the study protocols and scheduling subjects for testing. Tomorrow, they'd start collecting data, but for the rest of the day her goal was to get everything prepared so she could hit the ground running. Now her stomach was growling. The Memory Center's snack bar was closed for renovations, and she hadn't thought to pack a lunch. With thoughts of an assassin still fresh in her mind, she decided to squeeze in a jiu-jitsu workout over the break. The dojo was three blocks away, and she could pick up a to-go box from Mei's Noodles on the way back.

She passed Victoria on her way to the elevator. "I'm going out to lunch," Cristina said. "Care to join me?"

"Thank you, but I brought a sandwich." Victoria wiggled her fingers. "Toodles."

A crisp breeze kissed Cristina's cheek as she stepped outside. It was impossible to find parking during the lunch hour, so she decided to walk. Every so often, the sun peeked out between the clouds, warming her as she wriggled her way through a sidewalk packed with people in a hurry. She recalled what Dr. Campbell had said about the human brain being the most secure data storage ever created. In a way, that's how Quinn had treated her. Although he'd tried to erase Sabrina's memories, they'd remained behind. That's why he'd kept tabs on her: the formula for improving Recognate had been locked away in her brain. But why did some memories remain beyond her reach? And how had Quinn managed to wipe her mind clean in the first place?

She stopped short. She'd been so caught up in her thoughts she hadn't paid attention to her surroundings and had wandered into an alley between two medical centers. It used to be a busy shortcut to the dojo, but construction of an overhead connector bridge had dwindled foot traffic at street level. Now the alley seemed dark, empty, and foreboding.

Agent Jefferson's voice whispered in the back of her mind: *Your life may be in danger.*

Cristina tightened her grip on her purse, casting her gaze side to side. She should go back. Forget about the lunch workout. Beads of sweat formed on her scalp.

No, that was ridiculous. She forced herself to slow her breathing. Surely, no one would attack her in broad daylight so close to a busy street. And she knew how to protect herself. Hell, hadn't she held her own against Quinn and his goons?

As if trying to reassure her, a truck horn blared around the corner. She overheard two men yelling at each other. Cristina slipped her hand into her purse and pulled out her keyring, twisting it between her fingers until she found the attached canister of pepper spray, and started walking.

A sharp whiff of coffee grounds and cigarette butts trailed Cristina as she continued down the alley. Broken beer bottles stretched across the path. Bits of glass crunched beneath her shoes as she stepped over them.

The hospital walls loomed on either side of her, closing together ahead as if warning her to turn back. A chill ran down Cristina's back, and it wasn't from the cold weather.

Heart pounding, Cristina glanced back the way she'd come.

No one was there.

She swallowed against the lump forming in her throat and scanned the alley.

All she saw were dumpsters and a couple of battered traffic cones. But four yards back, a door was swinging shut.

Cristina chided herself for being paranoid. She'd probably just missed seeing a nurse or doctor taking the back entrance to the hospital. She glanced at a nearly illegible graffiti tag on the nearest brick wall, reminded of how someone with Alzheimer's might lose the ability to write. There was something beautiful about the painting, the control the artist had over the spray can.

If you want to use our lunch break to admire art, Sabrina whispered in her mind, *we could've gone to MassArt.*

The truck back on the street blared its horn once more. Cristina shook off her reverie and started walking again.

The sound of crunching glass echoed off the walls behind her.

Holding her breath, Cristina looked back.

A person dressed all in black, including a balaclava, was driving an electric scooter straight toward her at maximum speed.

Her muscles tightened. She frantically scanned for an escape route in the narrow alley.

Don't run, Sabrina warned her. *Take the offensive. Move now!*

Reflexively, she leaped forward, knocking the masked rider off the scooter. They both tumbled to the ground. Cristina rolled to her feet and whipped around, raising the pepper spray, finger depressing the button.

A gloved hand yanked her wrist and twisted it at a painful angle.

Spray shot out.

Cristina turned her head a second too late. White-hot pain bit into her eyes. A thousand red-pepper wasps stung her cheek. She held her breath to avoid inhaling the caustic spray.

A hand clamped over her mouth before she could scream. Her assailant's body pressed against hers, but all she could think about was that horrible pain boring through her eyeball all the way to the socket.

Block out the pain. Sabrina's voice shouted in her head, echoing off the flat bones of her skull. *You need to fight back.*

It hurts too much.

It will hurt a hell of a lot worse if you get stabbed or your neck is broken. Use your head.

Gnashing her teeth, Cristina used her head. She jerked her chin upward, throwing her skull backward. She heard a crunch and a grunt. The pressure over her mouth relaxed.

All at once, Cristina's thoughts were shoved aside as Sabrina took over. She burst free of her restraint and whirled around. Tears filled her eyes, blurring her vision.

She felt the air move. The assailant was rushing toward her.

She pivoted and raised her arm. What she guessed was a fist bounced off. She turned and punched. Her hand connected with bone.

The attacker howled. Cristina's body spun and kicked. Her foot connected with nothing but air.

The smell of sweat and leather assaulted her nostrils.

Cristina's body dodged right. A glove whooshed past her ear. Her hands shot out and caught the attacker's fist. She kicked again. This time her foot connected with flesh.

Her attacker grunted and jerked free. A moment later, feet pounded the pavement, followed by a thrumming sound. Cristina could barely make out a figure dressed in black zipping away on a scooter.

As the adrenaline wore off, the pain returned, and Cristina regained control. She managed to stagger over to the nearest wall and leaned against it. Her breathing came in ragged bursts.

"Hey!" someone shouted. Footsteps approached.

Cristina fell back into a fighter's stance, fists at the ready.

"Wait, I'm here to help." The voice was soft, reassuring. Cristina was able to focus enough to make out the woman's face. She was wearing scrubs with puppies and kittens on them. A pediatric nurse, maybe? "That looks bad. Did you get hurt anywhere else?"

"No." The burning sensation in Cristina's face was starting to lighten, but it still felt like she had lava in her eye. "Did . . . you see . . . who attacked me?"

"No, I couldn't see their face." The woman's hand hovered under Cristina's chin. "Let me help you inside. Our ER doctors can help."

As the woman guided her, Cristina closed her eyes and concentrated on breathing until the pain subsided.

"Should I call the police?" the woman asked.

Cristina nodded. "And tell them to call Special Agent Milton Jefferson at the FBI. I don't think this was a random mugging."

CHAPTER NINE

"All right, thank you," Detective Wilson said into the phone before hanging up. He turned to Detective Hawkins. "Trevino's doctor said Danny never missed an appointment, and the pharmacy confirmed his prescriptions were always filled at the same time. Neither one had reason to suspect drug diversion."

"Sanchez's psychiatrist said the same thing." Hawkins typed at his keyboard.

"Wait, Sanchez was taking meds too?"

Hawkins nodded. "Dextroamphetamine for ADHD."

"So, they were both taking amphetamines," Wilson said. "Could they have been abusing it themselves?"

"They would've requested early refills."

"Yeah, right." Wilson bumped his fist against his desk. "You said the medical examiner was suspicious of Sanchez's autopsy findings. What did toxicology show?"

"That's what I'm looking at right now." Hawkins typed a key. "Positive only for amphetamines, which is explained by the dextroamphetamine."

"It's going to take a day or two to get the report on Trevino, but at least we can rule out drugs."

"Maybe not. These kids are always finding new ways to poison their bodies. One day, it's cold medicine, the next it's detergent pods."

"True." Wilson leaned forward and pulled up the report he'd started writing on Trevino. "Did Sanchez's parents give you anything else? Names of friends or enemies?"

"Eduardo was a bookworm, obsessed with US history. He only had a couple of friends: a girl named Luiza and a boy from another school named Reggie."

Wilson sat up straight. "Reggie Horne?"

"Yeah."

"Trevino's mom said he and Danny were friends, but the witnesses made it seem like there was more to it."

"We could arrange interviews at the school." Hawkins locked his computer. "Besides Reggie, one of the teachers or other students might know something."

"Do it. I want to know all about Trevino's outburst."

Hawkins started making phone calls. Wilson's thoughts drifted to ones of another psychiatrist and he wondered, amidst the puzzles of this case, how her day was going.

CHAPTER TEN

As she sat in a private room at the Boston Police Department, Cristina rubbed the back of her head where she'd butted her assailant, grateful there'd been no bleeding. The pepper spray had burned her from the inside, but her injuries could've been much worse if Sabrina's training hadn't kicked in. Rinsing with the baby shampoo an ER doctor gave her had provided a small modicum of relief, but her eyes were still sensitive to the bright lights a half hour later.

Someone knocked on the door and opened it without waiting for her response. A tall man with a polished pate and wearing a black suit and tie entered.

"Special Agent Jefferson," she said with relief.

"Dr. Silva." He nodded curtly. "I'm giving you a ride back to your office. We'll talk on the way."

For the first few minutes of the drive in Jefferson's luxury sedan, they rode in silence, the agent focused on the road and Cristina shielding her eyes from the sun. After exiting Route 28 onto Tremont Street, he turned his head toward her, worry lines marring his forehead and bringing out the cooler undertones of his skin, and asked, "Are you okay?"

"Yeah." She massaged her shoulder and winced as her finger touched a bruise. "I'll be fine. Thank you for asking."

"Officer Truman read me the statement you gave him. What makes you think you were targeted?"

"They were clearly following me. And the way they moved, like a trained fighter—I was lucky to overpower them."

"Dr. Silva, you may have taken self-defense classes, but common criminals can still be skilled at combat. Some of them have military training."

"Not like this." She bit down on her cheek. "This was more like fighting a ninja."

"I understand you've been through a horrible experience, Dr. Silva, but—"

"You understand? You've had your own pepper spray turned against you?"

"Well, no." He cleared his throat. "But if you're worried you were attacked by the assassin, I assure you, that's not the case."

"How can you be so sure?"

"Because last night, a ReMind employee was killed in Nevada. And another died last week in Utah."

Some of her anger slipped away, replaced by concern. "Who?"

"Melissa Crawford, a pharmaceutical researcher, and Stephen Collins, a lab tech."

Pity gnawed at Cristina's heart. She didn't know the names, but the thought of more deaths shook her to her core. "What makes you think it's the same killer?"

"It's the same MO. He always kills at night, in a private location so as not to draw attention. He's never attacked in broad daylight."

"Okay, so maybe the assassin has changed coasts and I'm no longer in danger, but others still are."

"We have agents in other cities working to round up the remaining ReMind employees, though there aren't many left." Jefferson cocked his head. "But my primary concern is you. This mugging attempt clearly has you shaken."

"I'm telling you it wasn't a mugging."

"All right, I believe you." He waved a hand. "Boston PD is looking for witnesses, and I'll see what intel I can dig up on known criminals operating in the area. You said the attacker was wearing all black?"

"Including a balaclava. My eyes were burning so bad I couldn't see their face up close."

"Did you hear their voice? Were they wearing cologne?"

Cristina relived the scene, recalling the smells and sounds. "They didn't speak. When they screamed, it sounded like a woman's voice, but I can't be sure. All I could smell was the leather of their gloves and the pepper spray."

"I'll check the Bureau's and Interpol's databases, but my money's still on a garden-variety mugger."

"What kind of mugger uses an e-scooter?"

"Nowadays, quite a few." Jefferson straightened his tie. "Technically, they're illegal in Boston, but some areas have softened restrictions. As a result, we've seen an uptick in crooks using them as convenient getaways. It makes them easier to catch when we can trace the credit card they used to rent the scooters. But if they bought it outright, and in cash, they'll be harder to find."

"That's sounds more like an assassin than a common crook."

"If it was, they were way off their game. From what we've seen, if whoever's killing ReMind employees wanted you dead, you'd be already dead."

Cristina swallowed hard. "It's a good thing you're not a therapist."

"If I hear of any tangible threats, I'll contact you." He gave her a stern look. "But for now, take better precautions and don't venture out alone."

As they rode the rest of the way in silence again, Cristina couldn't shake the feeling Jefferson was wrong. Something about the assailant's fighting style felt familiar, but she couldn't put her finger on it. Still, there was nothing she could do about it but trust the FBI to do their job. Deep down, she wished she could call Wilson for help. He had a way of making her feel confident and secure even when the world was falling apart around her. But she'd burned that bridge, and no apologies could build it back up again. She told herself once again that she'd made the right decision. It was better for them to stay apart.

Keep telling yourself that, Sabrina murmured in the back of her mind. *But at some point, we must be willing to trust someone else. What good is living two lives if we're not really living either one?*

Cristina had no response to that. She caught her reflection in the side mirror, her red-rimmed eyes staring back at her. How could she trust someone else when she couldn't even trust her own mind?

CHAPTER ELEVEN

It was midafternoon by the time Detectives Wilson and Hawkins had finished with all but the last few interviews in the tiny resource room they'd taken over at Somerville Prep. So far, they'd learned nothing new. The other students told the same story they'd already heard. Danny Trevino had been a popular soccer player until a few weeks earlier, when he became sullen and withdrawn. They were rattled by Danny's behavior the last day they saw him alive, but none of them mentioned it to their parents and by the next day had already forgotten about it. The US History teacher admitted he'd made a mistake during one of the lessons and had been surprised by Danny's outburst but wrote it off as an idle teenage threat. While Danny tended to focus on the darker points of history, until that day, he'd been nothing more than a stellar student.

"You ready to keep going?" Hawkins asked as he stood up to stretch his legs.

Wilson nodded. "Call him in."

Moments later Scott Pierce entered and took a seat at the small table. His salt-and-pepper hair was cropped short. His biceps and pectorals bulged under his security uniform, suggesting he was in top physical form for his age. His slate-gray eyes darted side to side as he said in a gravelly baritone, "I know you're interviewing the whole friggin' school, detectives, but I don't got much to tell you, so let's make this quick."

"You understand you're not being detained," Wilson began. "You can end—"

"Yeah, yeah, I know the drill." Pierce snorted. "I wouldn't have agreed to meet with you at all if I'd done something wrong."

The security officer's attitude grated on Wilson's nerves, but he fought to remain professional as he pulled out a digital recorder. "I assume you've been informed of the death of Danny Trevino."

Pierce's bravado melted away. His cheeks sagged, accentuating the wrinkles. "Yeah. That was a damned shame. Danny was a good kid."

"We understand he became agitated in class three days ago and you calmed him down."

"I did."

Wilson leaned forward. "What did you say to him?"

"Nothing magical. He was pissed off at his teacher. I told him when I was his age, I thought all adults were idiots, and it wasn't until I was an adult myself that I realized I'd been right all along." Pierce grinned. "That made him laugh, and a few minutes later, he went back and apologized to his history teacher."

"That was it?"

"That was it."

Wilson glanced at Hawkins, who raised his eyebrows but said nothing. Clearly, his partner had the same thought: Pierce was giving them a load of bullshit. No way was that enough to calm a raging teen, not from what the other students had said about Trevino's threats. But why was Pierce lying? "The students reported Danny screamed—" he checked his notes "—'You're all going to die.' Did he talk to you about that?"

Pierce shook his head. "These kids say crap they don't mean all the time."

"Mr. Pierce, there have been over two hundred school shootings since Columbine. Every threat needs to be taken seriously. Did you report the incident to the headmaster?"

"Of course, I reported it." Pierce scowled. "Danny rattled off a bunch of those shootings by date. He said it was statistically likely our school would be next. That's why he said what he did. He wasn't threatening anyone. He was warning us that the threat was out there."

Hawkins tilted his head. "Did he identify a specific threat?"

"*Nah*." Pierce jutted his lower lip. "Look, I'm being real here. A few minutes after I started talking to him, he calmed right down. When I asked him point-blank if there was something we needed to worry about, he said he hadn't been sleeping well and he was sorry for shouting. He apologized and everyone was happy."

"So when he left that day, he seemed fine?"

"That's right."

Wilson tapped his finger against his chin as he sized up Pierce. Maybe the guy felt guilty for not doing more to get Trevino help and now he was minimizing what happened. Or maybe he was hiding something. "So let me get this straight: a student behaves erratically, he apologizes, and that's the end of the story?"

"I think they tried calling his mom, but she was at work and didn't answer. Danny had never made threats before, so I trusted he was telling the truth." Pierce spread his hands. "I know you guys are doing your job, but what's any of this got to do with his accident?"

"We're trying to confirm it *was* an accident." Hawkins tilted his head. "Have there been any other problems at this school lately? Any kids using drugs?"

Pierce scoffed. "You kidding? They all use drugs. Not Danny, though. His dad died from complications of alcoholism, so his mom made extra sure he stayed clean."

Wilson was surprised Mrs. Trevino hadn't shared that tidbit with him. "That seems like rather personal information. Did Danny share it with you?"

"Uh, yeah. These kids confide in me a lot."

Wilson's internal bullshit detector went ballistic. "Why?"

Pierce scratched at his eyebrow. "For all their money, these rich kids don't get much guidance at home. Their parents let them do whatever they want and don't give a crap about what's going on in their lives. I listen and I teach them how the world really works."

A weight dropped on Wilson's shoulders. After his parents died, he'd lived with an uncle who spent all his time at the tracks and casinos, leaving Wilson to fend for himself. He'd grown up quickly, but he'd always wished there had been one adult who would've been there for him. Danny's father was dead, and his mother was never around. Maybe Pierce had filled the gap in Danny's life. Or maybe there'd been something else between them. "So did Danny confide in you that anything else was bothering him?"

Pierce's cheek twitched, almost imperceptibly, but he shook his head. "Nothing."

Wilson glanced at Hawkins, who jerked his thumb toward the door. Nodding, Wilson stood and held out his hand. "Thank you for your time, Mr. Pierce. We'll call you if we need anything else."

Pierce shook his hand and left. Hawkins closed the door. "He's hiding something."

"I know. Let's run a background check on him back at the precinct," Wilson said. "In the meantime, let's talk to the last student."

From the first moment the detectives sat him down, Reggie Horne couldn't stop tugging at his jeans and glancing repeatedly at the assistant headmaster standing by the door to supervise the interview.

"You seem nervous, Reggie," Wilson said. "Something you want to tell us?"

"Of course, I'm nervous. Two White cops wanting to talk to one of the three Black kids in the school can only mean one thing." Reggie locked his gaze with Wilson's. "Something bad happened and I'm the scapegoat. It happened to Emmett Till in 1955, Hurricane Carter in 1966, and the Central Park Five in 1989."

"You know your history," Wilson said, impressed. "But you're not under suspicion of anything. We're hoping you can tell us about Danny Trevino."

Reggie's eyes widened. "Danny? You think he did something illegal? Shit, he just died. Let the dead rest in peace."

"We're not sure his death was an accident. We're hoping you can shed light on what happened."

The teen's mouth twisted into an O. He leaned back and folded his arms across his chest. "Why didn't you say so? What do you wanna know?"

"Tell us what happened the other day, when he yelled at his history teacher."

"Oh, yeah, that was scary stuff. I thought he was gonna pull out an AR-15 right there."

"Really?" Hawkins sat up straighter. "Everyone else has made it sound like no big deal."

"Maybe not to them." Reggie's lip curled. "But if I'd said what he said, they'd have had a SWAT team here in seconds."

Wilson glanced at the school administrator, who seemed fascinated by a spot on the ceiling. A bitter taste filled his mouth. He made sure the recorder was on and turned back to Reggie. "So tell us what you heard Danny say."

Reggie narrowed his gaze at the device for two seconds before saying, "Mr. Jenkins had handed back our tests. Danny was pissed because he got a ninety-three."

"What was wrong with that?" Hawkins asked.

"I got a hundred." Reggie shrugged. "We'd studied together the night before, so he thought we should've gotten the same grade. He accused Mr. Jenkins of not knowing anything about history. When the teacher said what answer he was looking for, Danny started yelling, saying he was wrong, and then Danny spewed a bunch of other historical dates."

"Did he say you were all going to die?"

"Yeah."

Wilson leaned forward. "What do you think he meant by that?"

"I don't know." Reggie stared down at the table. "He'd been saying weird shit for a couple of weeks, off and on."

"Like what?"

"He'd cut his finger two weeks ago and could still feel the pain like it just happened. We watched a documentary in class about the concentration camps and he remembered every detail the survivors described like he'd lived through it himself, to the point he insisted he *had* been there." Reggie jiggled his head. "Shit like that."

"Was he using drugs?" Hawkins asked.

"What?" Reggie's head jerked up. His eyes flashed, then he looked away. "No, he wasn't a junkie or nothing. But, you know, he took medication for ADHD."

"Yes, we know," Wilson said. "Was he abusing it? Or selling it?"

Reggie glanced at the assistant headmaster. "Not that I know of."

"Did he seem suicidal?"

"No. But a few times he looked scared."

"Scared of what?" Hawkins asked.

"He wouldn't tell me. But he had this look on his face when we were in school, like he wanted to escape as fast as he could."

Wilson drummed his fingers on the table, wondering why no one else had mentioned this. "Did you overhear his conversation with Mr. Pierce?"

"No, they went out in the hall."

"How did Danny look when he returned to class?"

"He wasn't angry anymore, but . . ." Reggie stared off into space.

"But what?"

"He was pale. I know it's a cliché, but it was like he'd seen a ghost. He wouldn't tell me why." Reggie wet his lips. "After school, we usually ride home together, but this time he took off. Said he needed some time alone."

Wilson's ear started to itch. "Did you see him after that?"

"No. That was the last time I saw him."

Hawkins shot Wilson a look that said, *This could all be bullshit.*

Wilson suspected Hawkins was right, but he considered himself a pro at detecting signs that someone was lying to him. Which meant he also knew when someone was telling the truth. Deep in his gut, he sensed Reggie was being honest.

"What about Eduardo Sanchez?" Wilson asked.

Reggie frowned. "What about him?"

"You were friends with him, even though he was at a different school. How did you two know each other?"

"We met at the library, started talking about video games." Reggie bumped his foot against the table leg. "We both like Minecraft and Fortnite. Sometimes we played against each other online. Eddie knew some badass hacks."

"So what happened?" Wilson leaned forward. "Why was he walking the train tracks?"

Reggie stopped torturing the table leg. The tendons stood out on his neck. "I don't know. He texted me that he had a fight with his parents and wanted to know if he could hang out at my place. But I said no. My mom was sick and needed my help. I didn't know he was going to kill himself."

"You're not in trouble," Wilson said instinctively, eliciting a twitch from Hawkins. Wilson chided himself. He knew better than to assuage a witness who might turn out to be a suspect, but he couldn't stop himself. Something about this kid was getting under his skin. He inhaled through his nose and tried to recover. "But you can see how it might look to a prosecutor, if our investigation reveals these boys weren't simply accident victims. Are you sure there's not something you want to tell us?"

Reggie dug his fingernail into the table and then shook his head.

Wilson bit his lip, still convinced the teen was telling the truth but also hiding something. Maybe he needed a nudge to open up. Watching Reggie's face carefully, Wilson asked, "What's Sack Man?"

Reggie's eyebrows shot up. "What?"

"Danny's mom said he was screaming about Sack Man the other night, but she didn't know if it was from a movie or a video game or what."

"Oh, yeah." Reggie fiddled with his shirt. "She probably meant Slender Man. It's a creepy game we played a couple of times. Hey, can I go now? I'm supposed to get some stuff for my mom at the store on the way home."

Wilson studied the teen's face. That was the first time during the entire interview Reggie's micro-expressions betrayed him. He was lying about Sack Man. But why? Wilson glanced at Hawkins, who nodded.

"You're free to go," Wilson said. "Do you need a ride?"

"No, I got my bike. Thanks." Reggie started for the door and stopped. He turned back to the detectives. "You really think Danny's death wasn't an accident?"

Wilson held Reggie's gaze. "What do you think?"

Reggie's jaw tightened as if he was about to say something more, but he turned and left.

"Well, looks like you were right," Hawkins said after thanking and dismissing the assistant headmaster. "There's more to this case than meets the eye. You think Reggie could've pushed Danny off the bridge?"

"No, but he knows more than he let on." Wilson pushed back his chair, the metal legs screeching against the floor tiles as he stood. "Let's keep an eye on him. Pierce too."

"I'll see what I can dig up back at the precinct."

"Do that. I need to head out." A smile teased at the corners of Wilson's mouth.

"Yeah, go ahead, lover boy." Hawkins grinned. "I guess you have eyes on someone a little prettier than Pierce."

"She's out of his league."

Hawkins gave a slow nod. "Be careful that she's not out of yours."

CHAPTER TWELVE

When Cristina drove home at the end of the day, her senses were on full alert. She triple-checked the rearview mirror each time she stopped at a traffic light, even though she'd already searched the tiny back seat for potential stowaways. Every time she turned at an intersection, she studied the cars behind her to ensure no one was following her. She jumped when a truck's engine brake engaged in the next lane. By the time she pulled into the parking garage for her apartment building, her jaw ached from clenching it.

You need to calm down, Sabrina nagged at her. *The whole afternoon, you kept thinking about ReMind and assassins. It drove me bonkers.*

After Jefferson dropped her off at the Memory Center, Cristina had gone straight to her office and tried to dig through the study protocols, but her mind repeatedly drifted to the attack near the hospitals. She couldn't bring herself to face anyone, not with her nerves on the verge of shorting out.

Cristina shook her head as she shut off the car engine and glanced in the rearview mirror. Her eye irritation had subsided, but an uncomfortable tingling remained when she blinked and the scarlet rings around her orbits made her look like a red panda. "What if Agent Jefferson is wrong and the assassin hasn't moved on to the West Coast?"

Then we deal with it. But we can't start becoming paranoid. Fear is the worst thing for neural recovery.

Cristina drew in a deep breath and slowly exhaled. As her limbic system calmed, she found she could think more clearly. "You're right. I trust Agent Jefferson to find out what's going on, and if there is an imminent threat, he'll help us neutralize it."

Good. Now, let's go distract ourselves with Netflix and calm down.

On the way up the stairs to her apartment, Cristina reflected on the handful of people in her life who knew the truth about her. They'd kept her secret safe, but that also put them at risk if anyone wanted to tie up loose ends. What she wouldn't give to make it all go away, to have one identity and set of memories so she could stop keeping secrets and live her life.

Her cat Grizabella mewled from inside the apartment as Cristina approached.

"Hold on, Griz," she said and fished for her keys in her purse. She'd need to warn those who knew the truth, even if some of those conversations might be painful after everything that happened. "Mommy will get your food as soon as I open this—"

The door flew open.

Cristina recoiled into a crouch, hands flying up to shield her face.

"*Oi, linda!*" Maria Carvalho stood in the doorway, beaming, arms outstretched. While in Rio searching for her past, Cristina had discovered she—*or, rather, Sabrina*—had a half sister. Maria had helped her recover Sabrina's memories and to get answers from Jose Kobayashi, the researcher who helped create Recognate.

Maria's smile fell away as she looked down at Cristina. "What's wrong?"

"What're you doing here?" Cristina clasped her chest as if the movement could slow her thumping heart. She stood and studied her sister, who was wearing a wool sweater, a scarf, and gloves. "And why are you dressed for winter?"

"It was early spring when I left Rio, and it's not much warmer here." Maria rubbed her arms. "I'm here to visit you, of course."

"But you weren't supposed to fly in until next week."

"I changed my flight. I wanted to surprise you."

"You surprised me, all right." Cristina rubbed her forehead. "How did you get in?"

"Wilson told me where you keep your spare key."

Cristina lowered her hand, stunned. "You talked to Wilson? When?"

"A few days ago." Maria pouted. "Was I not supposed to?"

"No, it's fine. Come here." Cristina pulled her sister into a hug. "But if I'd known you were coming today, I'd have picked you up at the airport and saved you cab fare."

"Oh, I got a ride."

"You did? From who?"

A dark figure stepped into view. Cristina dropped her purse.

Standing behind Maria was a man who was supposed to be dead.

CHAPTER THIRTEEN

DB studied the apartment building while perched on an electric scooter in the parking lot across the street. The black jumpsuit and balaclava were stuffed in a backpack, and she now wore high-rise jeans and a hoodie that allowed her to blend in with commuters.

Her cheeks burned as she fought to make sense of what had happened in the alley earlier that day. For two weeks since arriving in Boston, she'd gathered every scrap of information she could find about Cristina Silva: where she lived, where she used to work, what kind of car she drove. But it wasn't enough to explain why DB's employers wanted her to stay away from Silva, or why the name seemed so familiar. Once she learned Silva would be working at a memory center, DB realized she had to get closer, study the woman's movements, listen in on her conversations, to determine whether she could trust Silva to cure DB of her glitches once and for all. She'd tried to sneak into Silva's apartment to plant a camera, but the woman never seemed to leave the building, at least until that day, and a nosy building manager blocked her attempts. But following her to and from work was another matter.

When the doctor left the Memory Center in the middle of the day, DB's mind raced with possible reasons. Maybe she was simply going out to eat. Or maybe she had somewhere to be. Everyone had secrets, and DB was certain Silva had plenty. So, she'd followed Silva into the alley behind the hospital, keeping enough distance to avoid detection. Tracking her should've been as simple as walking through the park.

But a third of the way down the alley, a truck horn had distracted her. At that moment, a vision burst into her head. She was walking alone on a city street at night, the collar of an expensive overcoat turned up against the cold. A man stepped in front of her, masked in the shadows, lamplight glinting off the butcher knife he held. He demanded her purse. She saw herself handing it over even as she screamed at herself to fight back, to not be a victim. The man had snatched it and punched her in the face before running away.

Racked by adrenaline, fear, and helplessness over the vision, she'd ridden over broken glass, alerting Silva to her presence, and throwing DB off guard. She hadn't expected Silva to attack her, and it was all DB could do to fight her off. She clamped her fingers around the handlebar, wishing she could throttle the weak, pathetic version of herself in that vision or, even better, crush whatever was causing the glitches in the first place.

She gingerly touched the bridge of her nose and winced at the sharp bite of pain. At least it wasn't broken, and she'd managed to prevent the area where that bitch had head butted her from becoming swollen. No one got the drop on DB like that. No one who'd lived, anyway.

She kicked the scooter forward and zipped out of the parking lot. One way or another, she'd find out why Cristina Silva was so important to her employers and what she knew. And then DB would stop whatever was happening to her.

CHAPTER FOURTEEN

Wilson peered down the revolver's sights and locked on the shooting range target. The metal plating felt cold to the touch. He drew in a deep breath, blocking out all distractions, and said in the huskiest voice he could muster, "Feel lucky, punk?"

He fired three shots in succession.

The bullets found their marks.

Wilson grinned and removed the shooting earmuffs before turning to the woman in the lane next to his. "What do you think?"

"Nice shooting, Tex." The woman, wearing a suede jacket over a blouse and hip-hugging jeans, folded her arms across her chest. She was a detective with the Everett precinct he'd met a few weeks earlier on a cross-jurisdictional case. She jerked her head, making her shoulder-length auburn hair bounce. "But you need to compensate for the Model 29's recoil. You keep pulling to the right. And you're gonna get yourself in trouble with the Dirty Harry impersonations."

A tingling sensation spread across Wilson's cheeks. He looked back at the target downrange. Son of a bitch, she was right.

"But don't sweat it," she said as she donned her protective glasses and picked up a Beretta carbine rifle. "Clint Eastwood didn't know how to handle one of those either before *Magnum Force*."

"Is that true?"

She donned her muffs. "No."

She hefted the rifle's buttstock to her shoulder, aimed, and fired four rounds.

One shot went wide, but the other three hit dead-center.

"My dad owned a shooting range. I went every weekend since my fifteenth birthday." She winked. "Unofficially."

Wilson's nerve endings tingled as she returned the rifle to the clerk. He had to admit, he was having a good time. She was funny, smart, and had killer curves.

"Want to get out of here?" she asked as she returned. "I gotta be at a stakeout in a half hour so we don't have a lot of time." She rested one hand on her hip and tilted her head. "But I could show you some other things I learned on my fifteenth birthday."

Five minutes later, she was on top of him in the back seat of Wilson's Charger, her tongue exploring inside his mouth as she unbuttoned his shirt. His hands slid over her back, pulling her closer. An urgency swelled inside him.

She ripped her mouth away and pushed his head to the side before gliding her tongue along his neck.

A moan escaped his lips. He shut his eyes, electricity rippling over his skin as her lips and teeth teased him. Breathlessly, he said, "You're incredible, Cristina."

Her head popped up. She stared at him. "What did you say?"

"*Uh*," he began, but the thoughts failed to make their way to his lips as he realized his mistake. "I meant . . ."

Her gaze hardened. She sat back and let her hands fall to her sides. "Wendy."

"Right, Wendy." He massaged his forehead. "I, uh, meant to say that."

Her forehead crinkled. "Are you sure you're okay? You're sweating."

"I am?" He lowered his hand and stared at the droplets clinging to his fingers. "Um, you just got me excited. I could turn on the air conditioner and we can try again."

She dropped her gaze to his crotch. Her lip twitched. "It looks like you could use some rest."

His earlobes burned. He put his hand on her shoulder. "No, I really like you. It's . . . uh . . ."

"Don't worry about it." She climbed off him and adjusted her blouse. "But there's no point wasting our time when you've clearly got something you're trying to work out."

"But—"

She opened the door and stepped out. As she slipped on her jacket, she gave him a half smile. "When you figure out what you want, if you're still interested, call me."

"Yeah." He barely managed a nod. "I'm sorry, uh . . ."

"Wendy."

"Right."

She rolled her eyes and shut the door.

Wilson slumped on the car seat and rubbed both sides of his scalp with his fingers. Damn it. He was over Cristina. He was sure he was.

So why couldn't he stop thinking about her?

He started to button his shirt and stopped. Cripes, he'd worn the blue shirt he and Cristina picked out together at the Twin City Plaza to replace the ones whose buttons she'd ripped open. Maybe that was why she'd been on his mind. Although, he had to admit, she'd never really left his thoughts.

With a grunt, he moved to the driver's seat and started the Charger. He should go home and get some sleep. But with these intrusive feelings he was having, there was something he needed to do first.

CHAPTER FIFTEEN

"Get down!" Cristina shouted as she shoved Maria out of the way and charged into the apartment. Adrenaline surged through her body, electricity through her mind. She'd never reach the gun she kept locked in her nightstand in time. But, judging from the stunned look on the man's face, she had the element of surprise in her favor. She lunged toward him.

He reached inside his leather jacket.

Cristina spring-boarded off the couch. She rolled behind him and grabbed his arm. She twisted it behind his back and wrapped her other arm around his neck.

"What are you doing here?" she hissed in his ear. "How are you alive?"

"Let me go!" He tried to wriggle free. She tightened the headlock. He yelped. "*Que porra é essa?*"

"Cristina, what are you doing?" Maria entered the room, lips pursed. "Let him go."

"This is Federico Gomes." Cristina pinned the man's arm against his back. Federico had been an assassin sent by Quinn to kill Cristina and another Zero Dark agent who'd betrayed them, but someone had killed him first. "He tried to kill me, and he's supposed to be dead."

"That's not Federico." Maria pressed her fist against her lips, barely concealing a smile. "It's his brother, Bruno."

"Brother?"

"Let him go and see for yourself."

Cristina continued to restrain the man, frozen in place. It had to be a trap. But Maria wouldn't lie to her, would she?

"Please," the man said, wheezing. "I can prove it."

Hesitating, Cristina glanced at Maria, who nodded.

Slowly, Cristina released him.

As he backed away, rubbing his neck, Cristina noticed he had no scar on his cheek, and his eyes were a dark brown, whereas Federico Gomes had steel gray eyes that had haunted her for weeks after he'd shot at her.

"I'm going to reach into my jacket," he said, holding up one hand.

Cristina grunted.

He withdrew a high-end wallet from his pocket, dug through it, and held out a photograph. "This is a picture of the two of us together, from a long time ago."

Without drifting her gaze from his face or his other hand, Cristina took the photo and held it up to study it. Her stomach quivered. One man arched his arm over the other's back, laughing. The other bore a strained smile. They were young, in their early twenties. Both had the same babyface, but as Cristina studied them, she could see small differences around the nose, eyebrows, and cheekbones. And one was at least a couple of inches taller than the other.

"I'm the shorter one," Bruno said, as if reading Cristina's mind.

She squinted at him, and then back at the photo. His smile matched that of the shorter brother, showing a hint of teeth and accentuated crow's feet around the eyes. As she continued to study the image, she spotted a young woman laughing in the background. A woman whose face she knew all too well.

"Is that . . . ?" she began.

"Yes," he said softly. "That's you."

Cristina searched through Sabrina's memories until she found it. They'd gone to Tijuca National Park to hike through the rainforest together. A marmoset had stolen Federico's keys. Bruno and Sabrina thought it was the funniest thing ever, but Federico was furious. It had taken Bruno five minutes to calm his brother and get him to smile so Maria could take the picture.

"Okay," she said and returned the photo. "If Maria vouches for you, I believe you."

Tucking the photo into his wallet, Bruno looked Cristina up and down. "I know it's been many years since we saw each other but I can't believe you didn't recognize me."

"I guess Maria didn't tell you," Cristina said. "I was in an accident two years ago and suffered amnesia. I'm still having trouble remembering some things. I hope I didn't hurt you."

"I work in private security. Rough treatment comes with the territory." He squinted. "How extensive were your injuries? You look . . . different."

Cristina touched her face, recalling the modifications Quinn had made to her appearance. "It was pretty bad."

"And it involved my brother?"

"No. Well, yes, in a way, but . . ." She trailed off, unsure how much to disclose about Federico's role as a hitman for Quinn. "What do you know about his line of work?"

Shrugging, he said, "I know he worked for the Brazilian government. He and I stopped talking to each other several years ago, after I moved to the US."

"What happened?"

"A fight over a woman." He smiled sheepishly. "It's a cliché, *n'é?*"

Cristina caught herself smiling back. She shook it off and turned to Maria. "How is it I didn't know Bruno lived here?"

"That is my fault," Bruno said before Maria could answer. "I've spoken to few people back home since I moved here. A few weeks ago, after I learned of Federico's death, I reached out to Maria. When she told me that you were here in Boston, and she was traveling here to visit, it seemed the perfect time to reconnect." He made a face. "Though, I must admit, being placed in a chokehold wasn't what I had pictured for our reunion."

Cristina shielded her eyes. "Maybe I overreacted a bit. I take defense classes."

"*Meu Deus*, I just noticed." Maria rushed over and touched Cristina's cheek. "Your eyes are red."

"It's nothing." Cristina turned away. "Only a little pepper spray."

Maria frowned. "Tell me what happened."

It took Cristina several minutes to recount the attack behind the hospital.

"The streets are dangerous in Rio, but I thought it was safer here," Maria said when Cristina finished. "Have the police caught who did it?"

"Not yet, but I feel better now that you're here." Cristina held Maria's hand and said to Bruno, "Really, I'm sorry I attacked you."

"I understand," Bruno said. "And I am sorry for whatever my brother did to you. When I last spoke to him, he had become a different person. Do you know what I mean?"

A creeping sensation ran through Cristina's body.

"Well, I must be going. I was on my way out when you arrived." Bruno pulled a card out of his pocket and handed it to Cristina. "Maria is a good fighter—and I see you are too. But if you need extra protection, I can help."

The card read: *Pantera International, Private Security*, and had a local address and phone number at the bottom. "Pantera? That means panther," said Cristina.

"Yes, because we are discreet and deadly." He winked. "Like the panther."

She tucked the card into her pocket and shook his hand. "Bruno, it's nice to meet you—er, see you. You know."

He smiled, sending a tingle along her skin. "Likewise, Sabrina."

Cristina shut the door behind him and turned to her sister. "You didn't tell him that I go by Cristina now?"

"I thought explaining that you have two identities was too much yet." Maria chuckled and stretched out on the couch. "He's a good man. You should accept his offer."

Cristina plopped down next to Maria and patted her sister's leg. "I'm sure he is, but for now, let's enjoy each other's company. How was your flight?"

"Too long and the food was terrible," Maria said with a moue. "But I have something more interesting to tell you."

A knock at the door preempted Cristina's response. She glanced in that direction and then turned back to Maria. "Were you expecting anyone else?"

Maria shook her head.

Muscles tensed, Cristina crept to the door and peered through the peephole. Her mouth fell open as she recognized the man standing outside.

Wilson.

CHAPTER SIXTEEN

Gary Wilson looked the same as he had when Cristina last saw him. Navy suit snug around his muscular shoulders. Dark hair lightly tousled with sideburns trailing past his ears. Hazel eyes like a wolf's: watching everything, revealing nothing.

"Hi." His toe traced a line back and forth on the ground. "Sorry to stop by so late."

"It's fine. I didn't expect to see you." As she stepped closer, she noticed beads of perspiration on his forehead. "Are you okay? You look a little pale."

"Huh? Oh, yeah." He rubbed at his neck. "I'm fine. Do you have a moment?"

"Is that Gary?" Maria called out. "Tell him to come inside."

"Maria's here?" he asked.

"Yes, she said she talked to you on the phone." Cristina gave him a cool stare. "It would've been nice if you gave me a heads-up."

His eyebrows squished together and then he blew out his cheeks. "Oh, uh, sorry. I forgot."

Cristina caught the warble in his voice and her hackles raised. She'd never seen Wilson so scattered. "Gary, what's going on? Why are you here?"

His brow shot up and his cheeks tightened. "Well, um, I wanted to tell you . . ." His gaze darted to the side. "I . . . uh . . . I wanted to make sure Maria got in okay, that's all."

"But you said you forgot—"

"Oh, man, I didn't realize how late it was." He forced a smile. "Tell Maria to give me a call if she wants to get together, okay?"

Cristina reeled from his rapid topic shift. "Sure."

"Thanks." He mimed tipping his hat. "Night."

She watched him disappear down the hall, puzzling over what had happened, and then shut the door and rejoined Maria on the couch.

"What was all that about?" Maria asked.

"I have no idea. Things have been weird ever since I broke up with him."

"You broke up with him? Why?"

"It's a long story and I'm not in the right mood to discuss it right now." Grizabella darted onto Cristina's lap and curled up. Cristina stroked the cat's head. "Tell me this news of yours. I'm all ears."

Maria gave her a puzzled look.

"That means I'm listening."

"Oh, okay." Maria shook her head. "I still don't understand how you speak like you were born here, even though you only lived in the US for two years. It would take me a decade to learn all these idioms and lose my accent."

"It's an effect of the Recognate." Cristina scratched under Grizabella's chin. "The new memories it created were all-immersive, instilling accent, personality, mannerisms—everything that made me a different person. Quinn fed me information that helped shape all that."

"But why did you wake in the hospital speaking English instead of Portuguese?"

"There have been several cases of people waking from comas speaking fluently in a different language. That's probably what happened to me."

Maria rubbed her chin. "I guess that makes sense. It seems so bizarre."

"You're not the one living it." Cristina squeezed Maria's hand. "But I'm grateful to have you. The biggest thing missing from Cristina Silva's life is family."

"Then you'll appreciate my news. Wait here."

Maria opened her roller bag and riffled through it. She returned holding a bundle of papers wrapped with an elastic band. "I was clearing out space in my apartment two days ago and found these in a box at the back of the closet." Maria handed the bundle to her. "Mother must have hidden them there so my father wouldn't see them."

Cristina removed the rubber band and sifted through the papers.

"They're love letters!" Cristina scanned the flowery writing. *Querida Gloria* was written on the first page of each letter.

"She must have thrown out the rest of the envelopes, but I found this in the middle of the pile." Maria held out a torn piece of paper with part of an address and a postmark stamped in one corner.

"What address is this?" Cristina asked. "It's not in Rio."

"No, it's in Maceió, a city in northeast Brazil."

"When did Mom live there?"

"Look at the postmark." Maria pointed. "It's dated thirty-five years ago."

Wings fluttered in Cristina's chest. "I'm thirty-five."

"That's why I couldn't find your birth records. You weren't born in Rio." Maria grinned. "If your birth records are in Maceió, we can find out who your father is."

CHAPTER SEVENTEEN

Over the course of the evening, Cristina's paranoia faded as she huddled on the couch with Maria, reading their mother's love letters together. Some were embarrassingly steamy. Each was signed with the initials FG. Cristina had immediately thought of Federico Gomes, but that seemed ridiculous since Federico had been close to Cristina's age.

"What's their father's name?" Cristina asked after reading the last letter. "Bruno's and Federico's, I mean."

"Felipe." Maria frowned. "You don't think their father is your father?"

"I don't know what to think."

"Perhaps you should talk to Bruno about it."

"How do I ask him if his father had an affair with our mother?"

Maria chewed on her finger. "Yes, that would be awkward. Maybe get to know him better first."

"I don't know. It's a little creepy that his brother worked for Quinn and . . ."

An image popped into her head, the same one that had started an avalanche of unexpected memories six months earlier. She was running through Rio with a bouquet in one hand and holding Federico Gomes's hand with the other. A warm rush of excitement filled her body before the image faded.

She pressed her hand against her chest and fought to catch her breath. The passion in that memory had been so intense. If Felipe Gomes had been her father, wouldn't he have put a stop to Federico and Cristina dating? And how could Federico have agreed to attack her when they'd been so close?

"Cristina?" Maria lay a hand on her shoulder. "Are you okay?"

Cristina drew in a long, slow breath and waited for the adrenaline to drain from her body before nodding. "I'm fine. I think it's unlikely that Felipe is my father, but maybe talking to Bruno will help me better understand Federico's motives."

And he's not hard on the eyes, Sabrina said.

Grimacing, Cristina thought back: *Put a damper on it. Especially if there's even a remote chance we're related.*

Sabrina fell silent, but Cristina sensed a bit of rebellion from her alter. She knew it had to be tough for Sabrina to take a back seat in her own body, only taking control through sheer force of will. If she could, Cristina would gladly give Sabrina back dominance, but she feared doing so would cause her to cease to exist. She clenched her fist. There had to be a way to stabilize their relationship. She only hoped Sabrina wouldn't do anything foolish in the meantime.

CHAPTER EIGHTEEN

The next morning, Detectives Wilson and Hawkins marched triumphantly into the precinct, dragging two gangly robbery suspects in handcuffs. One of the thugs spat on the ground as they approached Sergeant Davis's desk.

"Hey, show some respect." Davis glared at the hooligan. "They just finished waxing the floors."

"Have these two booked and processed." Wilson handed over a baggie containing a handgun and a can of spray paint. "Charge them with petty theft and illegal possession of an unregistered firearm."

"I told you," said the spitter. "I got a permit."

"Let it go, Ricky." The other thug rolled his eyes. "They don't wanna see the crap your cousin printed off his MacBook."

"Shut up."

"You shut up."

"Both of you, shut up." Hawkins glowered.

The perps clamped their mouths shut.

Wilson turned to Davis. "You got this?"

"Sure thing, Detectives." Davis whistled to a uniformed officer. "Take these two down to Central Booking."

A few minutes later, as Wilson sat at his desk in the detective pen, he spotted the file marked *Trevino, Danny.* The adrenaline rush of closing a case drained from his body, leaving him once again frustrated over his failure to get a solid lead on Trevino's death. Scott Pierce and Reggie Horne had proved to be dead ends. When Pierce wasn't working at the high school, he spent most of his time at home or with a Revolutionary War reenactment group. Reggie lived in a lower-middle-class neighborhood, working part-time at the local gas station to help his mother make ends meet, and seemed to be a model student. Yet for some reason the skin behind Wilson's ear kept itching every time he thought of them.

Wilson's thoughts drifted to Cristina. He berated himself for chickening out the previous night. He'd planned to tell her how he felt, but the way she glared at him for not telling her Maria was arriving early had deflated his sails. Now she probably thought he was an even bigger flake.

Forcing himself to concentrate on something he was better at than relationships, he opened Trevino's file, scanning the autopsy report. Cause of death: traumatic brain injury consistent with an accidental fall. Tox screen positive only for amphetamines. No evidence of foul play.

"You're not already flogging yourself over the Trevino case, are you?" Hawkins wiped at his mouth as he watched Wilson from his desk. "We did some good work. Take a moment to pat yourself on the back."

"I know, but something about this case . . ." Wilson threw up his hands. "I don't know. It's a feeling."

"You and your effing feelings. The crime scene photos didn't show any signs of a struggle. If Trevino was pushed, the perp covered their tracks like a professional."

Wilson's desk phone started ringing.

"Must be a hot tip," Hawkins said. "What'll it be this time? Someone's refrigerator is running, and they need us to catch it?"

"You should quit being a cop and go into comedy." Wilson snorted and answered the phone.

It was Sergeant Davis. "Detective, there's a woman reporting her son missing."

"Why are you calling me? Transfer her to Missing Persons."

"She said she saw the news about Danny Trevino's death and is worried her son may be in danger."

Wilson suppressed a groan. Keeping the death out of the news was impossible, but anytime something happened to a teen, parents feared it would happen to their kid. "They're repairing the bridge Trevino fell off, so—"

Davis cleared his throat. "She said her son knew Danny Trevino."

Wilson neck prickled. The connection was probably another red herring, but worth the time to find out. "Transfer her."

The woman introduced herself as Deborah Jackman. "Thank you for speaking to me, Detective. My son has been missing for four days."

Wilson's stomach clenched. The success rate of missing person investigations relied on early processing. The trail often ran cold past seventy-two hours. And the fact the missing person was a kid . . . "Ma'am, why are you only reporting this now?"

"Caleb turns eighteen next month. We don't need to know where he is at all times. It wasn't unusual for him to stay over at his friends' houses for a night or two, especially when he was studying for a big test." The woman sobbed. "But, this time, he didn't come back."

"Okay, Mrs. Jackman, I'll need your address. We'll send someone out there to speak to you and get some photographs of your son so we can send out a bulletin. But first, do you have any idea where he might've gone? Sometimes we get lucky, and a missing teen is someplace obvious the parents forgot to check."

"Uh, well, he spends most of his time at the library."

"Really? The library?"

"For the past two months, he's been studying every moment he can." Mrs. Jackman's voice became strained. "Honestly, it scared me."

"What do you mean?"

"Caleb was always full of life and energy, but lately, he became grouchy. Irritable. Even a little mean. He kept rattling off historical facts he'd memorized and calling my husband and I idiots, saying most of what we knew was wrong."

Her words struck Wilson with creeping familiarity as he recalled hearing a similar story about another teen. "Ma'am, how did your son know Danny Trevino?"

"They went to a summer camp together a few years ago."

"That's it? Nothing more recent?"

"No. Why?"

Wilson exhaled slowly. A dead end, as he'd feared, but now he was committed. "No reason, ma'am. I'll need your address."

Mrs. Jackman recited her address and then said, "Please send someone out as soon as possible, Detective. Caleb doesn't have his medicine."

"What medication does he take?"

"Dextroamphetamine."

Wilson's heart skipped a beat. He shot a glance at Hawkins.

"Mrs. Jackman," Wilson said. "Are you at home?"

"Yes."

"Then please stay put. My partner and I will be there shortly."

Wilson hung up and turned to Hawkins, "Get your coat. It looks like my effing feelings just panned out."

CHAPTER NINETEEN

When Cristina arrived at her office the next day, she found Victoria waiting outside in the hall, clutching a binder against her chest. Her blond hair stuck out from under a white beanie, and she wore a pair of thick-framed zebra-striped glasses. She had a black T-shirt on, but her white coat covered most of the design.

"New look?" Cristina asked as she unlocked her door.

"Yes, Dr. Campbell insists I wear this coat during business hours, but I like to flair things up a bit." Victoria leaned in and whispered conspiratorially, "A little rebellion never hurts anyone."

"I'll have to try that sometime." Cristina couldn't help but smile. She indicated the folders in Victoria's arms. "What have you got there?"

"Consent forms and background questionnaires for today's subjects. I've assigned them all randomized identifiers as Dr. Campbell ordered, so we're blinded to diagnosis and history until after we've obtained and reviewed their diagnostic data."

"Perfect. Let me see."

Cristina skimmed the forms after Victoria handed them to her. Her assistant had even organized them numerically and placed colored sticky labels to highlight basic demographics. "This is excellent work," she said, returning the files. "What about the rest of their histories?"

"I created a separate database matched to their identifiers. Once we finished collecting data, we simply have to run a program to cross-match and analyze everything."

"Impressive. It's hard to believe you've only been here for a week."

"I've always been a fast learner." Victoria shuffled the folders without dropping any and hugged them against her chest once more. "I picked up samba when I was four."

"Really? I love samba."

"I heard there's a club in Everett. We should go sometime." Victoria covered her mouth and dropped her gaze. "Sorry, that was presumptuous of me. You're my boss."

Feeling a pang of sympathy, Cristina asked, "Do you know anyone else here in Boston?"

Victoria shook her head.

"Well, I know how it feels to be alone in a new place." The prior day's events replayed in Cristina's head. She suppressed a shudder. "But now's not a great time for me to go out dancing. Raincheck?"

Brightening, Victoria touched her brow in an approximation of a British military salute. "Sure. That'd be great. Um, I'll go file these. Thanks, boss."

After Victoria skittered away, Cristina sat down at her desk. She noticed the photo of Jorge and Claudia was askew. With a sigh, she corrected it and then leaned back in her chair. Yes, she did know about being alone. When she first woke up in the hospital nearly three years ago, she didn't know anyone, not even her own name. She'd built a new life, but now, after losing her best friend and then Wilson, she was again alone.

You'll always have me.

A pit formed in Cristina's stomach. She could never be truly alone, not when she was sharing a brain with Sabrina. But was that a good or bad thing?

At least she had Maria. While going to a club was out of the question, it certainly wouldn't be a bad idea to get out of the house a bit more. And there was someone else she knew, someone who could provide answers she desperately needed.

She picked up the phone and dialed. A moment later, a rough male voice answered. "Hello?"

"Hi Manny. It's Cristina." She wet her lips. "It's been a while."

CHAPTER TWENTY

Detective Wilson rang the doorbell on the two-story brick-faced house and glanced over his shoulder. The Stars and Stripes flapped lazily in the breeze. Neatly trimmed hedges lined the walkway, but the grass needed to be mowed. A shiny black SUV sat in the driveway.

"Nice place," he said to Hawkins.

"Fits with the neighborhood." Hawkins checked his notepad. "Both parents work in the financial district."

Before Wilson could reply, the door swung open. A man in his early forties stood in the entry, staring at them with glazed eyes. His unbuttoned shirt hung loosely from his stocky frame, half-tucked into the kind of jeans one wore when they weren't expecting company. He growled, cheeks reddening. "Didn't you see the No Soliciting sign out front?"

The detectives held up their badges.

"I'm Detective Wilson, Somerville PD. This is Detective Hawkins." Wilson tucked away his badge. "Are you the father of Caleb Jackman?"

"Yeah." The man wrinkled his brow. "I'm Ronald."

"Your wife is expecting us." Wilson tilted his head. "She didn't tell you?"

"Uh, I've been asleep." Ronald rumpled his thin hair. "Did, uh, did you find him? Caleb, I mean."

"No, sir. We came to get more information."

"Oh, right." Ronald stepped aside and motioned for them to enter. "Deborah's in the kitchen. We can go talk there."

The detectives followed him down the hall. Wilson wrinkled his nose at the acerbic cabbage fumes striking his nostrils. A woman at the stove whirled around as the detectives entered.

"Hello, Mrs. Jackman."

"Oh, you must be Detective Wilson. I'm Deborah. Thank you for coming so quickly. Please, have a seat." She motioned to a pair of metal chairs at a small glass table. "I'm making some *kapusta*. It's an old family recipe. I cook when I'm anxious."

As the detectives sat, Wilson surveyed the room. The flowered wallpaper, rustic furniture, and knickknacks lining the shelves reminded Wilson more of his grandmother's room at the retirement home than what he'd expected from the home's outward appearance.

"Would you like something to drink?" Deborah asked, wringing her hands. Her husband leaned against the refrigerator with his arms folded across his chest, appearing bored.

"No, thank you." Wilson pulled out his digital recorder. "Do you mind if I record our conversation?"

Deborah glanced at her husband, who shrugged. She turned back to Wilson and simpered. "Go right ahead."

After starting the recording, Wilson said, "Why don't we start by reviewing what you told me over the phone about your missing son?"

Deborah recounted the details of how she discovered Caleb had been missing and the changes in his behavior before then. Ronald nodded now and then, adding nothing.

When she'd finished, Wilson asked, "Do you have a picture of Caleb?"

"Yes, I got one ready after you mentioned it on the phone." She held out a framed eight-by-ten of a baby-faced teen mugging for the camera. Two of his bottom teeth were crooked. Acne dotted his forehead and chin. "It's a few months old, but it's the most recent we have. Lately, he'd lost interest in taking pictures."

Wilson snapped a shot of the photo with his phone. "Does anyone else live here?"

"Just the three of us."

Wilson kept an eye on Ronald's hands. The man's demeanor made him uneasy. In-home visits often provided important clues to an investigation, but they were riskier than conducting interviews at the station, where he had control over the environment. To Deborah, he asked, "Has your son ever run away before?"

"No, never." Deborah frowned. "Frankly, I don't believe he ran away now."

"Why not?"

"Well, he would never forget to take his medicine. He can't function without it."

Wilson leaned forward. "How long has Caleb been taking dextroamphetamine?"

"Oh, it must be . . ." She glanced again at her husband. "Five years now?"

"Something like that," Ronald said.

"Did he ever have any problems with it? Or seem like he wasn't taking it?"

"He missed a couple of doses here and there." Ronald yawned. "We could tell the difference. He was bouncing off the walls."

"Who's his doctor?" Hawkins asked.

"Rinat Lal."

Wilson tapped his chin. Caleb didn't have the same doctor as Danny Trevino or Eduardo Sanchez. Maybe he'd only hoped there was a connection. "Can I see the pill bottle?"

Deborah opened a kitchen drawer and removed a bottle, which she handed to Wilson. There were nine pills remaining. "Any chance he might've been selling them to friends or classmates?"

"No." Her brow furrowed. "Caleb would never do that."

Wilson exchanged knowing glances with Hawkins. Like many parents, Deborah Jackman saw her teen as the same innocent boy she'd always thought he'd been. If Caleb had been dealing amphetamines and crossed the wrong person, they would've retaliated. He tried another line of questioning, "Do you know of anyone who would want to harm your son?"

"No, no one. Caleb was very popular, at least until two months ago. He was captain of the lacrosse team."

"Then what happened?"

Deborah glanced at Ronald, who looked down at the floor. "We were about to update this house, get rid of all this old-fashioned decor. I mean, don't get me wrong, it allowed us to buy into the Powder House District for a steal, but it's hard to keep up appearances. We never entertain. So we hired a contractor, paid a deposit . . ." She twiddled her fingers. "And then Ronald got fired. We had to cancel the renovation and lost the deposit."

"No one's hiring." Ronald's cheeks reddened. "So we've had to cut back on expenses."

"And we may have said something to Caleb about how important it was that he do well in school." Deborah's thumbs jammed together as if they were at war with each other. "If he got a high enough GPA, he could earn a scholarship and we wouldn't have to worry about his college fund."

"Did that anger him?" Wilson asked.

"Oh, no, he took it to heart." Deborah scrunched up her face. "But that's when he quit the lacrosse team and started studying all the time and disappearing for hours, sometimes a day or two at a time." Her lips twisted. "I guess there is such a thing as too much studying."

"His teammates must've been upset that he quit lacrosse," Hawkins said. "Could one of them have tried to get back at him?"

"No." Deborah touched her lips. "At least, I don't think so."

"Did he ever mention any bullies?" Wilson asked. "Or have any unexplained injuries?"

Again, Deborah glanced at Ronald, who stiffened but continued to stare at the floor. Pressing her lips together, she turned back to the detectives. "No."

A creeping sensation started at the base of Wilson's skull and proceeded down his neck. There was more going on than pressure to perform. "Did Caleb study alone or with a friend?"

"Both."

"Did he have a girlfriend?"

"Nope." Ronald's lip twisted. "He wasn't into girls."

"He came out to us a few months ago," Deborah said. "I tried to be supportive, but Ron . . ." She flashed an angry glance at her husband. "He had more trouble accepting it."

"Don't start, Deborah," Ronald said.

"I can't stay silent anymore." Her lips quivered as she fought back tears. "You screamed at him. And now he's gone."

"Don't blame me. Caleb and I worked things out." Ronald scowled. "If anything, it probably involved that new boyfriend of his."

"New boyfriend?" Wilson asked.

"A boy at another school." Deborah dabbed at her eyes. "Oh, what was his name?"

For the first time, Ronald's eyes met Wilson's, angry sparks flashing beneath heavy lids. "His name's Reggie. Reggie Horne."

CHAPTER TWENTY-ONE

"Cristina . . . Cristina." Manny Feldman's voice had a playful jag to it. The sound of him clucking his tongue carried over the phone. "Do I know a Cristina? No, I'm not sure I do."

"Manny . . ."

"Oh, wait. Is this the Cristina who was supposed to come over for dinner four weeks ago, canceled at the last minute, and then disappeared from the face of the earth?"

Cristina flinched. "I'm sorry, Manny, things have been kind of rough and—"

"Eh, don't sweat it. I'm messin' with ya." Manny chortled. "But is everything okay? Beatrice and I were worried something might've happened to you."

"It's . . ." Cristina considered what to say. Wilson had told her that Manny had been the Silvas' mechanic. In fact, it had been Manny's insistence that Cristina wasn't the same woman he knew that convinced Wilson to believe her story. A few weeks after stopping Quinn, Cristina had found the courage to contact Manny directly in hopes of learning what she could about her namesake. She'd given him the short version of how she'd been given Cristina Silva's identity and how she now had two separate identities warring inside her. To her surprise, he and his wife, Beatrice, treated Cristina and Wilson like their own children, inviting them for summer cookouts and regaling them with stories about the real Cristina Silva. But then when the schism between Cristina's and Sabrina's thoughts again widened and she broke up with Wilson, she'd fallen out of touch with the Feldmans as well. "My . . . condition got worse for a while. I'm still trying to resolve it, and I was thinking you and your wife might be able to help."

"Sure, whatever you need. How about dinner here?"

"That would be wonderful. When?"

"How about tonight?"

"Oh, I wasn't expecting—"

"It's perfect timing. I'm closing the shop early, and Beatrice is making her famous *Accra* fritters. You don't want to miss them."

Cristina grinned. Manny didn't take no for an answer. "All right, but my sister is staying with me for a few days. Is it okay if I bring her?"

"I'd be angry if you didn't. Come by at seven."

Cristina's heart felt lighter as she turned to her computer. Maybe she and Sabrina weren't alone, after all. She sent Maria a text message to be ready for dinner by six-thirty and then prepared to dig into a busy day of research. That evening, her two worlds would finally meet.

CHAPTER TWENTY-TWO

"There he is." Detective Hawkins pointed at the entrance to Somerville Prep, where Reggie Horne was exiting the building, a backpack slung over his shoulder. The teen kept his head low, a hoodie shrouding his face, not talking to the other students as he trudged along the sidewalk. Exhaust smoke billowed around them as teens peeled out in their sports cars. Hawkins turned to Wilson. "What do you think? Should we follow him, see if he leads us to Caleb?"

The hair itched behind Wilson's ear as he watched Reggie ambling toward the parking lot. The Jackmans had said that Caleb dated Reggie for two months before he began acting strangely. Caleb never brought Reggie home to meet them, so they only knew him by name. At least, that was their claim. From the way Ronald Jackman described Reggie and spat his name, Wilson suspected Ronald might've been within striking distance of the teen at least once.

Wilson scratched behind his ear. Earlier that day, Hawkins had told him that, like Danny Trevino and Caleb Jackman, Eduardo Sanchez came from an upper middle-class family, and was being treated with amphetamines for ADHD. Two months before getting hit by a train, Eduardo had dug into his schoolwork and his grades skyrocketed, but he became moody and irritable, like the other two boys.

Now, two were dead and one missing, and all three knew Reggie. What did it mean? Were they part of a suicide pact? Wilson had called Reggie's mom, but she'd only had a few minutes to chat before leaving for work. Mrs. Horne told him her son took no medications and never did. His grades had also improved this year, but unlike the three other teens, Reggie continued to be a happy, easygoing kid. Yet the teen Wilson now watched didn't look happy at all. He hunched over, eyes darting side to side, like someone afraid of being caught.

"No, let's go talk to him," Wilson said, unbuckling his seat belt. "I think we can get through to him."

"I hope you're right."

When the detectives approached and called his name, Reggie jumped, dropping his backpack. He clutched his chest and fell to one knee.

"Are you okay?" Hawkins asked.

Waving frantically, Reggie dug a hand into his pocket.

Hawkins reached for his pistol, but Wilson stopped him. The way the teen was wheezing and gasping, Wilson understood what was happening.

Reggie pulled out an inhaler and took two deep breaths. His chest rose and fell more easily.

"My cousin has asthma," Wilson said, holding out his hand. "When we were kids, he had to use an inhaler all the time. His was triggered by cold."

"Mine's pollen and stress." Reggie used Wilson's hand to pull himself upright. "Sucks when I have to give a speech." His gaze bounced from one detective to the other. "What do you two want? I already told you everything I know about Danny."

"What about Caleb Jackman?"

Reggie stiffened. "Who?"

"Don't start lying now, Reggie. Caleb's parents told us about the two of you."

Avoiding Wilson's gaze, Reggie said, "Fine, what about him?"

"Do you know where he is?"

"No. Why?"

"His parents reported him missing." Hawkins gave the teen a stern look. "It would save everyone a lot of trouble if we knew where to look for him."

Reggie held up his hands. "Really, I don't know."

"So if we get a warrant to search your phone, we won't find text messages from him?"

"Nope."

Wilson bit his inner cheek. The kid's defiant confidence meant he'd already deleted his messages. They could still get them from the telecom provider, but he decided to try a different tactic. "There are two possibilities here: Caleb ran away or someone abducted him. He's in danger in either case."

Reggie squeezed his hands into fists and gazed at the ground.

Making a show of checking to ensure no one was within earshot, Wilson leaned closer to the teen and lowered his voice. "His father didn't like the two of you dating, did he?"

Reggie flinched as if he'd been slapped.

"Did he ever threaten you to stay away?"

Eyes wide, Reggie darted his gaze toward Wilson, but just as quickly looked away.

Wilson asked, "Did he take it out on Caleb?"

The teen continued to study the sidewalk, but this time he nodded.

"Caleb's not in trouble," Wilson said in a soothing tone. "It's not illegal in Massachusetts for a teen his age to run away. And it's not illegal to protect a friend. But it's not safe for him to be out on his own. If you tell us where he is, I promise we'll protect him."

"He didn't tell me where he was going, but there's a few places his parents wouldn't know nothing about."

Wilson jerked his chin at Hawkins, who pulled out his notepad and pen.

Reggie locked his gaze with Wilson's. "You gotta promise me nothing'll happen to him."

The pleading look in Reggie's eyes sent shivers from the nape of Wilson's neck to the holster of his gun. How horrible was Caleb's father to make this kid so afraid? Or was there still something else he wasn't saying, something that connected Caleb to Danny and Eduardo besides their friendship with Reggie Horne and a diagnosis of ADHD? He would've liked to question Reggie further but the clock for finding Caleb was ticking.

Setting his jaw, Wilson said, "Don't worry. He'll be in good hands."

CHAPTER TWENTY-THREE

Manny Feldman's one-story colonial home stood on a quiet Framingham cul-de-sac. The hedges were neatly trimmed, and the smell of fresh-cut grass lingered in the air. Pretty white shutters framed the windows. With Maria beside her, Cristina rang the bell and Manny appeared, wearing a button-down and dress pants.

"Hi, Cristina." He held the door open for the two women. "And you must be Maria. Nice to meet you."

"You, as well," Maria said. "You have a lovely home."

"That's my wife's touch." He grinned and held up his hands. "These are meant for fixing cars, and occasionally tilling a vegetable garden."

Pleasant smells of scallions, Habanero pepper, and frying oil drifted into the hallway lined with family photos. They entered the living room and took seats on a sectional sofa facing a simple brick fireplace.

A woman joined them, wearing a light sweater and jeans that hugged her lithe frame. A warm smile stretched across her face as she extended her arms to Cristina. "*Bonjou, machè*. It's been too long."

"Hello, Beatrice." Cristina hugged her and then indicated Maria. "This is my sister, Maria."

"Welcome to our home." Beatrice brushed off Maria's offer of a handshake and pulled her in for a hug. "It's an honor to meet someone from Cristina's family. Well, Sabrina's." She shook her head. "It truly is confusing, isn't it?"

"Yes, it is," Maria said. "How are you able to keep it straight? You knew the other Cristina Silva, didn't you?"

Beatrice grimaced. "Yes, such a pity. She was a good person, our Cristina. But it's not as difficult as you think. There is a passing resemblance to your sister here, but they really didn't look alike."

"Did you ever find a photo of her?" Cristina asked. To Maria, she explained, "She and their son, Julian, used to date."

"No, we searched for Julian's prom photo," Manny said. "But it must be stored away somewhere. He's been in Sierra Leone with Doctors without Borders for the past three months, so we haven't been able to ask if he knows where it went."

"We'll keep looking," Beatrice said and patted Cristina's hand. "You told Manny you needed our help. What can we do for you?"

Cristina cast her gaze downward, trying to sort out her feelings. This was more difficult than she'd expected. "For the past two years, I've believed I was her, and then I learned I was someone else. Yet even though most of what I remember was fabricated, it feels more real than my real memories—if that makes sense. I'd hoped you and your husband could tell me more about the actual Cristina, so I can sort out in my head what's real and what's not."

"But will hearing our stories make things clearer?" Beatrice asked. "Or make you more confused?"

The question dug under Cristina's skin. She was so good at analyzing others, yet she couldn't see herself clearly. "I'm not sure, but I think I have to try. And hearing your stories with Maria here may trigger some memories about Sabrina that we still haven't been able to recover."

"I'd love to hear some happy stories," Maria said, flashing a warm smile as Manny filled their glasses with wine. "They'll be new to me."

"Oh, we have plenty of stories," Beatrice said. "Manny, tell them about the time Cristina and Julian tried to learn jiu-jitsu."

Manny leaned forward and said, "Get comfortable. This one'll knock you off your feet."

DB crouched outside the colonial house. The on-demand car she'd rented waited a block away. It had been easy enough to follow Dr. Silva there, thanks to the tracker she'd planted on the doctor's Mini Cooper. She peered through the picture window, watching the four people sipping drinks and chatting. From the Feldmans' flabby bodies and the way they positioned themselves in the line of fire, they were clearly civilians, with no combat experience or training. But since Silva rarely left her house other than for work, there had to be something important about this couple.

The woman who arrived with Silva, on the other hand, was a different story. She carried herself like someone who knew how to hold her own in a fight. There was something familiar about her, too, but DB doubted they'd crossed paths. She resembled Silva, especially around the eyes and cheekbones, which meant she was probably a relative. Maybe a sister, though her research showed Cristina Silva didn't have a sister. DB pressed her lips together as she admired the woman's supple frame. She could work with that.

She withdrew the Sig Sauer from her waistband and started searching for a back door or window the owners forgot to close. Once she knew how these people fit into Silva's story, and why her employers wanted her to stay away, she could eliminate the lot of them.

Dama Branca never left loose ends.

CHAPTER TWENTY-FOUR

Wilson and Hawkins drove to an East Somerville neighborhood with run-down buildings and bullet holes in the stop signs, stopping at a dilapidated brick storefront. Faint red letters on a worn-out sign read Golden Goose Bookstore. Its boarded-up windows were covered with graffiti, some declaring Stephen King dead and others insisting he was immortal.

"This is some prime real estate," Wilson said as they exited the Charger and approached the building. "I'm surprised no one's snatched this place up."

"Makes a great hideout for a runaway," Hawkins said.

"Yeah. Too bad we had to check three other hidey-holes first."

Fresh footprints led up to the front door. Hawkins pointed at the lock. It had been broken and repositioned to appear intact.

They both drew their guns.

"Detectives Wilson and Hawkins, Somerville PD," Wilson announced, his entry heralded by creaking floorboards and a lungful of musty air. Dim light filtered in through broken windows. He tried the light switch. Nothing. He switched on his flashlight and panned it around the room. "Caleb Jackman, if you're in here, your friends and family are worried about you. Reggie Horne told us where to find you."

Something scurried behind empty bookcases.

Wilson touched his lips and pointed. They crossed the room, Hawkins moving to the opposite side. They raised their guns before circling the bookcases. A floorboard creaked under Hawkins's feet.

"Leave me alone!" a boy shouted. A hardcover book flew from behind a desk, missing Hawkins's nose by inches. "I can't go back!"

"You're not in trouble, Caleb." Wilson spotted a tuft of dark hair poking up over the desk. "Come on out and we'll go someplace we can talk."

Another book bounced off a wall. "I'm not going anywhere!"

"You don't have to go home." Wilson noted a pile of dirty sheets and pillows on the floor past the desk. "We'll get you somewhere with a clean bathroom."

Caleb sucked in rapid breaths.

"Your mom said you forgot your medication. We can get it from her and—"

"Don't call my parents!" A stapler exploded at Wilson's feet. "I don't want them to see me like this."

"Okay, we won't," Wilson said. They could easily rush the teen but there was the chance he wasn't alone. If they wanted answers, they needed to coax him out gently. "Caleb?"

"Did you take care of him?" Caleb asked in hushed tones. "Is he gone?"

Wilson frowned. "Your father? If he hurt you—"

"No, not him." Caleb took ragged breaths and then whispered, "Sack Man."

The name hit Wilson like a punch to the gut. He evened his breath. "Who is Sack Man?"

"Who is . . . ? Oh, no. No, no, no." Caleb slapped his hand against the desk. "You didn't get rid of him? Oh, shit. He's still out there. Oh, shit. Oh, shit."

Wilson scanned the store again, then started toward the desk. "Caleb, I'm coming in. I need you to—"

Caleb popped out from behind the desk and dashed between the detectives, shoving Wilson out of the way as he raced for the door.

"Stop!" Wilson chased after him and caught the teen's shoulder.

Caleb spun around and punched at Wilson's chest.

Wilson grabbed his wrist and twisted it behind Caleb's back.

"Let me go!" The teen fought but it was no use. Wilson had him pinned. "Sack Man can't know that you found me."

"Who? Who is Sack Man?"

"I can't tell you. He'll kill me." Caleb twisted his shoulder forward, trying to wrench his arm free of Wilson's grip. "He said he'd kill my parents if I tried to leave or called the cops."

"Stop fighting." Wilson tightened his hold.

"It's over." Hawkins moved to block the door. "You need to come with us."

"You'll keep my family safe?" Caleb asked, tears rolling down his cheeks.

"Yes."

"All right. But keep Sack Man away from me."

Wilson released Caleb's wrist. "We will, but you need to tell us everything you know about him."

Caleb's body coiled. He eyed the door.

"Running won't help." Wilson gave a stern look. "If there's someone threatening you, we need to stop him, before he hurts anyone else."

"Okay." Caleb bit his knuckle. "I'll tell you everything, but you gotta get me outta here. He could be back any minute."

"Wait." Hawkins held up one hand. "Was he here recently?"

"No, but he comes at night. He—"

Gravel crunched outside.

"It's him!" Caleb broke free and dashed to the back of the store. "Don't let him bite my neck."

"I'll check it out," Hawkins offered.

Wilson found Caleb cowering under the desk, rocking and covering his head with his hands. A purplish bruise blossomed on his shoulder. Wilson could make out a smaller lesion on the boy's cheek.

"It's okay," Wilson said. "No one's going to hurt you. Let us get you out of here."

Caleb stopped rocking and squinted up at Wilson. "You promise?"

Wilson nodded.

As Caleb stood, Wilson spotted a plastic baggie on the ground. Inside was half of a white tablet. "What's that?"

"My ADHD meds."

"You mother said you left them at home."

Caleb shrugged. "I took a few pills with me."

"Uh-huh." Wilson pocketed the baggie. Maybe the kid was telling the truth, but maybe he wasn't. They could sort it out back at the precinct.

The floorboards creaked.

Wilson drew his gun.

"It's me," Hawkins called out. "Noise was a stray cat. No sign anyone else was here."

"Let's go." They escorted Caleb to Wilson's car. After securing the teen in the back seat and shutting the door, Wilson said to Hawkins, "Call the precinct and tell them to get the Department of Children and Families to meet us there. Suspected child abuse."

CHAPTER TWENTY-FIVE

"The sensei said, 'You can't wear your shoes on the mat,'" Manny said, chortling. "And that's when Cristina asked, 'What do you mean? I already did!'"

Maria and Beatrice broke into caterwauling laughter. Cristina forced a smile, trying to appreciate the anecdote, but she realized Beatrice had been right. Even though the names were familiar, the story felt foreign, like picturing her life in a funhouse mirror. Only not so fun. She nibbled an Accra fritter and glanced around at the photos of Manny, Beatrice, and their son. A deep ache spread through her chest. All Cristina had was the portrait of Jorge and Claudia Silva and a handful of childhood photos Maria had given her.

"You said you were putting things into storage?" Cristina asked. "Why?"

"To better organize the house," Beatrice said. "We're thinking of moving."

Cristina's glass slipped in her hand. "Moving? Where?"

"We don't know yet. Maybe back to Haiti. Jacmel is quite lovely." Beatrice took a sip of her wine. "Or perhaps another island."

"But why?"

Manny held Beatrice's hand. "I've long promised Beatrice we would go see her family, but now, with these new immigration policies . . ."

"They may not let us back in." Beatrice's cheeks sagged. "And any-time a neighbor dislikes the way we mow our lawn, they threaten to call ICE."

"I've heard this from friends who moved back to Brazil in recent years." Maria set down her empty plate and turned to Cristina. "Even those who got their US citizenship fear deportation. Perhaps you should reconsider my invitation to come back with me. We desperately need more psychiatrists."

It would be a relief, Cristina thought, to move far away from all the madness of the past year. She and Maria could search for their family connections together. It would be a fresh start.

We already got one of those. Look how that turned out.

Cristina shivered. Leave it to Sabrina to jolt her back to reality. "I can't pick up and relocate to another country—even if, technically, I'd be returning home. Aside from Maria, there's nothing left there for me, and my life is here. I started this new job, and I have my apartment—"

"And you have Detective Wilson, right?"

All three women turned to stare at Manny.

His cheeks reddened. "Did I say something wrong?"

Shaking her head, Cristina said, "Gary and I broke up. It was too much for him, trying to deal with my baggage."

"I told you not to bring it up unless she did," Beatrice whispered to Manny, but not softly enough.

"Are you sure it was too much for *him*?" Maria asked, brow fur-rowed. "Wilson seemed like he could handle a lot. And I saw the way he looked at you."

Cristina's ears burned. "What are you saying?"

"*Meu amor.*" Maria patted Cristina's hand. "I've known you for most of your life. No matter what name you call yourself, some things never change. It's always been hard for you to fully accept someone into your heart. And the last time you did, he betrayed you."

The burning sensation faded, replaced by a prickling on her skin as she pictured Quinn's face, recalling how many times he fooled her, luring her into his web. Did Quinn's betrayal taint her relationship with

Wilson? Was she so jaded that she saw only the harm he might cause her? Maybe Maria was right, and Wilson wasn't the one who couldn't handle her baggage.

"Well, that ship has sailed." Cristina lifted her glass and downed the wine in one long gulp. "It's time to move on."

After a moment of awkward silence, Cristina realized Maria was watching her, a tiny smile teasing her lips. "What?"

"Nothing. It's . . ." Maria glanced at the Feldmans and her smile broadened. "When I spoke to Wilson last week to find out where you kept your spare key, he didn't sound like someone who had moved on."

Something stirred deep inside Cristina. "He didn't?"

Maria shook her head.

Cristina's heart thrummed inside her chest.

"Look at you," Beatrice said. "You're practically glowing."

"Well, what do you know?" Manny tossed back his wine and grinned. "Looks like you learned something useful tonight, after all."

DB knelt in the hallway shadows with the Sig Sauer pressed against her cheek. After listening to their conversation for the last ten minutes, she'd learned nothing useful, only nonsense about men and immigration.

As she watched the man sip his drink, however, she felt a sense of familiarity. The way he talked with his hands. The way he scratched his cheek when he laughed.

She rubbed the heel of her hand against her forehead. That was impossible. She knew no one in Framingham, had never been there before today.

But then, as the aroma of the fried snack they were eating wafted into her nose, her mind shifted to another time, another perspective. She saw herself sitting on that couch, chatting with the couple, nibbling on a fritter. A young man sat at her side, the same one in the photographs hung on the hallway walls. He grinned at her, rested his palm on her thigh, sending a pleasant tingle to her core.

Anger bubbled under her skin. This had to stop. She cast away the vision.

She drew in deep breaths, willing herself to regain control. An assassin didn't allow emotions to overcome her. Whether real or imagined, her connection to these people was eroding her confidence, affecting her ability to do her job. That meant she only had one option. She needed to erase them, like her memories.

Gripping the P226, she assessed the layout of the living room. The older couple were easy targets. The one who looked to be Dr. Silva's sister could be more of a threat. The most dangerous was Silva, as DB had learned the other day at the park.

But DB still needed Silva alive, to answer questions. She calculated her trajectories. With one good leap, she could incapacitate Silva, take out the sister, and then kill the other two. She reared back on her haunches, like a panther about to strike.

She clenched her jaw. It didn't feel right.

Why was the man so familiar? Silva was more than she seemed. Perhaps the same was true for this seemingly innocuous dinner party.

DB cast one more glance at the quartet, who were now laughing and eating their fritters. She resolved to learn everything she could about Cristina Silva, starting with those who were close to her, and she slipped out the back door.

CHAPTER TWENTY-SIX

In the interview room, Wilson set a bottle of water in front of Caleb Jackman and took a seat across from him. The boy had calmed down on the ride back to the precinct, but his gaze still darted side to side. His hand shook as he lifted the bottle to his lips, making the bruise on his arm more visible.

"A caseworker is talking with your parents." Wilson watched Caleb guzzle the water. "They said it was okay if I ask you some questions in the meantime."

Caleb wiped his mouth with his sleeve. "Okay."

Wilson tapped his finger on the table. He didn't want to interfere with a child abuse investigation, but he needed to know if this situation connected to his other case. He pointed at Caleb's shoulder. "Where did you get that bruise?"

The teen's brow furrowed as he looked down at his shoulder. "I don't remember."

"Caleb, I told you, you're not in trouble. You can tell me the truth."

"I'm not lying. I'm having trouble remembering a lot of stuff."

Wilson clenched his jaw as he glanced at the camera on the wall. It was a bad idea to ask leading questions, especially with kids, but he didn't have much choice if Caleb was going to play dumb. He leaned forward and said, "Tell me about Sack Man."

Caleb's eyes widened. "How do you know about him?"

"You told us. Back at the bookstore."

"Oh. Right." The teen's lips turned white as he pressed them together. His eyes grew damp. "He's a monster. I didn't want anything to do with him, but no matter where I hid, he found me."

The back of Wilson's neck prickled. "Can you describe him?"

Caleb scrunched up his face in thought and then shook his head. "He wears a black hood, and all I could see were his eyes. Evil dead eyes. He told me I had to do what he said, or he would hurt me and then kill me. I believed him because he said he killed Danny."

A jolt ran through Wilson's chest. "Danny Trevino?"

Caleb nodded.

"Your mom said you met Danny at summer camp."

"She did?" Caleb stared at the table as if the answers were scrawled there among the graffiti. "I guess she's right. I don't remember. But we met again through Reggie. We all hung out together a few times."

"What did you do together?"

"Just . . . stuff."

Wilson laid the plastic baggie containing half a white tablet on the table. "Stuff like this?"

Caleb stared at the pill, shoulders tensing.

"Even generic amphetamines have specific markings on it. This doesn't." Wilson pointed at the tablet. "So do you want to tell me what this is?"

"It's not what you think."

"Try me."

Caleb swallowed. "It's supposed to improve memory. It's called RAM Boost."

"Where did you get it?"

"There's this shop over in Assembly Square. They sell all kinds of supplements and vitamins." The water bottle crunched as Caleb squeezed it. "The woman who owns it promised it would help me ace my exams."

"What's this woman's name?"

"I don't . . ." Caleb shut his eyes tight and tapped on his forehead. "Dr. Wakefield. I think."

Wilson jotted down the name. "Was Danny Trevino taking RAM Boost?"

Caleb nodded.

"What about Eduardo Sanchez?"

The color drained from Caleb's face. "You know about him too?"

Wilson said nothing.

"Yeah, Eddie took it too."

Lifting the baggie up, Wilson asked, "So what happened when you took this?"

"It worked like she said. We could remember anything we read or heard." Caleb lowered his chin. "But then Eddie started acting weird."

"Weird how?"

"He got angry all the time, and said he remembered the pain of being born. He thought he was being followed. Hunted. The last thing he said to us before he died was that Sack Man was coming for him." Caleb shivered. "Then Danny called me a week ago. He said he'd lost control at school, and he was afraid Sack Man was going to get him. He tried to get away, but . . ." He trailed off, casting his gaze down at the table, his lower lip trembling.

Wilson shook his head. He'd been right that the three cases were connected. Eduardo's and Danny's deaths and Caleb's disappearance. His initial suspicion of drugs had been close to the target, but not the way he expected. "Did you actually see Sack Man kill Eddie or Danny?"

"No."

"Is Sack Man real?"

"I don't know." Caleb's forehead creased with deep lines.

"Why did you say not to let him bite your neck?"

"Because that's what Sack Man does. He eats naughty children."

The hair lifted on the back of Wilson's neck. "What else can you tell me about him?"

Caleb gazed off into the distance, his lips moving but no sound coming out.

"Caleb?"

"I'm trying to remember the past three days, but I can't. There are bits and pieces, little flashes, but I don't even remember leaving my house."

"Is it because you stopped taking this?" Wilson indicated the baggie.

"No, I was still taking it. I think." Caleb massaged his forehead. "I don't know. There's . . . holes in my memory."

Wilson's cheeks cooled. "What kind of holes?"

"It's like there's a rodent inside, eating away at my brain. Like, I can't remember how old I am, or my address, or . . ." He stared at Wilson with a faraway look. "What was the question?"

Realizing he'd get nothing more out of the boy, Wilson took the baggie and left the interview room. He found Hawkins in the recording room.

"You got all that?" he asked.

"Yeah, let's look into this Dr. Wakefield." Hawkins jerked his chin at the video monitor, where Caleb sat, head down. "What was all that about his memory?"

"I don't know. It could have something to do these pills, or he could've been making it up, so I'd stop questioning him."

"I'll tell DCF they should get a good medical exam on him. Maybe a psych exam too. What about this Sack Man? Think it's bullshit?"

"No, he believes what he said, but I'm not sure what to make of it. Either Sack Man is a drug-fueled hallucination pulled from his nightmares of the boogeyman"—Wilson twisted the tablet inside the baggie—"or someone out there is killing these kids."

CHAPTER TWENTY-SEVEN

The next day Cristina dove into her work at the Memory Center, hoping to distract herself from renewed thoughts of Gary Wilson. Yet, as she scribbled notes about her first subject for the day, a retired cop with Alzheimer's, she found her mind drifting to a harbor dinner cruise she once took with Wilson. As the sun sank into the sea, setting the sky ablaze with color, she'd told him about the mistakes Sabrina had made by trusting Quinn. Wilson held her hand and listened, never once judging. The memory faded into twilight, leaving her chest hollow. How had she let their connection slip away?

Her pen ripped a hole in her notepad. She laid down the pen and rubbed her temples.

When their relationship had started getting serious, she felt Wilson could've been *the One*. When she and Sabrina started dissociating again, she knew eventually it would be too much for him, but he would never abandon her. Gary Wilson was a man of his word, and if he promised to stand by her for better and for worse, he would, even if she descended into madness. She couldn't do that to him. He didn't deserve it, after all he'd already done for her.

And so, she'd ended it. She'd convinced herself it was the best for them both, and that he'd move on. But from what Maria had said, he hadn't gotten over her.

And the truth was, she wasn't over him either.

"Dr. Silva?" Victoria asked through the open door to Cristina's office. She was carrying another stack of folders. "Are you okay?"

Not wanting to put her frustration on display in front of her assistant, Cristina sat up straight and rearranged her expression into something that appeared more determined. "Yes, I'm fine, thank you. Are those the afternoon cases?"

"Yes, I was about to start setting up the EEG lab."

"You can leave them here. I'll take care of them."

"Are you sure? Dr. Campbell wants to do neuroimaging on all of them after we collect the brainwave data, and he wants it all done before close of business."

"Don't worry. I'll handle it as soon as I finish writing these observation notes."

"Okay." Victoria laid the folders on Cristina's desk. She turned to go, stopped, and looked back over her shoulder. "Listen, if you ever want to talk, I'm happy to lend an ear. Whenever I'm lost in this labyrinth of life, a friend is what I need to guide me out of it."

Cristina nodded. "Thank you. I'll keep that in mind."

After Victoria left, Cristina scoffed at herself. Even her research assistant better understood what she needed than she herself did. There were only a handful of people who knew about her dual identity, and one of them always managed to provide unique insight. It had been too long since Cristina talked to her.

She picked up the phone and dialed.

Three rings later, a familiar female voice answered: "DigiFend Security and Investigations, my name is Devi Patel. How can I help you today?"

"Devi, it's me."

Pause. "Cristina? It's so good to hear your voice. I heard you found a new job."

"Yes, as did you. I'd love to hear about it." Cristina smiled. "How about lunch?"

CHAPTER TWENTY-EIGHT

The MBTA Orange Line rattled past as Detectives Wilson and Hawkins pulled into the parking lot next to a Nissan Pathfinder. Across the way, pedestrians hurried to the high-end Assembly Row, whereas on this side of the street the detectives were greeted by a café, a smoke shop, and a storefront.

"You sure this is where Caleb said he got the pills?" Wilson asked, studying the colorful sign that read NatureBoost Vitamin Shoppe in bright yellow letters. Pyramids of bottles were displayed below a few hand-printed posters announcing: 20% Off Sale! A wicker chair sat in front of the open door. "Looks like a place my grandmother would've gone to get her knitting supplies."

"It's the only vitamin shop in Assembly Square." Hawkins checked his notes. "And it's owned by Allison Wakefield, Doctor of Pharmacy."

Wilson considered their plan as he surveyed the shop. DCF's take had been that Caleb was abused by his father and that trauma caused him to believe Sack Man was real and trying to kill him. They'd placed him in protective custody with a plan to start him in counseling the next day. The story made sense—except for the fact Eduardo Sanchez and Danny Trevino also said they'd seen the Sack Man. It had to be more than a childhood fear. And then there was the RAM Boost.

Wilson had turned the pill over to the crime lab for analysis, but that analysis would take a day or two. The skin behind his ear itched. At least a few of the answers they sought had to lie inside the vitamin shop. He was sure of it.

As they entered the shop, an electronic chime melody sounded overhead. Odors of incense and lavender assaulted his nostrils.

A woman with dark hair tied in a ponytail emerged from a doorway at the back of the store. She wore a white lab coat emblazoned with the words Allison Wakefield, PhD, ND. "May I help you?"

The detectives flashed their badges. "Detective Wilson. This is Detective Hawkins. Somerville PD. We'd like to ask you some questions."

Dr. Wakefield's smile faded. "I don't understand. My permits are all in order."

"No, ma'am. We need to ask you about Caleb Jackman."

"Who?"

"He says he obtained a supplement from you that would help improve his memory recall." Wilson gave her a pointed look. "RAM Boost."

Her face twisted into a full-on scowl. "I certainly never gave it that name."

"But you know what we mean."

"Yes, of course, but it's only a mild nootropic."

Hawkins wrinkled his nose. "A what?"

"Nootropic. Anything that affects cognition, whether a supplement or a prescribed drug, is a nootropic. Even caffeine. My supplement, MCH-21, is as harmless as a cup of coffee."

Wilson took an immediate dislike to her tone. "So why would anyone buy it?"

Her eyes flashed, but her voice stayed cool. "I said it was harmless. I didn't say it doesn't work. Four out of five of my clients report significant improvement in both short- and long-term recall."

"That sounds pretty effective. Where can I order some?"

"You can't. I make it right here."

Wilson cocked his head. "You create *and* sell your supplements?"

"I used to work for Big Pharma, but I like the idea of being my own boss." She arched an eyebrow. "Why the interest in MCH-21? Are you having memory problems?"

"My memory's fine, and I'm hoping yours is, too, so you can answer our questions. Let's start with how this drug works."

"It inhibits melanin-concentrating hormone neurons." When the detectives stared at her blankly, she held her hands out like she was typing on a keyboard. "You only have so much data storage on your computer. Every so often, you must delete files you no longer need so you can make room for new ones. Do that enough, and the storage space becomes fragmented and less efficient. You follow?"

The detectives nodded.

"Your brain works the same way. MCH neurons clear out data while we sleep. Sometimes the data isn't important, but sometimes it is, and remaining memory fragments lead to confusion, poor concentration, or emotional instability." She folded her fingers into a fist. "This drug turns off those neurons, so the data remains. Whatever you learn, you continue to retain."

"Like photographic memory?" Wilson asked.

"There's no such thing." Wakefield sniffed. "But this is one step closer than our biologic limits allow."

"Wouldn't messing with those neurons cause side effects?"

"Yes, if not done carefully. But the human brain is quite adaptable. And when I say my clients report improvement, I don't mean they're suddenly able to memorize everything on Wikipedia. The effects are mild." She crossed her arms. "You still haven't said why you're interested in my supplement."

"Two teens believed to have died by suicide were taking your supplement," Hawkins said. "A third ran away from home, claiming he'd been abducted by the boogeyman."

Wakefield's eyes widened and then she shook her head. "That's impossible. First of all, I don't sell my supplements to minors. And second, MCH-21 doesn't cause suicidal behavior."

"How do you know it's safe?" Hawkins asked.

"Because I have a grant from the National Center for Comprehensive and Integrative Health to run safety trials, and there have been zero toxic effects. Like I said, it's safer than a cup of coffee."

Recalling his conversations with Mrs. Trevino and the Jackmans, Wilson said, "From what I understand, these kids had massive memory boosts right before they began experiencing mood swings and became socially withdrawn."

Wakefield shrugged. "Perhaps they were simply being teenagers."

The detectives stared at her.

"Well, it wasn't from MCH-21," she said. "As I said, I don't sell to minors."

"So if we review your sales records," Hawkins said, "we won't find entries for Caleb Jackman, Danny Trevino, or Eduardo Sanchez?"

She typed on her computer. After a few minutes, she shook her head. "None of those names are in my system. If they were taking MCH-21, they didn't get it from me."

"Any idea how they could've gotten it?"

She rubbed her lip and stared at the counter, then made eye contact with each detective in turn. "A few months ago, someone broke into my lab and stole a third of my supply."

"Did you report it?" Wilson asked.

"Of course. The police located a suspect but couldn't find enough evidence to make the charges stick."

"Do you remember the suspect's name?"

"Hold on, it'll come to me." She massaged her forehead, then looked up and snapped her fingers. "I remember. Reggie. Reggie Horne."

CHAPTER TWENTY-NINE

The midday summer sun beat down on Cristina as she stepped out of her Mini Cooper onto the sidewalk. Fenway was only a few blocks from her office, but with thoughts of the assault near the hospital still lingering in her mind, she decided not to take any chances.

Cristina adjusted her skirt and headed inside the restaurant. The sounds of twangy bouzoukis and chittering tambourines assaulted her as soon as she stepped inside. Smells of paprika, olive, and meat hung heavily in the air. As she approached the check-in desk, she could hear people shouting and laughing over clinking plates and silverware.

A thin woman with blond hair tied back into a ponytail, who couldn't have been older than nineteen, smiled as she approached. "Welcome to Athena's. Do you have a reservation?"

"Uh, yes, I'm meeting someone." Cristina gave her Devi's name.

"She's waiting for you. Please follow me."

Cristina followed the hostess through a sea of round tables covered in blue-and-white-checkered tablecloths. Nearly every table was full. Azure flags hung from the ceiling, framed with grapevines. Waiters danced from table to table carrying trays loaded with souvlaki and gyros.

A woman waved from a booth in the back corner. The hostess led Cristina there, handed her a menu, and then left. As Cristina slid into the booth, a wave of nostalgia washed over her. Devi Patel had been the office manager for Cristina's private psychiatry practice—well, until Cristina learned Devi had been hired by a rogue Zero Dark mercenary to spy on Cristina. But in truth, Devi was one of the few people Cristina trusted. Having to let her go had been harder on Cristina than selling the practice, but it didn't surprise her that Devi's computer skills helped her quickly find a new job.

"You cut your hair," Cristina said as she settled into her seat, pointing out Devi's short bob hairstyle. "I like it. It nicely frames your face."

"Thank you." Devi smiled. "It's good to see you. It was a nice surprise when you called."

"I should've called sooner."

"No worries." Devi waved her hand. "After what you suffered, I wouldn't blame you if you never wanted to see me or anyone else from that part of your life again."

A waitress sashayed over, laid a bowl of hummus and a plate of pita wedges on the table, and then traipsed away.

"I ordered an appetizer for us," Devi said. "Dig in."

"Thank you. I love hummus." Cristina plucked a pita wedge off the plate and dolloped the chickpea mixture onto it. "It smells delicious."

"Athena's is the best in town."

Cristina savored the hummus as it rolled over her palate. "Yum. I agree. And you're right. For a while, I did want to distance myself from everything that happened last winter, but that's not really possible, is it?"

Devi nibbled on a pita wedge and said, "To control the mind is like trying to control a drunken monkey that's been bitten by a scorpion."

Cristina boggled at her.

"It's a Hindu proverb. It means we can't control where our thoughts will lead, especially when they've been scattered or traumatized. You can try to shut out the past, but eventually it either sneaks in or stumbles past your defenses."

"When did you become so self-reflective?"

Devi shrugged and scooped some more hummus. "I've taken up meditation."

"I could've used some of that insight when I was still seeing patients." Cristina slumped against the back cushion, recalling a lunch conversation at another restaurant months earlier. On that occasion, Devi had provided insight into Cristina's relationships that proved invaluable. "Actually, that's why I wanted to see you. I was hoping you could help me with something."

"I'm in your debt, Cristina. Your testimony kept me from serving time in prison for obstructing a federal investigation. And even if that weren't true, you were always kind to me. Whatever you ask, I'm happy to do it."

Cristina took a sip of water. The sound of the glass clunking against the table as she set it down somehow seemed louder than the din of the restaurant. "I'm starting to think I made a mistake."

"You mean closing the practice?"

"No, that was the right thing to do." Cristina brushed her hair out of her eyes. "I mean breaking up with Wilson."

"You two broke up?"

The family at the next table turned their heads to stare at them.

Devi waved sheepishly. When the people returned to their own conversation, Devi said in a lower voice, "What happened? You two were like Rose and Jack."

Cristina grimaced. "The ship sank, and Jack drowned."

"*Oops*. Bad analogy. But you know what I mean."

"Yes, I felt the same way until my condition worsened." Cristina updated Devi on how trying to integrate with Sabrina only grew a bigger rift between them. "I thought I was doing him a favor by freeing him of my tangled life. But Maria thinks Wilson isn't over me, and I'm starting to realize I'm not over him either."

"Are you ready to order, ladies?" The waiter, a young man with dark hair and a thin mustache, stood at attention next to the table.

"Uh, I'm sorry," Cristina said, fumbling with the menu. "We were so busy talking I forgot to make a decision."

"Two orders of chicken souvlaki, extra tzatziki, and two vissinadas," Devi said and handed her menu to the waiter. "And a side of Greek potatoes, please."

The waiter bowed and scurried off.

"I hope you don't mind my ordering," Devi said. "I thought you could use one less decision right now."

"No, really, thank you."

Devi leaned closer and said in a low voice, "Do you remember I once told you to stop listening to your head so much and to listen to your heart?"

Cristina nodded.

"Well, now you have double the reason. You've got two sets of thoughts in your head, and they're different enough you're bound to get conflicting answers to your question." Devi locked her gaze with Cristina's "So don't listen to either one. Instead, ask your heart: How do you feel about Wilson?"

The question hung in the air long enough Cristina felt like she could hold it in her palm. She searched inside herself and at last said, "When I'm with him, I feel complete, like the two halves of my life come together and there's no Sabrina and Cristina. Only me."

Devi steepled her palms together. "You have a complicated life, Cristina. There's no denying that. But there isn't a tree in the world that the wind hasn't shaken."

Cristina puzzled over that. "Another proverb?"

"No one can escape adversity. There will always be challenges." Devi tapped her forefingers together. "The question you must ask is do you wish to face them alone?"

Before Cristina could answer, the waiter appeared and placed a plate of chicken skewers and vegetables in front of her. A heady mix of enticing aromas wafted into Cristina's nose, but she was too focused on her friend's question to eat.

"Maybe you should've been the counselor instead of me," Cristina said as Devi dug into her food. "Or, at least had an advice column."

"You mean, like *Dear Devi*?" Devi speared a chicken chunk with her fork. "Perhaps, but it's like that peacock over there."

Cristina followed Devi's gaze to a painting on the wall of a colorful peacock.

"That's a pointillist painting," Devi said. "It's made of thousands of tiny dots. Up close, all you see are amorphous blobs. It's meaningless. But for someone outside, who can see the whole picture, it makes sense."

"So, you're saying I'm in too deep to see my own situation as it really is."

Devi shrugged and sipped her sour cherry drink.

It made sense. She understood now what she had to do. As she picked up a chicken skewer, she said, "Thank you, Devi. Again."

"I still owe you." Devi dabbed at her lips with a napkin and smiled. "Anytime you need help, give me a call."

CHAPTER THIRTY

"Man, I don't know what you're talking about," Reggie Horne said, his voice arcing upward in pitch. He dug his fingers into the wooden table in the Somerville PD's interview room. "Who's Allison Wakefield?"

Wilson shook his head as he sat across from Reggie. "I like you, Reggie, because you're honest with me. If you lie to me, it'll break my heart. But if you lie to a jury, that's big-time trouble. My partner's digging up the police report on the NatureBoost Vitamin Shoppe theft, and I already know your name's going to be in it."

Reggie puckered his lips and studied the tabletop, then threw up his hands. "All right, yeah, they tried to pin that on me, but I had nothing to do with it. I swear."

"So why did they suspect you did?"

"I went to the shop a couple of times, trying to buy something that would give me an edge when it came time for exams. Danny and I both had a chance at valedictorian. If I got it, I'd be a sure bet for a scholarship."

Wilson cocked his head. "That sounds like motive."

Reggie's eyes widened. "Jesus, I wanted that scholarship, but I wouldn't do anything to Danny over it. He was my friend."

Wilson waited to see if Reggie would crack or change his story, but he didn't. He looked scared, but not guilty. "All right, I believe you. Tell me what happened when you went to the vitamin shop."

"That bitch wouldn't sell anything to me." He glowered. "She said she didn't sell to minors, but I hung outside her store a couple of times and saw Penny Finkelstein and Thomas Murphy walk out with full shopping bags. They're both a year younger than me."

"Did anyone see you loitering around the store?"

"Yeah." Reggie flicked his finger against the table. "Maybe."

Wilson sucked between his teeth. He wanted to ask the kid straight out if he stole the pills, but that would shift the interview to an interrogation, giving the kid the chance to lawyer up or shut up. "Let's assume you didn't steal those pills. How did Caleb and the others get hold of them?"

"Danny got them, but he never told us where."

"Do you think he stole them?"

"No."

"But you know who did."

Reggie flinched but remained silent.

"Look, you don't have to answer. You're not under arrest." Wilson steepled his hands. "But if you know something, anything, that could help us learn what happened to Danny and Eduardo, now would be the time to tell me."

Reggie traced his fingertip over the wood grain. "You're not gonna believe me."

"Try me."

"It's the same thing I told the cop who arrested me. I went back to the store after they closed. I was going to tag her store with some quotes by Ta-Nehisi Coates. Knowledge is power, you know?" His lips twisted. "But I got as far as the parking lot before I chickened out. As I started to leave, I saw someone sneaking into the store. A man."

"What did he look like?"

"He was kinda big. Around your height, but a little bulkier."

"What about his face?"

"I don't know. He was wearing a black hood."

Wilson's mouth went dry. "A black hood?"

"Yeah."

"What did he do once inside?"

"I didn't stick around to find out. The next day the police came. I tried to tell them what I saw, but they didn't believe me." The teen's eyes welled with tears. "No one did. Even my mom thought I was making it up."

"Well, I believe you. Did you ever see this man again after that night?"

"No, but before he . . . died"—Reggie sniffled—"Danny told me he saw someone following him home from school. A man in a black hood. He called him Sack Man."

Wilson clenched his jaw. "You told me before you didn't know anything about Sack Man."

Reggie wiped his nose on his sleeve. "I know."

"Are you still taking RAM Boost?"

"Me? No, I mean, I took it a few times, but it didn't do much. I retained some facts but not like what it did to the others. They became living computers. Rattling off historical trivia. Reciting complex mathematical formulas. You name it."

"And then what happened?"

"One day, Danny and Eduardo started getting mean. They thought they knew everything. And they kinda did." Reggie kicked the table leg. "But they blew up anytime someone challenged them, jumped at every sound, and insisted someone or something was after them."

"Sack Man."

He nodded.

"What about Caleb?"

"He was dealing with other things, his dad most of all. I tried to help him, even offered to confront his dad, and make him listen to reason. But then Caleb started getting angry at me, screaming that it was all my fault, that he was bad, and Sack Man was going to punish him." Reggie lowered his head. "And then he ran off."

Wilson sat quietly reflecting on this information before asking, "Did you experience anything like what the others did? The anger or paranoia?"

"No, but since everyone thought Danny and Eduardo had been

lying about Sack Man or going crazy, I was afraid the same thing would happen to Caleb—or me if I told anyone about the guy in the black hood. So I kept it to myself." Reggie's lower lip trembled. "I should've said something. About Caleb's dad and about Sack Man. If anything happened to Caleb, I don't know what I'd do."

"He's safe now. No one's going to hurt him."

"Are you sure?"

Recalling Caleb's state of fear and confusion, Wilson suppressed a shiver. "I'll check on him. You're free to leave, but if you think of anything else, call me."

When Wilson got back to his desk, Hawkins looked up from a case file. "Hey, you should see this."

"Just a minute."

Wilson picked up the phone and dialed.

A voice on the other line said, "*Department of Children and Families.*"

"This is Detective Gary Wilson, Somerville PD. I need to speak to the investigator handling the case for Caleb Jackman, the teen brought in last night."

After waiting on hold for two minutes, he heard a female voice say, "Detective, I'm Sarah Watson."

"I wanted to see how Caleb's doing. He was pretty disoriented."

"Well, your guess is as good as mine."

His stomach clenched. "What do you mean?"

"I was just about to call you. Caleb went missing sometime this morning."

CHAPTER THIRTY-ONE

After finishing lunch and leaving the restaurant, Cristina offered her friend a ride home, but Devi preferred to walk as she worked only three blocks away. They hugged each other and then Devi strolled away as Cristina headed to her car. Her bright mood darkened as she noticed someone had parked a black motorcycle much too close to her Mini Cooper, making it difficult for her to maneuver out of the parking space. She looked around for the bike's owner, but no one seemed to be paying it or her any attention. The bike was much bigger than the e-scooter ridden by the assailant from the alley and looked expensive, with sleek lines and curves, twin exhausts, and charcoal-colored rims.

It's a Harley-Davidson Fat Boy. Sabrina's inner voice carried a tone of awe and respect. *Looks like the 30th Anniversary Limited Edition. It's got a Milwaukee-Eight 114 engine with tons of torque. I've always wanted to ride one of those.*

Cristina rolled her eyes, still unable to believe Sabrina was a motorcycle junkie, while Cristina could barely ride on the back of one without shutting her eyes. Just another mystery of her messed-up brain.

"We have to get back to work," she said under her breath, as she climbed into the Mini Cooper. "If we can go the rest of the week without being attacked again, we can go to the bike show this weekend."

When she returned to the Memory Center and headed to the elevator, she heard someone yelling upstairs. She glanced at the receptionist, who returned with a look that said: *You don't want to go up there.*

Summoning her courage, Cristina took the elevator up to her floor and stepped off to find Dr. Campbell waiting outside her office with his arms crossed and his face twisted into a scowl.

"Where have you been?" Dr. Campbell said as Cristina approached.

"I was having lunch with a friend." Cristina checked her watch. "It's still five minutes to one. I'm supposed to have an hour break."

"That's assuming you've completed all your morning work." Dr. Campbell glowered at her. "Like setting up the EEG lab for the afternoon cases."

Cristina's heart sank. In her haste to meet with Devi and her jumbled thoughts about Wilson, she'd completely forgotten about the case files Victoria left on her desk. "I—I didn't—"

"Do you have any idea how important it is to stick to our timeline?" His voice rose to a near-shriek. "I promised our investors we would have data for them by the end of the month. If they pull out, I may have to shut down the Mnemosyne project, and that would be very bad for all of us."

She dug her nails into her palms and said, "I'm so sorry. I meant—"

"She didn't know." Victoria appeared from around the corner. She shot Cristina a reassuring glance and then marched up to Dr. Campbell. "I placed the folders on her desk without realizing she'd already left for lunch."

He loomed over her like a volcano about to erupt. "This is your fault?"

"Yes, I take full responsibility." Victoria lifted her chin and squared her shoulders. "But I think you should also know I've taken the liberty of setting up the lab over lunch and rescheduling the earlier cases for later this afternoon. I'll stay late to finish them so that we won't fall behind schedule."

The anger drained from Dr. Campbell's face. "You will?"

"Yes."

He glanced at Cristina, who remained rooted in place, unsure if he might still unleash a torrent on her for the mistake. But instead, he said in his usual, cheery voice, "I apologize for the outburst, Dr. Silva. I'm sure you can appreciate the stress of running a business, especially one that deals in human lives."

"Uh, yes," Cristina replied, still reeling from his sudden mood swing. "And it's okay."

"Well, carry on, then." Dr. Campbell nodded to both women and then walked briskly away down the hall.

"Thank you," Cristina whispered to Victoria as she unlocked her office and invited her assistant inside. "But you didn't have to take the fall for me."

"You'd do the same for me, I'd wager," Victoria said with a dismissive wave. "And I've had a few extra days to learn how to redirect Dr. Campbell's tirades."

"I hadn't realized we were working for Dr. Jekyll and Mr. Hyde," Cristina said with a shudder. "He seemed so self-regulated at my interview."

"The other assistants warned me he gets like that whenever his pet project is threatened."

"Mnemosyne? What is that, exactly? He never mentioned it to me."

"It's top-secret. You have to be invited to work on it, and the researchers involved can't even discuss it with each other. I heard they're searching for a way to restore memory, but that could be rumor." Victoria fumbled with the folders off Cristina's desk. "Anyway, we've got enough work without worrying about that."

"Here, let me help you with that." Cristina took an armful of the files. "I'll stay with you to finish those late cases."

"Nonsense. You've got a lot going on in your life, right?" Victoria shrugged. "It's not like I have anything better to do right now."

Cristina felt pangs of sympathy and regret at the reminder that Victoria knew no one in the city and even Cristina had shunned her offer to hang out. Maybe her relationship with Wilson wasn't the only one she needed to reconsider.

"You're right, I have something I need to do tonight," she said as she helped Victoria carry the folders to Victoria's desk. "But later this week, how about I take you up on that offer to go out?"

Victoria's face lit up like she'd won the lottery. "That sounds lovely. I promise we'll have a smashing time."

Although she smiled in response as they continued to Victoria's workstation, as Cristina's thoughts drifted to Dr. Campbell's top-secret project and Victoria's comment that *I heard they're searching for a way to restore memory*, she couldn't shake a creeping feeling of *déja vu*.

CHAPTER THIRTY-TWO

Wilson remained on the phone with the DCF case worker, Sarah Watson, for nearly half an hour, trying to make sense of what had happened. According to Sarah, Caleb had become more agitated and confused after they left the precinct, so they took him to the emergency department. The doctors there examined him and documented multiple bruises on the teen's body.

"What you saw on his face and shoulder were the tip of the iceberg," Sarah said. "When we asked who hurt him, he said he didn't remember, but all indications point toward his father."

"What indications?" Wilson asked.

"We interviewed both parents separately, and though neither admitted anything, the mother suggested the father has a temper. And when I mentioned the father to Caleb, he acted like he didn't know who I was talking about. His mind suppressed the memories of the abuse, even of the abuser, as a way of protecting him from reliving the pain."

"He didn't say anything about Sack Man?"

"No. What's that, a video game?"

"Never mind." Wilson bit his fingernail, wondering why Caleb would change his story. "Did you get a psych eval on Caleb while you were at the ER?"

"Yes, and they said he showed signs of amphetamine withdrawal. Fatigue, ravenous appetite, irritability, poor attention, and memory problems."

"His mom said he stopped taking his amphetamines."

"The psychiatrist said that wouldn't explain it. He must have been using crystal meth or something equally potent for some time."

"Did they do a drug screen?"

"Yes, but it was negative."

"So you're telling me he was using methamphetamines the whole time he was living under his parents' roof, and then, during the three days he was in hiding, where he could do anything he wanted, he stopped taking them?"

After a pause, Sarah said, "I see your point. Maybe his parents bought the drugs for him. I know it sounds absurd, but we've seen it before. In any case, we believe that's why he snuck out of the foster home this morning. To score more drugs. The foster parents said he was raving all night long about someone trying to kill him, screaming that he was losing his mind."

"Why didn't you detain him in the hospital overnight?"

"The ER doctors gave him a sedative to calm him down. Besides, they didn't have a bed available, and this foster family has experience with troubled teens."

"Clearly not enough." Wilson squeezed his fist. "Did he leave any clue as to where he could've gone?"

"Like I said, the foster parents called twenty minutes before you did so we're still gathering information. I've already sent an investigator to the home."

"Okay, let me know what you find."

When he hung up, he caught Hawkins watching him. "What?"

"I've got something I want to show you, remember?"

"Oh, right." Wilson massaged his forehead. "Sorry."

"The kid ran off?"

"Yeah, and they said he was drug-seeking."

"You mean that RAM Boost stuff?"

"No, amphetamines."

Hawkins furrowed his brow. "We didn't find amphetamines in his hideout."

"Exactly." Wilson shook his head. "Did they finish the analysis of that pill we found?"

"They're still running it, but so far no narcotics."

"Reggie said RAM Boost didn't affect him, but it made all three of the other teens irritable. I don't care what Wakefield says, there's something wrong with her supplement. Let's get the Drug Enforcement Agency involved." Wilson stood and pulled up a chair next to Hawkins. "What did you want to show me?"

Hawkins pushed a case file over. "On the twenty-fourth of June, Dr. Wakefield reported a break-in at her store the previous night. The only thing missing was a batch of her memory supplements. Investigators reviewed security footage and saw Reggie Horne had been casing the joint for a few days prior."

"Did they see anyone else on video?"

"No, that's the weird part." Hawkins pointed out a paragraph in the report. "Someone covered the camera lens on the night in question."

"There was no footage of Reggie near the shop when the break-in occurred?"

"Only daytime."

"Did they find his prints?"

"Nope. They went off the fact he'd been loitering outside the store."

Heat rose up Wilson's neck. "That's not enough for an arrest warrant. Who was the investigator?"

"Joey Malone."

"How the hell did he get a warrant?"

"He went to see Judge Marshall."

"Marshall? He's practically a Klansman."

Hawkins closed the file. "Well, the kid got lucky because the DA dropped the charges. She must've seen through the racial profiling and realized there wasn't enough of a case."

"But what happened to the investigation? Malone didn't keep looking for suspects?"

"Captain Harris reassigned him to work on a missing person case."

Heat rushed up the back of Wilson's neck. "I can't believe this shit is still happening."

"What shit?"

"When I was still a rookie, I was partnered with a ten-year veteran named Hank Jackson. Hank was a role model for me, you know? A real fountain of knowledge, experience, and raunchy jokes."

Hawkins nodded. "I knew a guy like that in the Army."

"Three weeks in, we got dispatched to investigate an armed robbery suspect. When we arrived, I spotted a young Black man brandishing a gun as he was about to enter a hardware store. Hank drew his pistol and started shouting." Wilson's throat grew parched. He took a swig of coffee. "The guy panicked and turned toward us. Hank fired. The guy dropped his gun and collapsed."

Wilson's chest tightened. The incident had happened years ago but talking about it made it as fresh as if it had happened yesterday.

"Did you find the stolen goods on him?" Hawkins asked.

Wilson shook his head. "He didn't even have a gun. It was a power drill he was trying to return to the store."

"Oh, man." Hawkins dipped his head. "Did he die?"

"No, he survived to file a lawsuit against the precinct. Hank insisted he'd attacked us." Wilson took another sip of coffee, but it mixed with bile and seared his throat. He set the cup aside. "Our sergeant warned me of the damage a story like that could do to the precinct. Of what it could do to my career."

Hawkins sat quietly while Wilson massaged the tension from his neck.

"I didn't care. What Hank did was wrong. I spoke to the man's lawyer and offered to testify." Wilson pressed his knuckles against his chin, reminding himself of the pressure he endured to conform. "The judge was a friend of Hank's uncle. He dismissed the case before it even went to trial."

"That really sucks," Hawkins said.

"That's not the end of it, though." Wilson's stomach clenched.

"Months later, I learned the man Hank shot had killed himself after losing his job and receiving threats from other officers to keep his mouth shut."

Hawkins's eyes widened. "Shit."

"The sergeant found out about my deal with the guy's lawyer, but by then I'd already helped take down a few big crime lords and earned a recommendation for Detective. Still, I'd burned a bridge at that precinct, so they transferred me out. Even though they kept it under wraps, the sergeant at my next assignment knew, making him less willing to listen to my side of the story when it came to my alleged affair with a witness and—well, you know the rest." Wilson bristled. "And now they're doing the same thing to Reggie as Hank did to that guy. Reggie claimed he saw a man wearing a black hood break into the NatureBoost shop, but no one believes him."

"That wasn't even in Malone's report," Hawkins said. "If Reggie's telling the truth, that man could've obscured the security camera. But why steal a bunch of vitamins?"

"Unless there's more to them than Wakefield let on." Wilson drummed his fingers on the desk. "Can you search the databases for someone using the alias *Sack Man*? Cross-reference with local gangs and drug rings."

"Sure." As Wilson stood, Hawkins cocked his head. "What are you going to do?"

"First, I'm going over to the foster home." Wilson buttoned his jacket. "And then I need to have another talk with Caleb's parents."

CHAPTER THIRTY-THREE

Cristina was exhausted by the end of the workday. Dr. Campbell had tasked her with performing thorough neurobehavioral profiles on each subject, noting the course of their psychiatric symptoms and prior treatments before collecting EEG data. With eight subjects for the afternoon, she'd had only a two-minute break after each one before moving on to the next. At least she'd been able to finish her part on the last two before it was time to leave. Victoria would remain to finish the brainwave testing.

"Are you sure you don't want me to stay?" she'd asked after entering her notes into the computer system. "I can if you need."

"Go, already." Victoria rolled her eyes and laughed. "Don't make me regret my decision to help you."

As she headed for her car, Cristina thought about the decision she'd made earlier that afternoon. When she got home, she'd call Wilson and invite him out for a drink. She needed to clear the air with him and find out if he felt the same as she did. She was prepared to do some heavy apologizing, but from what Maria had told her, it might not take much convincing.

After she pulled her Mini Cooper out of the Memory Center's parking lot, she changed the XM Radio to a Brazilian channel. Soft Bossa Nova beats filtered through the speakers as Marissa Monte sang "Ainda

Lembro." Cristina tapped her fingers on the steering wheel and guided her car onto the Riverway.

I love this song, Sabrina purred in the back of Cristina's mind. *We used to listen to it all the time, me and Bruno and Federico. We should have dinner with Bruno.*

Gritting her teeth, Cristina hit the Skip button on the radio. The music changed to João Gilberto's "Chega de Saudade."

Why'd you do that?

Minor guitar chords thrummed as she stopped at a traffic light, working their way under her skin. "I know it was years ago, but I'm having trouble with the idea you and Federico Gomes were so close."

Why?

"Why? He was a Zero Dark mercenary. He tried to kill me. And now you want to spend time with his brother?"

Bruno's different. He was always far more charming than Federico, and he's got an honest job.

"Are you sure it's not because he's also the more attractive one?" Cristina drummed her fingers on the steering wheel. "I could sense the thrill down our spine when he flexed his big forearm muscles."

Sabrina fell silent.

Cristina trilled her lips. Maybe Bruno *was* different, but Sabrina was hardly a good judge of character. She'd been the one in love with Quinn, after all.

As the light changed and she started forward, she glanced in her rearview mirror. Her skin crawled as she spotted the obsidian motorcycle directly behind her. "Isn't that . . . ?"

A Harley-Davidson Fat Boy Limited Edition. Yes, it is.

Her gaze drifted up to the rider, who was wearing a full helmet with a reflective visor and a black bodysuit. She couldn't make out any distinctive markings. It had to be a coincidence. How many Harleys were there in Boston, anyway?

At the next intersection, she veered onto Boylston Street and glanced back at her mirror. The biker was still a car's length behind her.

Northbound traffic typically passed through Boylston on the way to Storrow Drive over rush hour. She tightened her grip on the steering wheel and accelerated, pushing the speed limit.

The motorcycle kept pace.

Wrong move, Sabrina said. *If you want to know if you're being tailed, change lanes and slow down, see if he passes you or not.*

Cristina swallowed the lump of fear in her throat and did as Sabrina suggested. She shifted into the right lane, eased up on the gas, and pretended to look for her turnoff.

The bike roared past.

Exhaling with relief, she resumed her original speed. She chided herself for letting fear control her. It wasn't a bad idea to be alert, but she didn't have to be paranoid.

But it's not paranoia if they're really after you.

She stopped at another traffic light next to a gas station. "Fio da Memória" by Luisa Maita came on the radio, electronic beats and synthesized chords pulsating through the Mini Cooper. She almost didn't need to look in her rearview to know. The goosebumps on her arms were enough.

The black motorcycle was behind her again. The driver made the sign of a cross on his chest, but there was something odd about the way he did it.

Cristina didn't have much time to think about it as the light changed. She accelerated past the Fenway gardens toward the turnpike overpass.

The bike fell two cars behind.

"You need to take control," Cristina said aloud. "You're better at this than me."

I can't. You're blocking me out somehow. Looks like you're in charge, as usual.

"Damn," she said as she started across the overpass. "What do I do?"

First of all, stop turning your head to look in the mirror so much. If they are following you, it's a dead giveaway you know something's up.

Cristina forced herself to watch the road ahead. Cars whizzed by in the opposite direction.

The electronica beat drove to a crescendo.

After you cross the turnpike, take the exit. Casually, like you always intended it.

The turnpike stretched below them. Holding her breath, Cristina veered into the right lane and steered onto the offramp toward Commonwealth Avenue.

She shifted her gaze to the mirror.

The motorcycle had followed her.

"Shit. Now what?"

At the next intersection, calmly turn around and go the other way, like you took the wrong exit.

Cristina fought against her shaking hands to keep the Mini on course. She glanced at the mirror, her gaze dropping to the biker's waist.

A gun was holstered there.

Massachusetts Avenue appeared ahead. She slammed the gas pedal to the floor.

Cristina, slow down. What are you doing?

She propelled the car into the intersection without stopping. She passed the divider and swerved left to cross onto Commonwealth, heading back the way she'd come. A car coming the other direction on Mass Ave. slammed on their brakes and horn at the same time. Centripetal force jammed Cristina against her seatbelt.

Que merda! Are you nuts?

Cristina fought to straighten the steering wheel and urged the Mini forward. She checked her side mirror. The motorcycle shot up Mass Ave. past Commonwealth and disappeared.

Her nerves rattling, Cristina slowed to the speed limit. She checked her mirrors twice more, but the biker didn't reappear. As she approached the turn that would take her to Storrow Drive and then toward home, she tensed, half-expecting the bike to leap onto the road in front of her. But it didn't. She made it onto Storrow Drive without incident.

What happened back there?

"I thought I saw a gun." Cristina shut off the radio. "But maybe I imagined it."

You didn't imagine it. But that's not the issue. Tension crept through Cristina's head as Sabrina whispered: *Why didn't he use it?*

CHAPTER THIRTY-FOUR

The moon rose over the city as Wilson drove away from the foster home in Winter Hill, puzzling over how all the different pieces in this case fit together. He'd spent an hour interviewing the foster parents and inspecting the room where Caleb had stayed. According to the caregivers, Caleb was initially sedate and quiet on arrival, but an hour after going to bed he began screaming about Sack Man transforming into a giant snake, biting his neck, and injecting a deadly venom that was now eating away at his memory. The foster parents managed to calm him back to sleep, only for him to wake yelling again an hour later. This continued throughout the night until shortly before dawn, when he bellowed that Sack Man was coming and he had to escape. The parents went to check on him, but he appeared to have gone back to sleep, so they returned to bed. Later, when he hadn't gone downstairs for breakfast, they went back to his room, where they discovered he'd tucked the covers around pillows to make it look like he was asleep and snuck out the bedroom window.

It hadn't taken Wilson long to comb the room for clues as it was little more than a closet with a bed, a door, and a window. But he found nothing more than footprints on the carpet.

Until he examined the window. The lock was rusted and broken, but the foster parents insisted it had been working the previous night.

Wilson opened the window to find a short stretch of roof that had seen better days. He climbed onto the roof and stared down. It was too far to jump, but an old ladder leaned against the side of the house. He wondered how Caleb could've known about the ladder, since it wasn't visible from inside the room, and as the room faced the back, he couldn't have spotted it when they drove up.

The most curious part, though, was when he bent to inspect the window. The inner frame was scratched, as if someone had picked at it until the lock broke. But the scratch marks were on the *outside*, not the inside.

Wilson checked for fingerprints but found none. Could Caleb have called someone to help him escape? Or had he been taken?

Now, as Wilson drove to the Powder House home of Ronald and Deborah Jackman, he made a mental list of questions he needed to ask. Wilson doubted they would be eager to talk to him. He'd already called Reggie, but the teen insisted he hadn't heard from Caleb and sounded genuinely worried that something had happened to him. So the Jackmans were Wilson's best bet for answers.

Wilson rang the doorbell and cooled the heels of his dress shoes for five minutes before Ronald answered, looking even more disheveled than he had the last time: shirt half-untucked, bare feet, two days' beard growth. The man's eyes wobbled as they attempted to focus on Wilson, his face growing as dark as his beard. "What do you want? Caleb's not here, no thanks to you."

"I know." Wilson leveled his gaze with Ronald's. "He's gone missing."

Ronald's eyebrows shot up. "What, again?"

Wilson nodded.

Smacking his lips and scowling like he'd eaten something sour, Ronald stepped back and waved Wilson inside. "You'll need to talk to Deborah too."

The smell of cabbage was no more, the kitchen instead stinking of stale beer. Deborah looked up from a chicken dinner, her eyes growing as wide as her plate. "What happened?"

"Caleb's missing again." Ronald plopped in a chair.

Deborah's fork clattered down. "Oh, God. Please sit down," she said to Wilson. "Can I get you anything?"

"No. Thank you." Wilson took a seat at the end of the table.

"What happened?"

"It looks like he escaped through a window at the foster home sometime this morning."

"That sounds like Caleb." Ronald dug into his chicken.

"Escape?" Mrs. Jackman's voice quavered. "You make it sound like he's in jail."

Wilson ignored the comment. "Has he contacted you?"

"The only ones who've spoken to us are you and that Sarah Watson." She sucked in her lower lip. "You don't have any idea where he is?"

"We've got officers looking for him. But there's information I need from you." A notification pinged on Wilson's phone. He swiped it away. "Tell me about Sack Man."

Ronald gagged on the beer he was drinking. "What?"

"Caleb said a monster named Sack Man would hurt him if he didn't do what he was told. The social worker thought he was referring to you."

Ronald's face turned a deep crimson. He rose out of his seat, fists clenched. "I didn't abuse my kid, all right? Yeah, I was probably too hard on him but—"

Wilson held up his hands, as if he could ward off the bigger man through sheer force of will. "I want to find Caleb, and I'm sure you do too. So tell me, is Sack Man a real person or not?"

Ronald unclenched his hands and sank back into his chair. "No, he's not real. He's something Caleb created to put a name to his fears. That's what his doctor said, anyway."

"Caleb talked about Sack Man to his psychiatrist?"

"Yeah, a few weeks ago. Dr. Lal said sometimes teens with ADHD develop anxiety as they worry about entering adulthood. They start seeing their demons as real, because it's easier to deal with something they can picture than disembodied fears." Ronald shrugged. "Or something like that."

"Did Dr. Lal prescribe a drug for anxiety?" Wilson asked.

"No."

"Was Caleb taking anything else besides amphetamines?"

Deborah shook her head.

Wilson pulled up the medical report that Sarah had forwarded him and showed it to the Jackmans. "The doctors in the ER felt Caleb was suffering severe amphetamine withdrawal. They said that could only happen if he was taking high doses. So I need to ask you again, did you suspect that Caleb was abusing drugs?"

Ronald started to shake his head. Deborah swallowed and said, "I did." When Ronald glared at her, she added, "Recently, in the last few weeks. The way he's been acting, the anger and isolation, the crazy things he was saying—how could I not? You didn't see it because you were too busy getting drunk."

Ronald's ears reddened. "That's enough, Deborah."

"No, Mrs. Jackman," Wilson said, shooting Ronald a warning look. "Tell me, did you know Caleb and his friends were using a memory supplement?"

"No," she said.

"All three of his friends claimed they saw someone called Sack Man." He hesitated to mention the rest, but they needed to know what was at stake. "Two of them are dead."

Deborah's hand flew to her mouth. "Oh, my God."

Ronald stared silently, either stunned or asleep with his eyes open. Wilson wasn't sure which.

"Either they all were taking something that caused them to have the same hallucination." Wilson gave them a hard look. "Or someone named Sack Man has been tormenting them. If he's real, and Caleb is with him now, he's in danger. That's why I need you to be straight with me. Have you seen your son with any adults who seemed suspicious or a little bit off?"

The Jackmans exchanged looks, faces pale. At last, Ronald pushed away his plate. "Right after school started, Caleb asked me to pick him up at Somerville Prep. He'd gone to hang out with Reggie. When I got there, Reggie was gone, but Caleb was talking to this older security guard. He said the guy was making sure he was safe until I arrived, but it seemed like more than that. Caleb looked uncomfortable, like he couldn't wait to get away from the guy."

Wilson's skin crawled. He knew exactly who Ronald meant. "I'll look into it. In the meantime, I've also dispatched officers to check the bookstore where we found Caleb last time, and we're running another BOLO with his photo."

"Please, find our boy." Deborah's eyes were wet with tears. "We've made mistakes, I know, but we don't want anything to happen to him."

Wilson buttoned his jacket. "We'll find him."

As he climbed into his car and started driving, Wilson thought about the last thing Mrs. Jackman had said, about making mistakes. Had he made a mistake, letting Cristina go? Sure, she'd been the one who broke up with him, but he didn't put up much of a fight, did he? Why not? Because he was hurt? Was he really that fragile? Or was it because he knew he didn't deserve her?

He stopped at a red light and pulled at his hair. This wasn't working. He couldn't stop thinking about her, and it was interfering with his ability to concentrate, to do his job.

The light changed. As he resumed course, he was determined to confront his feelings head-on, once and for all.

CHAPTER THIRTY-FIVE

The moment Cristina burst into her apartment, she called out for Maria. When no one answered, she withdrew the Glock she'd started carrying after the attack by the hospital from her backpack and turned off the safety.

Something moved near the couch. She widened her stance and aimed the gun.

Grizabella popped out, mewling.

Cristina exhaled and lowered her weapon. "Sorry, Griz."

The cat padded over and rubbed against her leg. Cristina scratched under the feline's chin. A moment later, she heard a squeak from the bathroom. The door opened. She lifted the pistol.

Maria appeared, head and body wrapped in towels. Her gaze fell on Cristina and she threw up her hands. "*Que merda!*"

"Sorry to you too." Cristina exhaled and dropped the gun back into her backpack. "Why didn't you answer when I called out?"

"I must not have heard you over the shower." Maria's brow wrinkled with worry lines. "Why are you so jumpy? You seem like you're expecting *Tropa de Elite* to raid us any moment."

Cristina pressed her lips together, the vibrations of her purring cat trailing from her palm throughout her body. She considered brushing the question off with a joke, but that wouldn't be fair to Maria. Her sister deserved to know the truth about potential dangers.

"Sit down," she said as she stood and led Maria to the couch. "There's something I have to tell you."

Her sister listened as Cristina described the biker and the chase on Commonwealth Ave. with wide eyes. When she finished, Maria asked, "Was it the same person who attacked you the day I arrived?"

"I don't think so. The motorcyclist seemed bigger." Cristina shrugged. "But I couldn't tell for sure."

"Should we accept Bruno's offer of protection?"

"No, I'm going to call my contact at the FBI. And we should stay in tonight."

"That's okay. I came here to see you, not the city."

As Maria returned to the bedroom to dress, Cristina dug her phone out of her backpack. So much for that conversation with Wilson. Well, she could call him tomorrow. First things first.

"I need to speak with you," she said when Special Agent Jefferson answered the phone. "It's urgent."

"Dr. Silva?" Jefferson's voice was gruff, as if he'd been interrupted in the middle of something. "It's rather late for a—"

"Someone followed me home today," she said, cutting him off. "On a black Harley-Davidson. And they had a gun."

The silence stretched like a cat. "Tell me everything," Jefferson finally said.

When Cristina finished describing the sequence of events, Jefferson cleared his throat. "Can you give me a description of your pursuer?"

"I couldn't see their face, and the bodysuit was padded. I think it was a man, but it could've been a large woman."

"Any markings on the bike or helmet?"

"No."

"Did you get the plate number?"

"I couldn't see it."

Annoyance crept into his voice. "I'm sure it's frustrating when a patient tells you they have pain but can't tell you where it hurts or how it feels, am I right?"

"I don't treat chronic pain, but, yes, I understand. I wish I could provide more details, but that's all I have. I was concentrating on escape." She chewed on her thumbnail. "What about the bike? Could you find out who bought a 114 Limited Edition Fat Boy?"

"I can check, but Harley's a popular brand. A single dealer sells a thousand bikes per year. Is there anything at all that stood out to you? Anything that might help me know where to start looking?"

Cristina replayed the scene in her mind, again seeing the biker behind her, following her onto Commonwealth. She kept picturing the soulless reflection on the visor, the sheen on the bike as it idled behind her, the glint of metal on the gun . . .

"Yes, there was something," she said at last. "He made the sign of the cross, but he did it in a weird way."

"What do you mean?"

"He did it backward, right to left. And he used his left hand."

"Catholics sign left to right, and almost always use their right hand." Excitement edged into Jefferson's voice. "Are you sure that's what you saw?"

"Yes, I'm certain. Does that mean something to you?"

"I'm not sure yet, but I'll see what intel I can find. In the meantime, I suggest you vary your route. Don't leave at the same time every day. Make yourself a harder target."

"Of course. Standard operating procedure. Please call me the moment you learn anything."

As Cristina hung up, Maria returned wearing a nightgown. "Did you speak to the FBI?"

"Yes, my contact there is going to see what he can dig up." Cristina made room for Maria to sit down on the couch next to her. "But be alert. Let me know if you see or hear anything suspicious."

Maria placed her hands on Cristina's shoulders and met her gaze. "If anyone tries to hurt you, I will kill them with my bare hands."

Cristina tilted her head forward, so their foreheads met. "And I'd do the same for you."

CHAPTER THIRTY-SIX

When DB returned to her temporary apartment, she did a visual sweep. Everything looked the same as when she'd left that morning. Throw pillows on the suede couch. Half-full glass of water on the coffee table. Motion detectors in place, green lights indicating they hadn't been tripped.

It had been a frustrating but productive day. The doctor's unexpected lunch date nearly threw off her plans, but she'd used the opportunity to sneak a listening device into Silva's backpack undetected. Now, DB strode over to the kitchen, set her purse on the counter, shoved aside Armani's Sig Sauer, and found a pair of Bluetooth ear buds. She stuck an ear bud in each ear and activated an app on her phone.

A second later, she heard Silva's voice: "... *I'm going to call my contact at the FBI now. But I'm afraid we're going to have to stay in tonight.*"

DB grinned. Silva's voice came through crystal clear. Too bad it had only a range of around five hundred meters, but that had been why she'd rented an apartment only a block away from Silva's. And she'd already learned the doctor was working with the FBI. How rich was that? No wonder her employers were so interested in Silva.

"*That's okay. I came here to see you, not the city.*"

This voice was different. Not the doctor's but maybe it was the woman who'd accompanied Silva to the dinner party. If Silva shared her secrets with this woman, DB could be the proverbial fly on the wall.

A minute passed without any conversation, then DB heard Silva speaking to someone, but only Silva's voice, so DB guessed she was on the phone.

"*Someone followed me home today on a black Harley-Davidson. And they had a gun.*"

The muscles in DB's shoulders tightened. She didn't own a Harley. But if it wasn't her, then . . . ?

Her cheeks cooled. She dropped the phone and reached for the Sig Sauer.

"Don't."

The voice was deep, husky, and masculine, and punctuated with cold metal pressed against her neck, right where it met her jaw.

She held still. "I knew it. Why'd they send you?"

"To clean up your mess. You need to leave Boston before you fuck things up."

"Fuck up what, exactly?"

His hot breath blew in her ear.

"Why were you stalking Cristina Silva?" she asked.

The pressure of the gun barrel against her neck flickered. She smiled inwardly. She'd hit a nerve. He wasn't acting under orders. This was personal.

When he didn't answer, she asked, "What if I refuse?" She kept her voice steady as she calculated the angle she'd need to ram her elbow backward and disarm him. "If our employers wanted me dead, you would've already shot me. Which means they want me alive, and you always follow orders. Don't you, *Sack Man?*"

The gun wobbled again. "How do you know who I am?"

"Don't be an idiot. I'm supposed to terminate everyone connected to Quinn, including his deep undercover mole. But I was planning to leave you alone, so long as you stayed out of my way." She turned to face him, unsurprised when he didn't try to stop her. "What's it supposed to mean, anyway? The name. Is it because you *bag* your prey?" She made air quotes.

He snarled. "You wouldn't understand."

"No, actually, I wouldn't care, but the fact you do means so would our employers." She lifted her chin. "Walk away and I won't say a word to them."

His eyebrows met, jaw set. His suppressed HK45 remained aimed at her chest. At last, in a low voice, he said, "It seems we're at an impasse."

Adrenaline coursed through her veins. "So how do you want to handle this?"

They held each other's gaze. His cheek twitched.

DB's mouth flooded with saliva. She licked her lips.

The corners of his mouth drifted upward, baring his teeth. He holstered his gun.

She grabbed him by the neck and dragged his head down, so his lips met hers, hot and salty.

His hands found her waist and slid down over her hips.

A moan escaped her lips as his tongue probed her mouth. She tugged at the hem of his shirt. He lifted his arms.

She yanked the shirt up and over his face, twisting viciously. Wrenching his head back, she dragged him to the ground, the fabric muffling his groans.

"Here's how we're going to play this," she whispered in his ear. "You stay out of my way don't ask any questions, and I won't gut you from your clavicle to your pubis. Do we have an understanding?"

His head jerked twice in what she assumed was a nod. She released the shirt. He sat up and ripped the shirt off his head, gasping for air.

"Now," she said, pushing him back down and climbing onto him, "let's finish what we started."

CHAPTER THIRTY-SEVEN

The next day, Cristina left home early and took the longer route to work, watching for anyone suspicious. She didn't note anyone following her, but that provided little comfort. It only meant her stalker was being more careful to avoid getting caught.

As she was settling into her office chair, preparing to dive into her work, she noticed the picture of Jorge and Claudia Silva askew. The cleaning crew must have knocked it over and tried to replace it. Biting her lip, she adjusted it. Better. At least one thing in her life needed to be properly in place.

After a few minutes of reviewing her notes from the prior day's neurobehavioral assessments, Cristina realized she hadn't yet seen Victoria, who up to now had seemed incredibly punctual. Wondering how things turned out with the remaining EEG studies, she took a stroll over to her assistant's desk.

Victoria's chair was empty. Perhaps she was already downstairs in the lab.

When she reached the first sublevel, however, the EEG lab was also empty, save for the jumbled equipment and monitors. Cristina logged in to the network to find Victoria had kept her promise and entered all the data before leaving the previous night. There didn't seem to be anything more for Cristina to do down there, so she headed back upstairs.

On the way to the elevator, she stopped another researcher in the hall and asked if she'd seen Victoria.

"She had a doctor's appointment," the woman said before resuming her brisk pace. "Said she'd be in this afternoon."

Cristina puzzled over that as she rode the elevator up to her floor. Why hadn't Victoria mentioned a doctor appointment the day before? Was she sick?

That's your problem. You're always worrying about everyone else.

The hairs on Cristina's arms bristled. "Excuse me for caring."

You don't get it. The problem isn't that you care, it's that you don't care enough.

"Give me a break."

If you really cared so much, imagine if you shared the Recognate technology with Dr. Campbell. Maybe it's useless for memory restoration, but what about replacing unwanted traumatic memories?

"Okay, before you go all *Eternal Sunshine of the Spotless Mind* on me, memories shape who we are and how we act. There's too much potential for abuse. Look at what Quinn did."

This is different. Quinn wanted profit. If we developed a real treatment, we could make it free to everyone. We'd only be doing it to help people.

"Isn't that what Dr. Kobayashi intended before Zero Dark corrupted his research and killed him?"

Sabrina fell silent. Their argument was a painful reminder that Cristina and Sabrina really were two different people, with different opinions and feelings. Even if they had a magic pill, how could they ever reconcile that?

The elevator door opened.

"Look," she said as she stepped into the hallway. "We have to be careful. It's because of experiments like you're proposing that we're in this mess."

Sabrina whispered back: *It's because of experiments like this you exist.*

The overhead fluorescent light buzzed.

Cristina fought to breathe. She hadn't realized Sabrina thought like that. But she was right. Until two years ago, there was only Sabrina. Did Cristina have the right to be in control, to be making decisions for them? Did she even have a right to exist?

"It's funny," a familiar voice said as she rounded the corner, "I missed those one-sided arguments."

Cristina froze in the hallway, her heart hammering. Her knees wobbled as she caught sight of the man standing outside her office, wearing a dark suit and a lopsided grin.

"Wilson?"

CHAPTER THIRTY-EIGHT

A light breeze blew as DB watched Manny Feldman from behind the hedges while he tended to his garden. After her encounter with Sack Man, she'd questioned the strange sense of familiarity she'd felt while spying on Feldman during the dinner party. She readied her pistol while he whistled, head bowed, back arched away from her.

His phone rang. He set down the shears and answered.

"Hi babe, all done with yoga?" He tilted his head, listening. "Lunch with Brigit and Luanna? No, I'll make a sandwich for myself." He listened again, nodding to himself. "All right. Have fun. Love you."

He tucked the phone back into his pocket, knelt over his plants, and reached for the shears on the ground next to him.

DB stepped out from the hedges, aimed the Sig Sauer at his chest, and thumb-cocked the first round.

Feldman looked up at the click. He raised his hands by his head. "May I help you?"

Her eyebrows raised at his calm tone. "You're at gunpoint and you're not afraid?"

"If you were here to kill me, I assume I'd already be dead."

"You will be if you don't answer my questions."

His mouth tightened. Fear flashed in his eyes but quickly passed. He squinted. "Who are you? You seem familiar."

She took a step closer. "I do? How?"

His face paled. "Oh, my God."

"You know me?" Her pulse spiked. She aimed for his forehead. "Tell me. Who am I?"

He blew out a long breath. "Your name is Cristina Silva."

Cristina's chest rose and fell as she stared at her visitor, unblinking. The last thing she expected when she started work that morning was to find Gary Wilson standing at her door. A bit of scruff clung to his chin and cheeks, adding to his charm, but he had bags under his eyes. Her heart thumped in her chest.

Stay cool, she told herself.

"Hi." He leaned against the wall, his gaze unwavering.

She gazed back, breathless. "Hi."

He jerked his head toward her office door. "Can we talk inside?"

"Oh. Sure." She approached, fumbling in her pockets for her keys. As she unlocked the door, she caught a whiff of his musky cologne. A tiny thrill ran down her back. She managed to open the door and motion him inside before following him in.

He scanned her office. "It's nice. A little smaller, but brighter, more open."

"Thanks." This wasn't how she'd planned this conversation. Damn him for throwing her off-balance by showing up unannounced. Any more awkward small talk and she would go nuts. "What are you doing here? Shouldn't you be at work?"

"I was up most of the night searching for a missing teen. I asked for a few hours off to see my doctor."

"Doctor?" She narrowed her gaze. "Gary, what's going on?"

He fiddled with his jacket buttons. "Uh, can we talk in private?"

"Certainly." She shut the door and motioned for him to sit before claiming her own chair. The way this was going, she wasn't sure her knees would hold out much longer.

It took a moment for him to settle into the chair across from her desk, as he tried crossing and uncrossing his legs, placing, and removing his arms from the armrests, and finally leaning forward, resting his hands on his knees. She waited patiently, though her curiosity was skyrocketing.

"You look fantastic," he said at last. His lower lip jutted out. "That's not how I intended to start."

"No, it's fine." She gave him a reassuring smile, encouraged by his compliment. "You look good too."

He grinned in return, but the smile fell away. "Look, I wanted to say, I'm sorry. I must have really messed up to drive you away. The worst part is, I don't even know what I did." He tried to smile, but it came out looking more like he was in pain. "Typical guy, right?"

She gawked at him. "You've been blaming yourself this whole time? Gary, you did nothing wrong. You were nothing but kind and understanding. I was the one who couldn't handle it."

His gaze narrowed. "So it wasn't me, it was you?"

"That's not what I mean." She brushed her hair out of her eyes. "I was getting worse. I mean, look at me. Not only am I broken, but I'm literally split in two. One day, you would've reached the point where you'd be begging to be free, but you wouldn't do it because you're a man who believes in commitment and honor." She shook her head, wanting to silence herself, but if she didn't admit the truth, her fear of it would consume her. She looked him in the eye. "I knew that you wouldn't leave, even if it was destroying you. Our relationship would suffer, and that would hurt both of us. So I let you go before that could happen."

He didn't move, didn't blink. Then he leaned back, folded his arms across his chest, and made a popping sound with his lips. "Wow."

"I'm sorry, but I—"

He cut her off with a wave of his hand. "You really thought I had no idea what I was getting into? You thought I couldn't handle it? Have you met me?"

She was speechless.

The corner of his mouth quirked. "Just because you're a neuroscientist and a psychiatrist, you don't know how everyone else thinks. It

only took me a month to get used to your shifting memories and conversations with yourself. I appreciate you were trying to look out for
me, but it wasn't your choice to make."

Heat rose up the back of her neck. Everything he said was true.
Out of fear of losing control over her own life, she'd taken charge of his.

"You're right," she said softly. "I had no right to make the decision for you. I should've talked to you about how you felt. I should've
trusted you."

He stayed silent, gaze narrowed, long enough she feared he would
laugh at her and walk out. But instead, he shrugged. "Next time, give
me a little credit, okay?"

"Next time?"

"We could start fresh. After all, you're a different person than when
we met, and a breaking-and-entering investigation wasn't the ideal cir-
cumstance, anyway." He leaned forward and held out his hand. "Hi,
I'm Gary Wilson."

Cristina's heart thumped in her chest. This was what she wanted,
right? So why did it feel like the wrong time? Was it fear whispering in
her ear again? Jutting her chin, she took his hand, feeling a jolt of anticipation running up her arm. "Hi. I'm . . . uh . . . " She trailed off.
Who was she, really?

Quietly, he said, "I'll call you Cristina, okay?"

Reluctantly, she let go of his hand. "You're sure you can forget what
happened?"

"Actually, that's why I'm here." His expression hardened. "I need
your help."

Cristina blinked at his sudden seriousness. "What kind of help?"

"I've got a case. A couple of teens died suspiciously, and a third has
gone missing after hallucinating about a boogeyman trying to bite his
neck." A muscle in his cheek ticked. "All three of them have been taking
a supplement that's supposed to boost memory."

"You're asking me to consult on your case?"

He nodded.

Was it a good idea to work with Wilson while at the same time trying to reboot their relationship? She rubbed her fingertips across her lips. Would it be crossing a professional line?

Oh, just help him. Sabrina's voice nagged from a remote corner of her brain. *I'm tired of listening to you second-guess yourself.*

Despite her irritated tone, Sabrina was right. Cristina had been over-thinking everything. Like Devi had told her, she needed to trust her gut, and right now her gut was telling her she needed to be there for Wilson, like he'd always been there for her.

"Tell me about this supplement," she said at last.

"It's called RAM Boost. Well, it's actually got some other name, but that's what the teens call it." He scratched his cheek. "Dr. Allison Wakefield, the one who created it, says it prevents the brain from erasing memories at night, improving long-term memory storage."

"That's theoretically possible. Researchers recently discovered cells that control skin pigmentation are also involved in mood, sleep-wake cycles, energy regulation, and memory." She tapped her temple. "They're called melanin-concentrating hormone neurons."

"MCH." He snapped his fingers. "Yeah, that's what she said. So, do you think this supplement can do what she claims?"

"That's not my area of expertise. But you could talk to my boss, Dr. Campbell. He's a neurologist and head of the Memory Center. I can get you in touch with him."

"Yeah, that'd be great."

"I'll see if he's free now." She reached for the phone.

He pulled out his cell phone and held up his other hand. "Hold that thought. It's Hawkins." He answered and then listened. He grunted a few acknowledgments and then said, "All right. I'll meet you there."

After hanging up, he stood. "I have to go."

"Right now?"

"This can't wait. They found that missing teen." His voice choked. "He's dead."

CHAPTER THIRTY-NINE

DB fought to maintain her composure as Manny Feldman's words sank in. A crow cawed from a bush behind the garden. A light breeze carried a trace of mint that triggered memories of a woman preparing herbal tea with honey.

She shook off the image and trained the P226 between Manny's eyes. "Cut the shit. There's no way I'm Cristina Silva."

"It's true. I thought you were dead. Maybe I'm dead and this is the afterlife."

"You're not dead. Yet." She gnashed her teeth. "Don't lie to me."

"Your hair is much lighter and they did something to your face. But your voice. Your posture . . ." He frowned. "You're not Cristina?"

Her grip on the gun faltered but she recovered. "No."

"Then why did you ask me who you were?"

"Because . . . because I . . ." She trailed off, unable to bring herself to say, *Because I don't know who I am.*

She forced her voice to level out. "You know I'm not Cristina Silva. I saw her here, with you, the other night."

His gaze narrowed. "What is it you want?"

"Tell me the truth. Do you really recognize me?"

"May I stand?"

She nodded.

He stood and brushed off his pants. "You're Cristina Silva. That's the truth."

She tightened her grip on the pistol.

"The woman you saw was made to believe she was you, after you died." He shook his head. "But obviously you did not die."

"You're saying I'm the *real* Cristina Silva?" Images flashed in her mind. Medical school graduation. Nights on inpatient wards, doing rounds. Sitting for her initial licensing exam. She pressed one hand against her forehead, trying to hold back the flood of visions. "And that bitch stole my life?"

"It's not her fault." He held out his hands by his sides. "She was forced into it."

"Well, she seems comfortable enough now. And you're rather chummy with her." She looked him up and down. "Who are you to her?"

"Me?" He laughed mirthlessly. "I'm a friend. Of yours, and now hers."

"You're not making sense." Her finger lingered over the trigger. "Tell me where I can find my parents. If I see them, talk to them, maybe it'll make sense."

His face sagged. "I'm so sorry. They're dead."

The world spun. "What?"

"I'm sorry, Cristina, but your parents died."

A jagged dagger stabbed through her chest. "How?"

"A car crash."

Hot white light. Crunching metal. Screams. An air bag slamming her chest.

Her heart fluttered. "Was it me? Was I driving?"

Manny gave a solemn nod.

DB covered her mouth. This wasn't possible. She already knew who she was. She wasn't some Massachusetts doctor. Her parents didn't die with her at the wheel. Someone else didn't step in and claim her identity.

Except it *was* possible. She knew ReMind had been working on a memory drug that didn't work the way they claimed. It delivered false memories.

DB's memories shifted to her lying on a hospital bed. The image was hazy, as if filtered through gauze, but she could tell there were other beds, other patients. A scientist was rounding, reviewing their charts, before injecting them with a blue liquid.

The landscape changed again, and now she was in a dark room with a projector, being forced to watch home movies. Someone else's home movies. When the movies finished, they showed her martial arts training videos. Combat instruction films. Clips portraying ruthless acts of violence and murder.

Her heart jumped and she snapped to the present. She dug her fingers into her cheeks. The weekly injections to prevent the glitches—that was the memory drug.

She pulled at her hair. Everything was a lie. She wasn't Dama Branca. She wasn't an assassin. That was what they made her to be.

Ice flowed through her veins, cooling the fire burning in her chest. She lowered her hand, traces of the white foundation she used to lighten her skin tone dotting her palm. Maybe it was time for the White Lady to retire. After she found out why they did this to her and what made the other woman special enough to win her identity.

"You're going to tell me everything you know about this poser," she spat. "I want to know who she is and what makes her tick."

"Why would I do that?" He lowered his hands to his sides. "I'm sorry for what happened to you, but you're not the Cristina I know."

"Oh, you don't have a choice. And you're not going to do anything to tip her off." She smiled coldly. "Or you and your lovely wife will join my parents six feet underground."

CHAPTER FORTY

An autumn breeze nipped at Wilson's neck as he stood next to the Foss Park pool, looking down at Caleb Jackman's lifeless body. The teen's clothes were still soaked, but the morning sun had already dried his pale skin. His blue eyes, frozen open, sent shudders down Wilson's spine.

"The caretaker pulled him out thirty minutes ago," Hawkins said, scanning his notes. "He'd started his shift a few minutes earlier, so he had no idea how long Caleb had been there. Best guess is sometime before sunrise, which means no one saw anything."

"What've you found so far?" Wilson asked.

"His cell phone was in his pocket." Hawkins held up a baggie. "New model. Should be water resistant."

"Let it dry out and we can see who he last called. Anything else?"

"Nope. If he had any cash on him, it's gone."

Wilson's gut twisted as he studied the frozen look of fear on Caleb's face. "Either he was tripping out or someone did this to him. Any sign of foul play?"

"There's a partial footprint near the pool. Looks like generic sneakers, though. No special markings."

"Let's run it anyway. What about drugs? Any pill bottles or baggies?"

"Nothing." Hawkins tucked away his notebook. "If I were a

suspicious man, I'd think someone swept this area clean. Drug deal gone bad?"

"Maybe." Wilson crouched next to the body and used a pen to turn the teen's head. "There's a fresh wound on his neck. Looks like an injection."

"Think he was shooting heroin?"

Wilson jammed his tongue against his teeth. Like with the Trevino kid, he had a feeling that didn't sit well with him. "Tell the medical examiner to let us know as soon as the toxicology comes back, and to check for hidden track lines."

"Got it."

As he stood, Wilson fought to keep his mind focused on the work at hand. Seeing Cristina again had left him feeling giddy. A weight had been lifted from his chest. Not only hadn't he done anything wrong, but she wanted to start over.

"You okay, partner?"

Wilson startled and realized he'd been staring blankly at the pool. Shaking his head, he said, "Yeah, just pissed we haven't caught this creep yet. Run another check on the local dealers. We owe it to these kids to find out what happened and prevent any more deaths."

Hawkins nodded. "What will you be doing?"

As Wilson studied the bruising on Caleb's face, the name *Sack Man* played over and over in his head. "There are two things that tie Trevino, Sanchez, and Jackman together: RAM Boost and Sack Man. And, according to Reggie Horne, Sack Man stole the supplements in the first place. Since we can't find this Sack Man, we need to focus on RAM Boost." He set his jaw. "Which means I need to have another chat with Allison Wakefield."

CHAPTER FORTY-ONE

After Wilson left her office, it had taken Cristina the better part of a half hour to set her mind straight. The idea of rekindling their relationship both thrilled and frightened her. His comment that she needed to have more confidence in his ability to decide whether he could handle her unique situation was a valid one. But could *she* handle it?

Especially with the possibility that someone was stalking her. Why hadn't she told Wilson about the biker following her home, or the masked assailant from the other day, or about ReMind employees being killed? For that question, at least, she knew the answer. If he knew of a potential threat against her, he would insist on being her knight in shining armor, standing sentry outside her apartment and risking his own life to track down the culprit. That made for an unbalanced relationship. She didn't want a heroic protector who saw her as a damsel in distress. Besides, she already had Special Agent Jefferson to cover those three threats, and the feds were better suited to handle them than local law enforcement.

Speaking of Jefferson, she wondered if his investigation had turned up anything on the biker. She pulled out her cell phone and dialed.

"Dr. Silva," Jefferson said on answering. "Your ears must've been burning."

"Did you find something?"

"Yes, but we shouldn't discuss this over the phone. Can you come to the field office in Chelsea?"

"I have a full schedule here at the Memory Center today."

"Tomorrow, then. I'll be here all day."

Her scalp prickled. "Should I be concerned for my safety until then?"

"Not if you maintain a low profile. Stick to work and home and keep tabs on anyone important to you. If you see anything suspicious, call me."

As she hung up, Cristina's chest felt hollow. There was someone important to her who could've been at risk alone at the apartment. Cristina dialed Maria's phone.

"*Oi, beleza.*" Maria's chipper voice sounded like music to Cristina's ears. "*Tudo bem?*"

"Yes, is everything okay there?"

"Completely boring. I'm going—how do you say—*stir crazy.*"

Cristina was at a loss for words. She understood how lonely it must've been for Maria to stay by herself all day, but she couldn't very well send her sister out sightseeing alone. Not with a stalker out there. "I'd invite you to join me for lunch, but I don't think public transportation is a good idea, and I don't trust Uber either."

"That's not a problem. I can ask Bruno for a ride."

Ooh, I like that plan.

Blocking out Sabrina's opinion, Cristina said into the phone, "Are you sure that's a good idea?"

"If you don't feel comfortable seeing him, I'll ask him to drop me off at the front door."

With a sigh, Cristina said, "Fine. I'll see you at quarter to noon. You have the address?"

"I do. *Até logo, maninha.*"

"Hey, what's with the *little sister* business? I'm the older one, re-member?"

Maria laughed and said, "*Tchau,*" before hanging up.

Cristina smiled to herself as she tucked her cell phone into her pocket. Lunch with Maria would help distract her from her worries about what Jefferson found out, and she could tell her sister about her conversation with Wilson.

But you need to get over this awkwardness with Bruno. The longer you allow Federico's specter to haunt you, the more power it will hold over you.

An artery throbbed in Cristina's temple. She hated to admit when Sabrina was right over things like that. She did need to face Bruno. But not right then. For a little while, she wanted to savor the feeling she had after seeing Wilson—the feeling that things might finally be going her way.

CHAPTER FORTY-TWO

The door chimed as Wilson entered NatureBoost. A bald man with flecks of red and orange dotting his gray beard was talking to Dr. Wakefield near the register. They both turned in Wilson's direction.

Wakefield's eyebrows met. She gave him a curt nod and said, "Detective."

"Oh, you must be Detective Wilson," the man said and fished around in his pocket before pulling out and holding up a badge. "Connor Delaney, DEA."

"I didn't expect them to send anyone so quickly." Wilson shook Delaney's hand. "Usually, it takes weeks for something to happen."

"I'm nearby at the Stoneham office." Delaney stuck his hands in his pockets. "I did a random compliance audit on Dr. Wakefield last year, so I figured this would be an easy case."

"Well, I don't want to interfere with your investigation, so—"

"Don't worry. I'm done."

"What?"

"All of Dr. Wakefield's numbers are in order, and I've already inspected the lab equipment." Delaney held up a device that looked like a bar code scanner. "I'm taking samples of MCH-21 back for full pharmacological testing, but Dr. Wakefield provided her own studies, and everything looks clean."

The back of Wilson's neck prickled. "So, you're saying there's nothing psychoactive in this supplement?"

"As I told you, Detective," Wakefield said before Delaney could speak, "MCH-21 is all-natural and completely harmless. Look." She picked up a bottle, opened the cap, scooped out a handful of yellow tablets, and popped them into her mouth. "Would I do that if I thought they were dangerous?"

"She's right," Delaney said. "We'll confirm on our own equipment, but as far as I can see, it's safe."

There was something off about Connor Delaney. Or maybe it was Wilson's distaste for feds. He said, "Thanks for coming out. Let me know if you find anything else."

"I will." Delaney tapped his forehead to Wakefield. "And thank you for being so cooperative, Dr. Wakefield. It made my investigation a lot easier."

"My pleasure." Wakefield smiled. "I'm always happy to help law enforcement."

As Delaney left, Wakefield turned to Wilson, her expression cooling. "Is there anything else you wish to accuse me of, Detective?"

Ignoring her abrupt shift in attitude and her question, Wilson said, "Speaking of your willingness to assist law enforcement, you were quick to accuse Reggie Horne of stealing your supplements, even though a light breeze could've knocked over the case against him."

"He was poking around here for days before the theft. And there were no other suspects."

"Because someone blacked out the security camera. Why would he have allowed himself to be seen outside your store if he was guilty?"

"He's a kid. Why do they do anything?"

Wilson cocked his head, sizing her up. He'd struck a nerve. "He accused you of discrimination. He claims you sold to other teens. White teens."

Her face reddened. She set her shoulders and raised her chin. "Even if I did, what does it matter? You heard Agent Delaney. There's no way MCH-21 had anything to do with what happened to those two teenagers."

"Three."

"Excuse me?"

"Another died this morning."

Her stony countenance crumbled. "Oh, that's terrible. How?"

"I'm not at liberty to say. But we know the victim was taking your supplement. Any idea how he got it, if you didn't sell it to him?"

"Perhaps whoever stole it had something to do with it."

"Can you think of anyone else who would've wanted to steal MCH-21? A rival store owner, maybe?"

"Plenty, but as to who would go so far as to actually steal it?" She shook her head. "No idea."

Trying a different tactic, Wilson asked, "Does the name Sack Man mean anything to you?"

Her expression didn't flicker. "No. Should it?"

"A witness saw a hooded man sneaking into your store after hours."

Closing her eyes and squeezing the bridge of her nose, she said, "Let me guess. That witness was Mr. Horne."

Wilson gave her his best poker face.

"Yes, I heard about this mysterious thief," she said. "But the detective who investigated the burglary found nothing to support the boy's wild claim. If you ask me, Reggie Horne is guilty. He probably sold my supplements to his friends, and the only reason he's not in jail is because the ADA had her own reasons not to pursue the case."

The skin behind Wilson's ears tightened. "You mean, because she's Black."

Wakefield shrugged.

Squeezing his fingers into fists, Wilson forced himself to stay calm. Wakefield reeked of racism, but he couldn't arrest her for her viewpoint, no matter how offensive it was. And, with the DEA ruling MCH-21 safe for consumption, he'd lost his best lead on what caused the change in the teens' behavior. Maybe they were doing other drugs. Or maybe whoever stole the supplement laced it with something hallucinogenic.

Either way, Wakefield couldn't be held responsible for something out of her control.

"If you think of someone who might've wanted to steal your supplements," he said at last, turning to leave. "Please call my precinct."

"No hard feelings," she said.

He looked back over his shoulder.

She smiled sweetly. "I appreciate you have a job to do. You want to protect the public, so naturally you needed to ensure my product is safe. Maybe for personal reasons, as well."

"What do you mean?"

"You seem to be struggling with this case. Maybe you could use an assist." The corner of her mouth crept higher. "You know, to keep track of all those little details."

Heat rose up the back of his neck. "I'm fine."

"Of course, you are, but everyone could use a little boost." She jiggled a pill bottle. "It can be our little secret."

He stared at the bottle, pushing his tongue against his inner cheek. The DEA considered the supplement safe. An edge could help him find the killer.

No, it was a bad idea accepting anything that could be construed as a bribe. Captain Harris was already breathing down his neck, waiting for him to screw up. There was no reason to make it easier for him. Wilson shook his head. "Pass."

"Suit yourself. But if you change your mind, the door's always open." The bottle disappeared as if Wakefield had cast a magic spell. She leaned over the counter and leered at him. "Like I said, I'm always happy to help law enforcement."

CHAPTER FORTY-THREE

After a lovely lunch at the Indian restaurant a block down the street, Cristina walked Maria back to the Memory Center. They'd chatted about Wilson and his proposal to reboot their relationship, and about Cristina's research, sticking to Portuguese to minimize the risk of eavesdroppers listening in on their conversation. It felt good to open up to her sister, knowing that whatever she said would be met with compassion and understanding. As they strolled arm-in-arm, Maria laughing and nuzzling up against her, Cristina tried to imagine what it must've been like when she—or, Sabrina, really—had been young. Her childhood memories were still spotty, and she could only recall glimpses of her time with Maria. An uncomfortable tightness spread through her chest. It was another crack that kept her from being complete.

Maria slid her hand down Cristina's arm and squeezed her hand. "Everything okay?"

The discomfort quickly faded. Maybe she would never recover those memories, but at least she could still create new ones. She returned Maria's squeeze and smiled at her. "Couldn't be better."

As the office elevator opened on Cristina's floor, she held the door for Maria. The moment her sister stepped off, a woman with short blond hair rounded the corner and crashed into her. A bunch of folders flew into the air, spilling their contents all over the tile floor. Maria lost her footing and fell onto her butt.

"Oh, bollocks!" Victoria scurried over to Maria and held out her hand. "I'm so sorry. I should've been paying more attention to where I was going. Are you okay?"

Maria accepted her hand and pulled herself up. "I'm fine, and it's all right."

"What a cock up," Victoria said as she surveyed the damage. "I'm such a wally."

"Are you both okay?" Cristina asked as she left the elevator.

"Only bruised my ego," Victoria replied.

"Here, let me help you," Maria said and crouched to pick up the files.

"Thank you so much." Victoria knelt next to Maria and scooped up an armful of the papers. "You're too kind. I could've handled . . ."

Their eyes met. Neither said a word for several heartbeats.

"Uh, Maria," Cristina said, unsure what exactly was happening. "This is my assistant, Victoria. Victoria, this is my sister, Maria."

"Sister?" Victoria's eyes widened. "Oh, bugger. I'm such a klutz. This is so not how to make a good first impression."

Maria smiled as she picked up the last of the files and stood erect. "Don't worry. Accidents happen to everyone."

"If, by everyone, you mean 99.9 percent of the time to me, then you're right." Victoria stood and took the papers. She nodded to Cristina. "I'll, um, bring these by your office soon."

"Wait, Victoria," Cristina said, an idea striking her. "You mentioned a club in Everett that plays samba. Is it open tonight?"

Victoria screwed up her lips. "No, only on weekends. Sorry."

"That's all right." Cristina shrugged. "We can rent another movie."

"Do you know much about the area?" Maria asked.

"Me? No, I'm new to the area." Victoria tittered. "I need a tour guide. Or a friend."

Maria looked down at the ground. "Tour guides show you what they want you to see. I prefer a friend."

Victoria smiled. "Me too."

Suddenly feeling like an unwanted guest, Cristina cleared her throat and said, "I need to get to my office. Victoria, I'll look for those files later."

"Yes, of course." Victoria turned back to Maria. "It was nice running into—I mean, *meeting* you."

Maria grinned. "Likewise."

CHAPTER FORTY-FOUR

When Detective Wilson arrived at the precinct and started toward his desk, he spotted Detective Malone by the coffee machine, chatting and laughing with another White detective. Wilson cringed as he thought of the shame and ridicule Reggie Horne had suffered thanks to Malone's incompetence. An urge rose in Wilson's gut to go over there and punch Malone in the face.

"Hey, check this out." Hawkins pulled up a chair next to Wilson and dropped a folder on his desk.

The violent urge faded. Wilson indicated the folder. "What's this?"

"Everything they got off Caleb Jackman's phone. His incoming text messages and calls were deleted, but there were two voice mails from Reggie Horne, asking where Caleb was."

Wilson shrugged as he flipped through the folder. "No surprise there. Reggie's probably a wreck right now."

"Yeah, but that's not the big news." Hawkins pointed at the middle of the next page. "His outgoing call history showed several calls and one text to an unknown number."

"What did the text say?"

"Something about meeting where the Revolution lives again." Hawkins rapped his index finger on the notepad. "Foss Park is where they host Patriots' Day events."

The hair on Wilson's arms prickled. "When was this?"

"The text is a week old, but Caleb made the calls at midnight two nights ago."

"Not long before he drowned. Can we trace the number?"

"Do you think I've been sitting on my thumb this whole time?" Hawkins chuckled. "It belongs to a burner phone bought five years ago, but I was able to track down the store where it was sold. Fortunately, the buyer used a credit card."

Wilson's fingertips buzzed. "Who was the buyer?"

"Prescott Pearson."

"Who's that?"

Hawkins flipped to the back of the folder, revealing a three-page printout. "You know him better as Scott Pierce."

"The security guard?"

"He's only been working at Somerville Prep for four years." Hawkins's eyes glinted. "Before that, he was a cop at this precinct."

Wilson felt dizzy as he stared at the headshot portrait in the printout. The officer in the picture had darker hair and fewer wrinkles but was unmistakably Scott Pierce.

"Good work." Wilson couldn't tear his gaze away from the photo. Pierce's dark eyes seemed to follow him whichever way he moved. "Why'd he leave the force?"

"Whatever the reason was, it got redacted from his file. All it shows is he quit a year after he made Detective, roughly nine years ago."

Wilson frowned. "That doesn't make sense. Was he here when you joined?"

"I didn't retire from the Army until six months after he quit the force."

"What about Captain Harris?"

"He's only been here five years."

Wilson tapped his finger against the photo. "Would anyone here remember him?"

"Just one."

Wilson followed Hawkins's gaze to the front desk. His stomach clenched. "No . . ."

A moment later, the detectives stood at Sergeant Davis's desk. The sergeant eyed Wilson like he was the coyote offering flowers to the road-runner. "What's up, Detectives?"

"How long you been on the force, Sergeant?" Hawkins asked.

"Twelve years."

Wilson held out the file. "Do you remember this man?"

Davis studied the photo for two seconds. "Scottie Pierce. Yeah, I remember him. He was a good guy. Big war history buff. Pisser what happened to him."

"What happened?"

"He busted this crook, Vinnie DeLuca. Guy was a real piece of work. Everyone knew he was dealing but no one could make anything stick." Davis's eyebrows danced. "But Scottie found a bag of speedball in Vinnie's apartment. Blew the whole case wide open."

"How'd he get a warrant to enter Vinnie's place?" Hawkins asked.

"That's the thing." Davis bobbed his head side to side. "Scottie pretended to be a maintenance inspector for the landlord, spotted the drugs, and then returned the next day with the warrant. Only Vinnie claimed Scottie planted the speedball. Scottie was alone in the apartment for an hour, and the drugs were hidden in a sock drawer. He admitted to snooping before getting the warrant, but by then he already looked guilty. After Internal Affairs did some checking and found enough evidence of tampering with other investigations, they were shitting their pants about a lawsuit."

"So—" Wilson connected the dots. "They ordered him to resign."

"DeLuca agreed not to sue as long as the charges disappeared. Once Scottie left, IA dropped the case against him."

"Sounds like you knew him pretty well," Hawkins said. "Did you ever see him after he left?"

Davis twiddled with his pencil. "We had drinks and bowled a few frames of candlepin, but he was a mess. Kept saying he had bigger fish to fry."

"What did that mean?"

"Hell if I know. But after a couple of months, he really did disappear. I never heard from him again."

Wilson scratched his chin. "What happened to Vinnie DeLuca?"

"He disappeared, too, about six months later. I guess he got tired of slumming in Somerville." Davis laughed at his own joke.

The detectives exchanged glances.

"Thanks," Hawkins said. "You've been a big help."

As they walked back to the detectives' pen, Hawkins asked, "What do you think?"

"It explains why Pierce created a new identity for himself, but it also paints a pretty dark picture." Wilson's gut twisted. "There's no good reason for Caleb to call a security officer at another high school."

"Unless Pierce is their dealer."

"Drugs are what got him in trouble in the first place." Wilson squeezed his fists. "If we've got an ex-cop dealing drugs to teens, we need to take him down before he hurts anyone else. I want to know everything he does for the next twenty-four hours. See if we can get a warrant for his phone records. The call from Caleb should be enough."

"Sounds like a plan."

"And then we should talk to Captain Harris. He may want to get the FBI involved early."

Hawkins's eyes widened. "Gary Wilson wants to call in the feds? Who are you and what have you done with my partner?"

"Very funny. I'm trying to do things differently now."

Hawkins tilted his head and studied his partner. "You okay? You look tense."

"It's this case, that's all."

"Nope. That's not it." For another two seconds, Hawkins continued to stare at Wilson as if he were trying to read his mind, then his eyebrows lifted, and he cracked a smile. "You saw Cristina, didn't you?"

"What? I . . . uh, yeah. I did."

"So that's what your *doctor* appointment was about. No worries, I get it. I'm glad." He clapped Wilson on the shoulder. "I'll handle the grunt work this weekend. Take some time off to rest and get your life together. I'll call you if anything comes up."

"Thanks."

As Wilson packed up his desk, thoughts of Cristina seeped into his mind. The weekend would be the perfect chance to show her he had no ulterior motives. But if he really wanted to make an impression, he'd follow up on his promise. He picked up the phone.

"My name is Gary Wilson," he said when the receptionist answered. "I'd like to make an appointment with Dr. Campbell."

CHAPTER FORTY-FIVE

After a brief chat in Cristina's office, Maria called Bruno to pick her up for a ride back to Cristina's apartment. Maria gave her sister a peck on the cheek and promised to text the moment she arrived home. Cristina spent the next hour digging through her research notes. So far, all their subjects experiencing delusions showed differences in electrical activity and metabolism in the brain regions processing sensory input, but those with brain injury or dementia appeared to have stronger differences in the regions controlling memory consolidation, particularly the hippocampus. This was consistent with recent studies she'd read, but their new data suggested focused research on that region could lead to a way to redirect the hippocampus to access buried memories instead of confabulating new ones.

Which could mean a way to unlock my lost memories.

Cristina chewed on her lower lip. That was the reason she was involved in this project, right? To recover Sabrina's memories and find whatever was keeping them from integrating. So, why did that idea scare her so much? Was it because she feared restoring Sabrina would make Cristina redundant?

"Dr. Silva," Victoria stood in the doorway, hugging a stack of folders, cheeks flushed, "I'm sorry for that whole fiasco earlier."

"Really, it's fine." Cristina set aside her discomforting thoughts and waved Victoria inside the office. "Is everything okay, by the way?"

"*Hmm?*" Victoria blinked.

"You had a doctor's appointment, right?"

"Oh. Yes. Right." Victoria placed the files on Cristina's desk and then brushed a lock of hair behind her ear. "It was nothing, only a routine checkup."

Cristina tilted her head to study her assistant. "Then why do you seem so giddy?"

The color on Victoria's cheeks deepened and she averted her gaze. "I, um, ran into your sister again as she was leaving. I mean, I didn't actually run into her this time, I just—you know, we talked a bit more."

"Oh." Cristina noted the way Victoria's voice lifted when she said *sister*.

"She asked me to see some of Boston's sights with her tomorrow. There's a new exhibit at the Museum of Modern Renaissance." Victoria waved her hands dramatically. "But I wouldn't want to do anything that might seem to be stepping outside my caste."

A jolt of worry shot through Cristina at the thought of her sister traipsing around the city with someone they barely knew. But Victoria had proven herself to be trustworthy, even taking the blame for Cristina's mistake the other day. And Cristina would be tied up in her meeting with Special Agent Jefferson. The tension drained away.

"It's no problem at all." Cristina smiled. "I'll be happy knowing Maria's in good hands."

"Oh, yes, my hands will take good care of her." Victoria blanched. "I don't mean like that sounds. I just mean—"

"I know what you mean." Cristina couldn't help laughing. "I hope you two have a good time. The Museum of Modern Renaissance is a good, unexpected choice. Maria loves art."

"Me too. Thanks for the suggestion." Victoria bounced on her toes. "And thank you for your blessing. I'll see you in the EEG lab."

After Victoria walked, or rather, practically skipped, out of the office, Cristina's grinned to herself. Victoria and Maria would make a cute couple.

"How come I didn't know Maria was into women?" she whispered.

It never came up, Sabrina replied. *And, frankly, I didn't remember. Or maybe she came out after I joined Zero Dark.*

Cristina's hand tightened around a pen. So many pieces still didn't fit. She needed to find out more about Sabrina's life, to put those random memory scraps in context. When she got home, she'd talk more to Maria, both about her new friend and about their childhood. But she had to admit at last that it was time to talk to someone else who might have answers. As hard as it might be for her, she'd have to talk to Bruno.

CHAPTER FORTY-SIX

The Boston FBI field office building reminded Cristina of the Chinese Yin-Yang symbol. One light-colored eight-story-high box nestled inside a larger, darker box, like two interlocking pieces. She understood the design offered reinforcement, but as she reflected on the dual nature of the agency, one public and one hidden, she wondered if the contrast had a deeper meaning.

As she entered, security officers screened her with a metal detector. Fortunately, she'd left her Glock in the Mini Cooper. She held still as they wanded her and hoped Maria would be okay by herself. Then she chided herself for being a nervous mother hen. Maria knew how to handle herself in a fight, and she had Victoria with her. Cristina couldn't wait to hear how the date went when she and Maria had dinner with Bruno that night.

One of the officers gave a thumbs-up and directed her to a reception desk on the other side of the lobby.

Her heels clicked on the floor tiles as she made her way to the desk, passing utilitarian black couches and a simple wooden table. A massive seal filled the entire back wall that read Department of Justice Federal Bureau of Investigation. Off to the side stood the Wall of Honor, displaying photos of agents who'd lost their lives. She stopped for a closer look, recognizing none of the faces except for one, recently added at the bottom: Charles Forrester.

A bitter taste filled her mouth. Special Agent Forrester had been blinded by ambition to the corruption in his backyard and ultimately killed by one of his own. How many others had Quinn inserted into official positions, and what was his master plan? Unfortunately, no one knew. The answer to that question died with him.

Shaking off her nerves, Cristina left the memorial and approached the service desk. A young man in a black suit and buzzcut greeted her.

"I'm meeting with Special Agent Jefferson." She assumed an authoritative tone. "He's expecting me."

"Of course. One moment, please."

The receptionist placed a call and then turned away, speaking softly into the receiver. After a moment, he handed her a visitor badge and pointed at the couches. "Wear your badge at all times. Wait here and Special Agent Jefferson will escort you to the interview room."

Cristina pinned the badge to her lapel and took a seat, preparing herself for her meeting with Jefferson. What had he discovered that he couldn't share over the phone?

After a few more minutes, Jefferson stepped off the elevator. The skin around his eyes crinkled as he spotted Cristina. His lips stretched, revealing white teeth that glistened against his dark skin. He crossed the room with long strides and held out his hand.

"Welcome, Dr. Silva." His grip was strong and warm. "Please, follow me."

As Cristina trailed behind him, he asked, "How is your new job working out?"

"Very well, thank you." They entered a small room not much bigger than a closet, containing only a small square table and two chairs. On the table was a water jug and a stack of paper cups. Surveillance cameras were mounted on two of the four walls, red lights indicating they were recording. "I think I made the right choice," she said.

Jefferson motioned for her to sit as he closed the door. She settled into one of the chairs and crossed her ankles. He sat across from her. "Would you like some water?" he asked.

"No, thank you."

He poured himself a glass and took a sip. "You know, I returned to Quantico for a year, to get some extra training. It was strange going from being a barracuda in a pond to a minnow in the middle of the Winnipesaukee. It gave me time to realize that's not what I wanted, so I returned here."

Cristina raised an eyebrow. "You're saying one day I'll get bored and reopen my own practice?"

"No, I'm saying you need to find what works for you. Maybe where you are is what you need, or maybe you're destined for something even bigger." The corner of his mouth twitched. "Like being an expert consultant."

"You want me to work for the FBI?"

"No." He narrowed his gaze and lowered his voice. "I want you to work for me."

"What?"

"I'll make sure you're protected, and with everything going on, I need your expertise—"

"Wait a minute." She held up her hands. "Protected from what? What's going on?"

His features hardened. He pulled out a folder and laid it on the desk. "I did some research. Roman Catholics cross left to right, but Eastern Orthodox cross right to left."

"So you're saying my bike pursuer is an Eastern Catholic? How does that help?"

"It doesn't. There are over sixteen million Eastern Orthodox. But most Catholics encourage use of the right hand to make the sign of the cross even if they're left-handed. Your description of the motorcycle driver using his left hand to sign rang a bell, so I checked the Dark Web to confirm my suspicions." He leaned forward and lowered his voice. "There's a mercenary who supposedly had a childhood neurologic condition causing him to be highly left-hand dominant, whether when using a gun or signing the cross. He was a deep cover operative for Quinn."

Cristina's throat constricted. "Who is he?"

"No one but Quinn knew his real name, but he uses the call sign Sack Man. Does that mean anything to you?"

"No."

Jefferson flipped the folder open to a sheaf of printouts. "Since Quinn's death, Sack Man has gone into hiding from what's left of Zero Dark, but his last known theater of operations was the Boston area. From the intelligence I've gathered, he wears a black hood so no one can identify him."

"If you don't have a face or name, how are you going to find him?"

"I've asked a few of my informants to put out job offers through the Dark Web." Jefferson made a sour face. "So far, nothing. Either he knows they're from us, or he's too busy with another job."

Cristina's skin grew clammy. "How does this help me? Now I know one of Quinn's men is after me and there's nothing you can do about it."

"If this man wanted you dead, I'm quite certain you'd be dead. There must be another reason he was following you. My guess is that you know something that can either help or hurt him."

Words uttered by a stranger months ago resonated in the back of Cristina's mind: *You saw something you shouldn't have. Something that made you a threat.* She swallowed hard. "I don't know anything other than what I've already told you."

Drumming his fingers on the desk, Jefferson screwed up his face, studying her. He stuck his hand in his pocket and then leaned forward. "I've activated a short-range jammer. It'll look like part of the routine maintenance they've been running this past week."

Cristina glanced at the mounted cameras. The recording lights were dark.

"We have eight minutes to speak freely without anyone becoming suspicious."

"What's going on?" she asked.

Without answering, he laid another folder on the desk and silently opened it before turning it around to face Cristina.

Her stomach heaved. It was an autopsy photo of a dead man with a bullet hole in his forehead. She covered her mouth with her hand and looked away. "Who is that?"

"Dominic Steadman. The field agent killed alongside Mateo Gonzalez."

"I don't understand. Why are you showing me this?"

He turned the page, revealing a series of images of the agent's skin. One showed a small tattoo of a scorpion. Another was a closeup of the bullet wound. And the third showed an annular scar.

Cristina leaned closer, running her fingertip over the photo of the scar. "I've seen something like that before. Where was this taken?"

"At the base of Steadman's neck."

The hairs on Cristina's arms lifted. "Jerry Peterman and Carl Franklin had scars like this on their necks. The medical examiner thought it was a coincidence."

"Peterman and Franklin both worked for Zero Dark, correct?"

She nodded.

"What I'm about to say cannot leave this room." Jefferson closed the file and folded his hands together. "I have reason to believe Agent Steadman also worked for Zero Dark."

CHAPTER FORTY-SEVEN

Footsteps echoed from the marble floor of the Memory Center lobby, causing Detective Wilson to snap to attention. He'd been waiting alone in one of the cramped chairs for ten minutes and had started to doze off. The previous night he barely slept, repeatedly waking from nightmares about a hooded man stuffing his memories into a sack and running off, always inches beyond Wilson's reach. Now, he scrubbed his face in a vain effort to appear presentable.

"Detective Wilson." A tall, wiry man in a white lab coat with a Jamaican accent held out his hand. "I'm Winston Campbell. I apologize for the lack of attention, but I don't require my ancillary staff to come in on weekends."

"I understand." Wilson stood and shook Dr. Campbell's hand. The neurologist had a strong grip. "Thanks for seeing me on such short notice, and for giving up your Saturday morning."

"I would've been here anyway." Campbell chortled. "I do my best work when no one else is around. Come with me."

Wilson followed the doctor up the elevator to an expansive office decorated with framed diplomas and certificates, models of the human brain, and brightly colored abstract art. A model of a motorcycle sat in a place of honor in the middle of the desk.

"Is that a Crocker?" Wilson asked.

"You have a very good eye. It's a 1942 V-Twin Big Tank. I'm a bit of a collector."

"So you ride?"

"Nothing quite so rare as this, but yes, I do." Campbell motioned to a plush armchair before sinking into a leather recliner behind a heavy wooden desk. He leaned back and steepled his fingers. "I understand Dr. Silva referred you to me, because you need help with a case?"

"That's right."

Wilson explained about the teens becoming irritable and possibly hallucinating after taking a memory supplement. Dr. Campbell repetitively clicked a pen as he listened. When Wilson finished, Campbell lay down his pen.

"Fascinating," Campbell said. "Who created this so-called supplement?"

"Dr. Allison Wakefield."

"Wakefield." Campbell nodded. "I met her at a Cognitive Neuroscience Society meeting. Brilliant woman, if not a bit backward in her views."

"Yeah, that's her."

"And she believes MCH-21 couldn't be involved?"

"Yes. But what do *you* think?"

"I suppose it's possible. Even prescription drugs that underwent rigorous testing can have unanticipated psychiatric effects. Take the leukotriene inhibitor montelukast, for example. It was once considered a safe first-line treatment for asthma, until the FDA issued a Black Box Warning that it could cause depression and suicidal thoughts. Because the FDA doesn't regulate nootropics, it's often difficult to know what problems they might cause until there's a lawsuit."

Wilson drummed his fingers on the arm of his chair. "That's what I thought."

"But I'm more curious about the actual effects of this MCH-21. You said the teens developed uncanny memory retrieval?"

"So their friends and families claim. I couldn't tell you for sure. By the time we found the last teen, he barely recalled his own name."

Campbell sat up straight. "Really?"

"Yeah, he said it was like he had holes in his memory." Wilson cocked his head. "That mean something to you? I thought it was the supplement wearing off."

"Even if this supplement had as strong an effect as you describe, and stopping it caused a withdrawal syndrome, I can't imagine how it would affect anything other than recently acquired memories."

"The ER doctors thought he was suffering from amphetamine withdrawal."

"A good thought, but memory problems usually develop during the course of chronic amphetamine abuse, not suddenly during withdrawal." Campbell ran his finger along his upper lip. "He described it as *holes* in his memory?"

"He said it was like a rodent eating away at his brain."

"Well, that's simply preposterous. I fear this teen was romping with you, Detective."

Wilson raised an eyebrow.

"That means he was yanking your chain." Dr. Campbell chuckled. "There's no drug that erodes memory selectively like that, and unless the medical examiner discovers he had a prion disease or blood clots in his brain, it's highly unlikely an otherwise healthy young person would experience progressive memory loss."

Something about the neurologist's tone caused the hairs on the back of Wilson's neck to prick up. Dr. Campbell seemed awfully quick to discredit Caleb's symptoms. "Why would he lie? He wasn't in danger of any criminal charges."

"Perhaps he wasn't lying. There are psychological conditions like conversion disorder that manifest as physical conditions. He may have believed he was losing his memory, and so, in effect, he was."

"The other two teens had similar symptoms." Wilson scratched his chin. "So you think it was all in their heads?"

"I'm a neurologist. Most of what I study is all in our heads." Campbell grinned at his own joke. When Wilson didn't smile back, Campbell cleared his throat. "But seriously, placebo effect can be quite strong. If these teens believed the supplement would improve their memory, perhaps it did—by unlocking their nascent abilities. And if one of them developed psychotic symptoms, the others could have as well, in a sort of mass hysteria effect."

Wilson's cell phone vibrated. He shook off his thoughts and checked the caller ID. Hawkins.

"I'm sorry, Dr. Campbell, but I have to take this." Wilson stood. "Thanks for your time. If I come up with anything else, can I call you?"

"Of course, Detective." Campbell grinned. "My door's always open."

After leaving the office, Wilson answered his phone. "What's up, Rick?"

"Autopsy report came back on Caleb Jackman. The only thing in his system was amphetamines."

"The ones he was prescribed." Wilson grunted as he jabbed the down elevator button. "Like the others."

"That's the thing. Because Caleb had been off his meds for several days, they ran more intensive tests. He had trace amounts of amphetamine, not enough to explain his psychosis."

The elevator doors opened. Wilson entered. "And amphetamine withdrawal wouldn't explain his memory loss. So he injected something else."

"The ME is running more tests on samples from the injection site. It'll take a few more days. But there's something else."

"What?"

"She didn't find any track sites, nothing to suggest he'd shot up before, except for a ring-shaped scar at the base of his neck."

The elevator dinged. "A scar from what?"

"Good question. Brenner says she's never seen anything like it."

A draft blew over Wilson's bare neck as he stepped off the elevator. He reached back to turn up his collar.

"Brenner's going to run an analysis of the scar tissue," Hawkins continued. "See if it's relevant."

"Great. Tell her to check his brain for any sign of damage too."

"Like what?"

"I don't know. Prion somethings or clots. What about Pierce?"

"He's kept to himself all day. I'm still working on getting his phone records."

"All right. Let me know if you find anything else."

As Wilson stepped outside, a chill bit deep into his bones, carrying with it the feeling of being watched. Lowering his hand to the pistol in his holster, he glanced behind him, to the side, and finally up.

A pigeon cooed overhead and flew off.

Wilson relaxed and strode to his Charger parked at the curb.

As he was entering his car, his phone rang. He didn't recognize the number.

"Detective Wilson," a female voice said. "It's Allison Wakefield."

"Dr. Wakefield. I didn't expect to hear from you on a Saturday morning."

"I remembered something that might help your case. I'd like to speak to you in person. Could you please come to the store?"

Wilson backed out of the parking spot and started driving. "I'll be there in twenty minutes."

CHAPTER FORTY-EIGHT

Cristina's temporal pulses pounded as she held Special Agent Jefferson's unblinking gaze. He had to be joking. That was it, right? Some sick FBI humor. Except nothing on his face suggested the slightest bit of mirth.

"I thought you weeded out all the moles Quinn planted in your agency," she said at last, fighting to control her nerves. "*Cleaned house* were your exact words."

"Yes, well, apparently we missed one." Jefferson twiddled his thumbs. "Steadman covered his tracks well, piggybacking his extracurricular operations onto official business so as not to raise suspicion. He channeled private funds to keep Mateo Gonzalez in hiding. The night they were killed was the first direct contact they'd had since ReMind was shut down."

"So this assassin didn't know your agent was a mole?"

"Or they did, and Steadman was a liability." Jefferson spread his hands. "It's hard to know for certain."

A thought crossed Cristina's mind. "Could Sack Man be the assassin?"

"It's possible, but the murders don't fit his style. And if he's gone rogue from Zero Dark and running his own operation, hunting down ReMind employees would draw their attention to him." A muscle ticked in Jefferson's cheek. "More likely, he's another target."

Cristina's breath caught in her throat. "But Zero Dark died with Quinn."

"Maybe it didn't. The assassin also killed a DEA agent and a US Marshal." Jefferson's eyebrows scrunched together. "Both had the same scars on the backs of their necks, and evidence suggests they worked directly for Quinn."

"What evidence?"

"I can't discuss that."

Cristina rankled. "Any idea what the scars mean?"

"Not yet. It could be a way of branding operatives."

"But if Zero Dark is still in operation, why would they eliminate their own people?"

"Groups like this are highly volatile. Whoever took control once Quinn died may be tying off loose ends to erase competition." Jefferson clasped his hands together. "I'm not sure how deep this goes, but you must use extreme caution. I have to assume the Bureau, and possibly other federal agencies, are compromised. That's why I'm using the jammer. And while the consultant offer was a ruse to throw off anyone watching, I want you to report only to me." He gave her a pointed look. "If you have even the inkling that someone is trying to undermine you, call me immediately and tell me anything you learn. As soon as we learn how far this goes and what they want, I will pull you out and make sure you're protected while we take them down."

Every muscle fiber in Cristina's body contracted. She wanted to fly away somewhere no one would ever find her. But that was impossible. No matter how far she ran, someone was always close at her heels. If she had kept running six months earlier, Quinn would still be hunting her.

"All right," she said at last. "But I need you to do something for me."

"Name it."

She straightened her back and looked him square in the eye. "Tell me everything right when you know it. No more sitting on information like this scar thing. If you're supposed to be the one person I can trust, then you need to trust me with knowing everything I need to survive."

He remained silent for a moment, pressing his knuckles against his lips. At last, he said, "If I withhold anything from you again, may God strike me down."

CHAPTER FORTY-NINE

When Cristina arrived at her apartment shortly after noon, she found Maria curled up on the couch, watching television. Whiny, irritating voices spilled from the surround sound speakers. Maria wrinkled her nose and shut off the TV.

"How can Americans stand this garbage?" Maria tossed the remote onto the coffee table. "Who wants to watch spoiled housewives cursing at each other and complaining about not having enough champagne on their private jets?"

Cristina hung up her jacket and sat next to Maria. "Funny, I heard the Brazilian version of the show was even worse." She smirked. "And I recall you saying you never missed an episode."

Maria waved her hand. "That's different. The fights in Portuguese are far more nuanced."

A chuckle passed Cristina's lips. She reclined on the couch as Grizabella padded in and jumped onto her lap. The cat's soft purrs soothed her jangled nerves. "Well, those shows will rot your brain in any language. Tell me about something more interesting, like how your date with Victoria went."

Maria blushed. "It wasn't a date."

"What would you call it?"

"Okay, I suppose it was a date." Maria nuzzled against the cushions and traced her finger along the seams. "It was nice. We went to the art museum. There were so many unusual paintings there. Victoria was very interested, or at least, she acted like she was."

Cristina smiled and stroked Grizabella's back. "Why didn't you stay out with her longer?"

"She has an appointment this afternoon to review her work visa with an immigration officer. Some form she forgot to complete. At least they're giving her the chance to correct it." Maria tucked her knees against her chest. "Besides, I knew you would feel safer if I were home when you returned."

Regret nipped at Cristina's chest. Her sister deserved to go out and have fun, not to stay at home like a prisoner. She brushed her palm across Maria's cheek. "I'm sorry. My FBI contact found some leads, so hopefully this will all be handled soon. Are you going to see Victoria again?"

A smile played at Maria's lips. "We're going out tomorrow night."

"That's good timing. Wilson invited me over for dinner then."

"So neither of us will be alone." Maria nodded. "Perfect. Are you still okay with Bruno joining us here tonight?"

Bruno's handsome face popped into Cristina's head.

"Damn it, Sabrina," she murmured. "Knock it off."

"What?" Maria asked.

"Nothing." Cristina shook her head. "Just your sister being rebellious. Yes, I want Bruno to come. Here. Come *here*." Her cheeks burned. "Damn."

Maria giggled and patted Cristina's hand. "Don't worry. I have confidence you'll be in charge tonight. But I'll be here in case Sabrina tries to do anything reckless. I know how to handle my sister."

Cristina forced a smile. But as Maria wandered off to the bathroom, her body tensed. In a low voice, she asked, "You wouldn't really do anything to ruin my chances with Wilson, would you?"

Of course not, Sabrina's voice shot back. *You trust me, don't you?*

Cristina's fingers dug into Grizabella's fur. The cat yowled. She startled and soothed the feline's back. "Sorry, Griz. Of course, I trust Sabrina. How could I not trust myself?"

She continued to pet her cat, staring blankly at the floor, doubt lingering at the edges of her mind.

CHAPTER FIFTY

The sign on the door announced the NatureBoost shop was closed, but as soon as Wilson pulled into the parking lot, Allison Wakefield opened the door and motioned him inside.

"Thank you for coming." She led him over to the back counter. "I've been thinking about what you said, and I might have an answer to your question."

"Which question is that?"

She cocked her head. "Are you serious or is that a memory joke?"

His jaw clenched. "Serious."

"You asked who might want to steal my supplements. Roughly five years ago, when I first opened this shop, a man became a frequent customer. He bought all kinds of supplements and vitamins, always paid in cash, and always high potency." She stopped and gave Wilson a hard glare. "I want to repeat that everything I sell in this store is safe. That being said, when mixed together, some can have psychoactive effects."

Wilson held his tongue, already sensing where Wakefield was going with this.

"One day, this particular customer managed to overhear me speaking to a director of neurologic research about my discovery of a way to use MCH antagonists to stimulate memory consolidation. He came back day after day, pestering me to let him be one of the first to try it." She shook her head. "When I told him no, he became belligerent. He threatened to smash everything in my store. I told him he was no longer welcome, and I'd call the police if he set foot in my shop again."

"Did he ever return?"

"Once, about four months ago." Her lip curled. "He'd dyed his hair white, put on a few pounds, but I recognized him instantly. He even tried using a fake name. I threw him out."

"Four months ago." The words triggered Wilson's memories. "That would've been shortly before the break-in. Do you think this man broke in and stole the MCH-21?"

She knitted her brow. "Yes."

"Okay, I'll need a statement." He riffled through his pockets until he found a pen. He tingled with anticipation. This was the break in the case he needed. "What was the fake name this guy used?"

Wakefield jutted her chin. "Scott Pierce."

CHAPTER FIFTY-ONE

DB stood at the edge of the lot, shivering despite the relatively balmy weather. She clenched her fists tightly as she stared at the charred ruins of what had once been a two-story saltbox house. The remains of the sloping frame rose up like a monument out of the scorched husk. Creeping vines had started making their way up the foundation walls. Clover poked out where there had once been grass.

The sign at the end of the driveway announced the lot was still for sale two and a half years after the house had burned to the ground. DB snorted. It didn't surprise her that no one wanted to rebuild on an arson site, especially when the previous owners had been subsequently murdered.

A light breeze ruffled her hair. She drew in deep breaths, searching for a feeling, any feeling, about this place. Manny Feldman had told her this had been her home. She'd spent the previous night searching through public records, discovering a criminal named Francisco Martins had been responsible for torching the house. She'd found the obituary for Jorge and Claudia Silva, whom she now knew had been her parents. At first, she refused to believe it, but then she saw their photo, and another glitch overtook her. It was the same vision she'd had before, where she was playing with a toy robot while a man watched a soccer game, only this time, when he turned around, he had Jorge Silva's face. And she knew it was true.

High up in a maple tree, a blue jay cawed. DB stared up at it, thinking about how much simpler it would be to be something other than human. No complex memories. No conscience. Only instinct.

Wasn't that what her employers had made her to be? They ripped out her past, everything that made her who she was, and left her with nothing but technical skills and a drive to follow orders. A cold-blooded killing machine.

So then why was she having these glitches? Were they real memories? Or was she losing her mind?

A ray of sunlight poked through the tree canopy and glinted off something half-buried next to one of the few intact wooden beams. She scanned the field for trip wires or landmines or anything else that might've been left as a trap but saw nothing suspicious. Curiosity threatening to consume her, she picked her way through the rubble over to the beam. She knelt on the bare ground and tugged at the object until it came free of the dirt.

Something fluttered in her stomach as she twisted it in her hands. Her eyes stung and she swiped at them with the back of her hand.

The metal head was caved in on one side, but she recognized it anyway. It was the toy robot from her vision.

Her breathing slowed as memories flooded back. She could picture every room in the house, from the contemporary kitchen with stainless steel appliances, to the upstairs bedrooms decorated in rainforest themes. She remembered her father tucking her in at night, always singing a ballad by Antônio Carlos Jobim before kissing her forehead.

She gasped. Her hand crept up to her face. Her cheeks were wet with tears.

This wasn't right. Dama Branca had no past. She felt no emotion. She never cried.

But what if she wasn't meant to be a killer? She tried to recall her first kill and couldn't. The more she tried to picture it, the more muddied it became. Could she still be something else?

She thought about the woman who'd taken her place. Every record she found, public or otherwise, identified the doppelgänger as Cristina Silva. Who was she, really? She had a sister, DB now knew, whose name was Maria. According to Feldman, the woman was a victim whose memories had also been stolen. So why was she still pretending to be Cristina Silva?

DB's grip on the robot toy tightened. She couldn't live like this. She needed answers. She needed to know who her double was and whose side she was on. If there was a chance that she could cure DB of the glitches, then DB would have to make sure that's what she did. And if she couldn't . . .

Well, the world didn't need two Cristina Silvas.

CHAPTER FIFTY-TWO

There was a knock on the door at ten minutes to five. Cristina crossed over to it and peered through the peephole to confirm the visitor was who they were expecting. She looked back at Maria, who was wearing skinny jeans and a silk ruffled-front blouse. Maria nodded at her. Cristina smoothed out a wrinkle on her midi dress and then opened the door.

Bruno stood in the hallway, wearing all black under his leather jacket, one hand behind his back. One corner of his mouth crept upward.

"You look beautiful," he said and moved his arm forward to hold out a bouquet of tropical flowers: anthuriums, birds of paradise, and ginger lilies. "Who will pay for the flowers and the burial, if I die from love?"

Cristina blinked.

"It's a poem by Vinícius de Moraes." Bruno's grin collapsed. "Perhaps I translated it incorrectly into English."

"No, it's lovely, and so are these." Cristina accepted the bouquet and ushered Bruno inside. "I wasn't expecting to hear poetry."

"My mother loved poetry." Bruno removed his jacket and set it on a chair. "As did my brother, Federico."

Cristina shivered at the mention of Federico's name. A vision popped into her mind of a man with nearly the same face, marred by a scar under one eye, firing at her from behind a snowbank. She flinched as if the bullet had struck her.

Bruno's face deepened with concern. "What did he do to you?"

"It's a long story, but he hurt some people and tried to hurt me."

His eyes locked with hers. His expression didn't flicker. At last, he dropped his gaze. "Did it have to do with the *Renascimento* project?"

Cristina's hackles rose. How did Bruno know about the secret Recognate drug trials on Rio's favela residents? Quinn had gone to great lengths to cover up the drug's failures—including murdering the subjects. Cristina turned to Maria, asking with her eyes: *Did you tell him?*

Maria shook her head.

"I know Federico introduced you to those researchers," Bruno said, inhaling sharply through his nose and arching his back. "And once you got involved with them, I lost you."

"Lost me?"

"If it's seemed like I've been avoiding you . . ." He released his breath in a huff. "It's because I have. I thought I'd prepared myself for the pain of seeing you again, but then you looked so different, sounded so different, and I thought, maybe . . ."

His eyes met hers again, only this time he projected regret and . . . something else. A memory resurfaced of her holding hands with a young man, running through the streets of Rio with a bouquet of roses. The man turned to smile at her. But this time, she noticed his eyes weren't gray, but brown.

"I wasn't with Federico." She could barely speak. "I was with you."

"Yes."

Cristina turned to Maria. "Why didn't you tell me this?"

"She didn't know about us," Bruno said before Maria could respond. "The relationship between our families is complicated. We agreed to keep our romance secret. But one person managed to find out about it."

The answer was written all over his face. "Federico," she said.

"I should never have let him involve you in his schemes. It was obvious to everyone but me that he wanted whatever I had." He dabbed at the corner of his eye. "He was my brother. I trusted he had good intentions. Maybe he thought by working with you, he would win your heart for his own, or maybe he didn't want me to have you. But once you got sucked into that program, you stopped talking to me. That's why I moved here." His lip quivered. "To forget."

Regret gnawed at Cristina's chest, even though she couldn't remember any of what he'd described. She searched in vain through her recovered memories, but there were still too many gaps she hadn't managed to fill.

He's telling the truth, though, Sabrina said in her mind. *That's why I've been so drawn to him since he arrived. I loved him—or, at least, I thought I did—until I bought into Quinn's promises of adventure and wealth. Bruno's a good man. I made a terrible mistake.*

The urge to cry anew clawed at Cristina's heart, but she had no tears to spare for anyone else. Not when she'd lost so much. Carefully, she said, "I was a different person then. I made some poor choices, but I've changed. A lot."

"I can see that." He tilted his head as he studied her. "You're now Cristina Silva."

"Yes."

He smiled thinly. "You seem like a good person."

"So do you," she said, and she meant it. Whatever reasons drove Federico Gomes to work for Zero Dark, Bruno didn't have the same motivations. She could only imagine how hard it must have been for him, when he clearly still had feelings for her despite the way she—*Sabrina*—had treated him. And it seemed Sabrina had rediscovered feelings for him, as well. But Cristina couldn't allow those feelings to interfere with her relationship with Wilson. Casually, she said, "And I hope you're hungry, because we ordered a feast from Churrasco Gostoso."

Bruno's grin widened. "I'm starved."

They chatted about random things while they ate: differences between soccer and American football, horrible Boston winters, and the more interesting celebrities who'd employed Pantera, Bruno's private protection firm. After his revelation about their past relationship, Cristina no longer had the courage to ask him about his father. And no doubt he had many questions, like why she'd changed her name and moved to Boston, but he respected her privacy enough not to ask them. That made him all the more attractive. Something stirred deep inside.

Thoughts of Bruno and Wilson tossed and turned in Cristina's mind. She didn't want to hurt either man, but she only had enough trust in her heart for one of them. As she pushed her steak around with her fork she avoided staring at his face, and she brooded.

CHAPTER FIFTY-THREE

For most of the following day, in between periods of worrying about an assassin and sorting through her feelings about Bruno, Cristina obsessed over her upcoming date with Wilson. Now, as she drove to his apartment, the doubts crept back in. Did he see it as a date? True, he'd invited her to his apartment, which typically carried certain expectations, but maybe there was another reason, like he wanted to consult her again on his case.

Get a grip, Cristina. It's too crowded in here with all these second guesses.

Catching her breath, Cristina turned her focus back to driving. Sabrina was right. It was a date. Just a date.

So why did that scare her so much?

By the time she arrived at his apartment, she'd managed to settle her nerves. It wasn't like he was going to do something ridiculous like ask her to marry him. And they'd already cleared the air between them. She opened her car door and stepped out into the cool night air. This would be a simple dinner between two old friends reconnecting. Yes, that was it.

As she rang his doorbell, she caught a whiff of onions and garlic. Her mouth watered. One of Wilson's neighbors must be a damned good cook.

The door opened. Cristina's heart jumped.

Wilson was wearing a sleek navy button-down and charcoal pants that hugged his hips in a most flattering way. The gold flecks in his hazel eyes sparkled. He grinned as he looked her up and down.

"That dress is gorgeous on you," he said. "Is it new?"

"No, but I don't wear it much." She smiled. "But I know that shirt."

His cheeks flushed. "Yeah, it's comfortable. I should wear it more often."

"Yes, you should." She waited patiently. When he continued to grin at her, she asked, "May I come in?"

"Yes, of course." He motioned her inside and shut the door.

She drank in the fragrance of fresh salmon. "Did you order from Richiamo?"

"Next best thing. I cooked it myself."

"You cooked?" Her jaw slackened. "I thought you barely knew how to operate the microwave."

"I watched some YouTube videos. It's a pretty simple dish, but it really tantalizes your tastebuds." He took her coat and draped it over the couch before escorting her to the dining table. After holding her chair, he scurried into the kitchen and returned with two plates of salmon in a cream sauce. He placed one in front of her and bowed. "Bon Appetit."

She inhaled the aroma of garlic butter. "It smells wonderful. Consider me impressed."

Wilson filled her wine glass and then settled into a chair across from her. As he cut into his salmon, he asked, "Was Maria okay with staying alone tonight?"

"Oh, she went out with my research assistant."

He looked at her quizzically.

"They met at my office. I think they'd make a great couple, actually. It's too bad Maria's only here for another week." Cristina scooped a forkful of fish into her mouth. Tastes of sun-dried tomato and spinach rolled over her tongue. "Wow. This is delicious."

"I'm glad you like it." He jabbed and held up a cream-covered spinach leaf. "The secret is not overcooking the spinach. Two minutes is all it takes. Otherwise, it tastes like sewage."

She stared at him.

He stopped eating. "What's wrong? Is it undercooked?"

"No, it's perfect. But I never imagined Detective Wilson would be playing Master Chef."

He flashed a lopsided smile. "Roleplaying can be a lot of fun."

She blushed at the innuendo.

His fork squeaked against the bottom of his plate. Looking down at his food, he said, "I talked to your boss, by the way, about my case. Interesting guy."

"Yes, you could say that. Was he helpful?"

"Somewhat, but something about him bothered me."

A prickly heat rose up the back of Cristina's neck. "In what way?"

"He was quick to poo-poo the idea that something could cause the teens to develop holes in their memory. Almost like he wanted to make sure I thought it was impossible so I wouldn't dig any deeper into it." He took another bite of salmon. "But I'm probably reading into things."

Cristina's stomach churned as she recalled Dr. Campbell's quick temper and the way he kept looking at her while discussing delusions and false identities. "You're an incredible detective, Gary. If something felt off to you, it probably was. Did he say anything else that seemed odd?"

"Other than it's hard to picture him as a motorcycle aficionado, no. But he was intent on pushing the narrative that the teens were having some kind of mass hysteria or placebo effect from the supplement. Maybe a converting disorder or something."

"Conversion disorder." Cristina took a sip of wine. "It's somewhat common, affecting roughly twenty out of a hundred thousand people. Had any of the teens been diagnosed with it?"

"No, they were all being treated for ADHD, but their psychiatrists didn't diagnose anything else."

"Then it would be highly unusual for all three of them to have it and go undiagnosed." She tapped her cheek in thought. "A placebo effect is more likely, but it doesn't explain the memory loss you described. I'm surprised Dr. Campbell so quickly wrote it off, especially given his interest in dementia and memory restoration." She caught Wilson staring at her with laser focus. "What?"

He shook his head and smiled. "I love hearing you talk about science."

She blushed and bowed her head to study the cream sauce but couldn't help smiling.

Suddenly, he wiped his mouth with a napkin and crumpled it up. "There's something I have to confess to you."

A quiver started in her stomach and worked its way through her abdomen. She looked up at him and saw the serious look in his eye. *Oh, God*, she thought. *Please don't say you worked for Zero Dark.*

He fidgeted with his fork, running his fingertip over the tines, and then said, "I've really missed you."

Relief washed over her, carrying with it a tidal wave of emotion. "I've missed you too."

He stood, crossed over to her, and lifted her chin. She could taste his lips even before they kissed. Electricity jolted through her as he pulled her close.

After a breathless embrace, he pulled his head back and looked in her eyes. "Is this okay? We're not moving too fast?"

Of course not, Sabrina whispered. *You've waited long enough. Grab him and kiss him.*

Cristina's muscles tensed. She wanted to do exactly that, but doubt crept into her mind. She didn't want to screw this up by throwing herself at him.

"Um." She bit her lip, hoping he didn't mistake her hesitance for lack of interest. "Maybe we should finish dinner?"

He blinked rapidly, eyebrows meeting. Slowly, he nodded. "Yeah. Good idea."

Walking stiffly, he returned to his seat, replaced his napkin on his lap, and took a bite of salmon.

Cristina's legs quivered as she forced herself to scoop creamy spinach into her mouth, unsure if they would make it through to dessert.

CHAPTER FIFTY-FOUR

As Cristina and Wilson finished their dinner, she marveled over the fact that, although they ate in silence, it didn't feel awkward. Instead, it was comfortable, like they knew each other so well words were unnecessary. And they shared plenty of glances and smiles that spoke volumes. Each bite of the salmon tasted better than the last—or maybe that was thanks to the wine.

After finishing the fish, Cristina reclined in her chair and held her belly. "I couldn't eat another bite."

"That's too bad." Wilson grinned. "You'll miss out on the tiramisu."

She jolted upright. "You made tiramisu?"

"That I bought. But I know it's your favorite."

She shook her head. "I'm going to have to let you embarrass yourself more often."

Wilson chuckled and started to clear the plates. "Pass."

"Wait, what time is it?" Cristina checked her phone. "I need to call Maria and make sure everything's okay."

"She's a big girl." He gave her an amused expression. "Since when are you her mother?"

"Since I found out someone's been killing ReMind employees and . . ."

She froze. Shit, she had said that out loud, hadn't she?

A muscle ticked in Wilson's jaw.

"Um," she began, "I had a lovely time. How about we catch a movie tomorrow?"

"Don't change the subject. Who's killing ReMind employees?"

She told him what Special Agent Jefferson had told her about the murders and about the FBI agent suspected to be a Zero Dark mole.

Wilson's forehead crinkled. "Why didn't you tell me about this sooner? I could've helped."

"We hadn't spoken to each other in weeks."

"What about the other day? You didn't say anything then." He scratched at the back of his neck. "I would've gone with you to meet with Jefferson."

"You were busy with your case." She dropped her chin. "I didn't want to pull you away."

He remained silent, long enough for Cristina to expect him to toss her out the door. After all, he'd asked her to trust him, and she'd kept the murders—and a lot more—from him.

But he didn't make her leave and he didn't yell or do anything other than cover her hand with his and gaze into her eyes. "You can trust me, okay? Whatever's going on in your life, I want to know. All of it."

As she met his gaze, she could feel the sincerity in his touch. She interlocked her fingers with his. He was right. She needed to trust him. She needed to trust someone, or she'd go mad.

"There's more," she said. "Someone followed me the other day. Some-one who used to work for Quinn."

Wilson clenched her hand. "Are you okay? Did they hurt you?"

"No, I think he was trying to learn my driving route. I managed to evade him."

"I don't believe this," He pulled out his cell phone. "I'm setting you up with a forensic artist. We'll put out a BOLO and, until we catch him, I'm going to assign a watch over you."

She plucked the phone from his grip and laid it on the table. "I al-ready spoke to Jefferson about it and he's taking care of it but thank you."

"Let me help you."

"You are helping me, by listening." She patted his hand. "But the FBI can handle this one. Anyway, the man who followed me wore a helmet so I couldn't see his face."

"You don't know who he is?"

Cristina looked down at her fingertips as she rubbed them together, wanting to go back in time and avoid this conversation altogether.

Wilson took hold of her hands. When she met his gaze, he didn't blink.

"Please." His tender tone made her stomach flutter. "Don't shut me out."

She became aware of her own heartbeat as his rough fingers slid over the backs of her hands. Her thoughts muddled together. She wanted to protect him, to keep him away from the madness of her life, but at the same time, she yearned for him to be a part of it.

He doesn't want to be protected, Sabrina murmured. *And he's already involved.*

Inhaling through her nose, Cristina nodded to herself. They had the chance for something real, but it had to be built on honesty. She wet her lips. "Jefferson thinks he's operating under a code name. Sack Man."

His eyes widened, face paled. "Did—did you say Sack Man?"

"Yes. Why?"

Instead of answering, he released her hand and grabbed a notepad. "Can you give me Jefferson's phone number?"

"Of course, but what's going on? Why are you acting so strangely?"

"Because my case involves a murdering lowlife named Sack Man. I think I know who he is." His expression hardened. "But if he worked for Zero Dark, I'm going to need the FBI's help to take him down."

CHAPTER FIFTY-FIVE

Following Special Agent Jefferson's advice to vary her driving route cost Cristina time the next morning as she ran into a traffic jam crossing the bridge over the Charles River. By the time she arrived at the Memory Center, she was ten minutes late. She scurried into the building, straightening her hair with her fingers on the way.

The receptionist caught her eye as she passed by and mouthed a warning. Cristina listened for the sound of Dr. Campbell yelling, but thankfully all she heard was the sound of her own heels on the tile floor.

As she rode the elevator up to her floor, she reflected on what Wilson had told her the previous night. While he couldn't name his suspect, what he could tell her was that the Sack Man he was pursuing was tied to the deaths of the three teenagers who'd been taking the memory supplement, and he wore a black hood like Jefferson had described. Wilson promised he would coordinate with Jefferson to catch Sack Man but cautioned Cristina to take extra precautions.

She unlocked her office and dropped her backpack on her workstation. The handgun inside clunked against the wooden desk. Once she'd settled into her chair, she glanced around her desk. Damn it. The cleaning crew had knocked her picture frame out of place again. With a grunt, she repositioned it.

"Oh, Dr. Silva, you're here." Victoria poked her head into the doorway. "Dr. Campbell was looking for you."

"Is he pissed because I was late?"

"No. At least, he didn't appear so, but perhaps that's because I said you were here early preparing the correlation analysis on the data."

Cristina frowned. "But I didn't—"

With a grin, Victoria produced a collated and stapled ream of papers. "I took care of it."

Relief washed over Cristina. "You are a lifesaver."

"Pish-posh. It's my pleasure."

Leaning back in her chair, Cristina asked, "How was bowling? Maria got in late last night and she was asleep when I left this morning."

"Oh, it was ace. That candlepin bowling is something else, though I prefer Skittles. Your sister is such a fast learner, and a ton of fun. I'm really glad you're okay with us hanging out."

"Why wouldn't I? If she's happy, I'm happy."

Beaming, Victoria headed toward the door, and then stopped. She turned back, her expression becoming serious. "I do have a question, though. When Maria showed her passport to buy our drinks, I noticed her name isn't Silva. It's Carvalho. Was she previously married?"

The back of Cristina's neck burned. There was another reason why she and Maria had different last names, but it wasn't one she could discuss with Victoria. Fortunately, there was an explanation that wasn't far from the truth. "No. We had different fathers."

"Oh, right. Of course, that makes sense." Victoria chuckled awkwardly and backed away. "I was just wondering. I'll see you in the lab."

After Victoria left, Cristina tapped her pen on the desk. She needed to write up her plan for the day's studies, but her mind was too jumbled to concentrate on it. She hoped Jefferson and Wilson could collaborate to capture Sack Man, and maybe the assassin, as well, but what if they weren't the only ones out there? What if Jefferson was right, and someone else was now in charge of Zero Dark? Would they send someone else after her?

Frustrated, Cristina tossed the pen across the desk and crossed her arms. She had a feeling she wasn't going to get much work done that day.

CHAPTER FIFTY-SIX

When Detective Wilson arrived at the precinct, Hawkins was nowhere to be seen. Wilson didn't have time to look for him, not with Cristina's revelation still bouncing around in his head. If Pierce was Sack Man, and he was using American history to connect with the teens, Wilson needed ammunition to figure out the guy's next move. Gathering up all his investigation notes, he marched to Captain Harris's office.

The captain looked up from his cup of coffee at Wilson's knock. His forehead wrinkled. "Something the matter, Detective?"

Wilson shut the door behind him and laid his notes on the captain's desk. "I think my case involves a terrorist."

Harris set down his cup and pressed his palm against his forehead. "Not another one. All right, tell me what you've got."

Wilson reviewed everything with Harris, except for his source of information. When he finished, the captain clucked his tongue. "So the FBI is already looking for this guy?"

"Yes."

"Give this Agent Jefferson a heads-up, but make sure he knows we're taking the lead on the homicide investigation." Harris smoothed the lapels on his uniform. "We need the community to know we're keeping them safe."

"Copy that, Captain."

As Wilson returned to the detectives' pen, he ran into Hawkins, who held up a computer printout and looked like he'd hit the jackpot at Mohegan Sun.

"I got the phone records for Pierce's burner phone and guess what?" He jabbed a finger at the top page. "He'd spoken to Caleb Jackman at least three times before the night Caleb died."

"That only confirms they knew each other," Wilson said. "We need more than that."

Hawkins flipped a page. "How about fourteen calls and text messages between Pierce and Danny Trevino?"

"Trevino?" A tidbit of conversation glinted at the outskirts of Wilson's mental spider web. He pounced on it. "Reggie said Danny seemed like he'd seen a ghost after Pierce spoke to him in the hall. If Pierce was dealing to these kids, maybe he threatened to cut Danny off."

"We could check his bank records for suspicious transactions."

"Get a warrant and do it. Let's also put a wiretap on his cell phone."

"Already done."

"What did the text messages say?"

"It looks like they met a few times at Prospect Hill."

"Another Revolutionary War site," Wilson said, pieces clicking together.

Hawkins nodded. "No details about why they were meeting, though."

"Try to get a hold of Danny's outgoing texts. I need to make a call."

Wilson hustled to his desk and dialed the number Cristina gave him. After several rings, Special Agent Jefferson answered. Wilson introduced himself and then got right to the point. "I understand you're looking for a mercenary who goes by the name Sack Man. I know who he is."

"How?"

"He's the primary suspect in a homicide investigation. The victims and a witness all described a man wearing a black hood."

"That sounds like our guy. He's extremely dangerous."

"Yeah, so I've heard."

"How did you know to call me directly?"

"Dr. Cristina Silva."

Jefferson sucked air through his teeth. "Detective Gary Wilson. I should've recognized the name. You were involved in Chuck Forrester's last case, weren't you?"

"That's right."

"Well, you're going to need my help with this one. Did you already petition for an arrest warrant?"

"No, my partner is preparing an application right—" Wilson noticed Hawkins standing next to him, making excited movements with his hand. "Standby, Agent."

"You're not going to believe this," Hawkins said when Wilson put Jefferson on hold. "Pierce got another call to his burner phone."

"Did you record it?"

"Sure did, but I'll sum it up for you. It was Reggie Horne."

Wilson's stomach hardened. "Reggie called him?"

"The kid told Pierce he wanted to take over RAM Boost distribution and demanded a meeting to talk it out. Pierce agreed."

"Where are they meeting?"

"Pierce said he was leaving his home and would text the location."

"Damn it. Put out an ABP with both Pierce's and Reggie's descriptions." As Hawkins hurried off, Wilson picked up the call with Jefferson. "We've got a situation. How fast can you get a team together?"

"Twenty minutes."

"Do it. Is this your cell?"

"Yes."

"I'll call you with the location."

CHAPTER FIFTY-SEVEN

When Cristina arrived at the EEG lab, there was no one else there. She found a note from Dr. Campbell directing her to the next sublevel. Curious, she followed his directions and exited the elevator into another stark white hallway. At the end of the hall, she encountered a small room set up like an airlock. A sign on the wall instructed her to remove all metal and electronic objects and place them into a bin. After she complied, a green light appeared over the opposite door.

The next room contained a massive machine that looked like something from an amusement park. Dr. Campbell was fiddling with a control pad. As Cristina approached, he glanced over his shoulder.

"Ah, Dr. Silva," he said, standing erect. "What do you think of our new upright functional MRI machine? They finished installing it last night."

"It's impressive." She admired its sleek angles. Unlike a traditional MRI machine that required a patient to lie down and hold still inside a tube for an hour, this one was open in front and had a small chair where a patient could comfortably sit. "I didn't know we were going to include MRI data in our delusion study."

"Oh, we're not. This is for the Mnemosyne project." His lips stretched outward, displaying a flawless set of teeth. "We're going to study the effects of various drugs on brain metabolism and function in regions that control long-term memory, specifically neuronal switches that we can reactivate to restore lost memories."

"Wow, that's incredible." Cristina felt a twinge of envy. Not only could a discovery like that bring international recognition to the Memory Center, but it could pose a solution to her own memory problem. "I'd love to work on something like that."

"I hope you would, because I want you to start next week."

"What?"

"Speaking to your friend, Detective Wilson, made me realize the key to activating those switches is to localize which ones are turned off in individuals with psychological suppression of memories. To do that, I need someone with a strong background in neuropsychiatry."

Cristina's knees weakened. She grabbed onto a nearby chair to hold herself upright. "I'm flattered, but there are other scientists more experienced than me who would kill to be involved."

Dr. Campbell's eyebrow twitched. "Yes, I'm sure that's true. But I doubt any of them understand displaced memories as well as you. Wouldn't you agree?"

The way his voice curled up as he said that last part and the way his gaze locked with hers made Cristina's blood turn cold. It sounded as if he knew more about her than he should. But how?

"I'll—I'll have to think about it," she said, searching for the right words that wouldn't make her sound ungrateful or suspicious. "I'm not sure I can juggle two major projects right now, and I don't want to give anything less than my best work."

His gaze narrowed and he seemed to be peering directly into her brain. But then his features smoothed out and he turned back to the control panel. "Of course. I fully understand. Mull it over and let me know what you decide. In the meantime, perhaps you could help me calibrate the machine?"

"Oh, um, sure." Cristina crept forward. "What do I need to do?"

"Sit here and get comfortable." Dr. Campbell directed her to the chair. He pressed buttons on the control panel. The machine started making a soft thumping sound. "This machine uses new technology to reduce the scanner noise. Studies found the louder equipment affected working memory and other neural processes. For this project to be successful, we need more natural conditions and opportunity to pair multimodal sensory input with memory acquisition."

"That makes sense. The limbic region is involved in both sensory processing and memory, and most of my patients showed improved recall when they tried familiar scents or tastes like rosemary." Cristina settled into the chair. She caught a whiff of something spicy in the air. "Or cinnamon."

"Yes, did you know that a recent study showed cinnamon improves hippocampal plasticity?" He pressed a few more buttons on the control panel.

Cristina's skin crawled as she recalled ReMind's CEO saying nearly the same thing six months earlier. In fact, one of Quinn's associates had used a cinnamon-based perfume. It had to be a coincidence, she told herself, but she suddenly felt like the machine was closing around her.

"Are you okay?" he asked, looking up sharply. "You show a spike in activity around your amygdala and thalamus, as if you were anxious about something."

"No, I'm fine. Just a little claustrophobia."

"I see." Dr. Campbell fiddled with the control panel once more and then held up a printout. "I'm going to ask you some questions. They're designed to help the machine recognize typical responses, so they shouldn't be too difficult. Are you ready?"

Cristina nodded.

"First, tell me your name."

The muscles in Cristina's neck tightened.

Dr. Campbell frowned. "That wasn't a trick question."

"Sorry." Cristina cleared her throat. "Cristina Silva."

As he studied the control panel, Dr. Campbell's brow furrowed. "Interesting."

"What is it?"

"Never mind. Let's move on." He scanned the paper. "What is your job?"

"Neuroscientific research." Cristina thought quickly. "But I also worked as a psychiatrist."

He nodded and tweaked one of the controls. "Where were you born?"

Again, she tensed. "Rio de Janeiro."

His gaze dropped to the monitor and then bounced back up to her. "I didn't know that."

"You didn't ask before."

"Touché." Dr. Campbell set the paper down. "Do you believe you're someone other than Cristina Silva?"

Heat drained from her face. "What?"

"Sorting out false memories from real, suppressed ones is a major part of the Mnemosyne project. If we can determine what neural processes are involved in confabulation, we can tease out which switches we need to activate to restore true memories." He hooded his eyes. "But I need to tune the machine to a baseline. So, please, answer the question. Do you believe you're someone other than Cristina Silva?"

The machine thrummed around her, matching her pounding heartbeat. How should she answer that question? If she told the truth, it would provoke questions she didn't want to answer. But if she lied, would he know?

There's a loophole, Sabrina whispered. *You're not someone else. I am.*

Her breathing eased. It was true. Everything she felt and remembered told her she was Cristina Silva, and Sabrina Carvalho was simply a guest in her mind. Even if that weren't technically true, it was the answer that felt right. Confidently, she said, "No. Are we done here? I need to check with Victoria on entering the EEG data into the database."

Dr. Campbell, who had been staring at the monitor, glanced at her out of the corner of his eye. He jutted his chin and said, "You may go. Thank you for your help. It was quite enlightening."

She nearly leaped out of the machine and strode to the door, resisting the urge to look back over her shoulder to see if he was still watching her. As she rode the elevator up, she recalled what Wilson had said about Dr. Campbell: *He wanted to make sure I thought it was impossible so I wouldn't dig any deeper into it.* Had he intentionally tried to throw Wilson off-track? And there was something else about him, something Cristina hadn't noticed until she'd been in that machine, watching the neurologist work.

He was left-handed, just like Sack Man.

CHAPTER FIFTY-EIGHT

Detective Wilson had spent the last twenty minutes searching through reports on the Trevino, Sanchez, and Jackman teens for references to common meeting points, anywhere that might give him a head start on where Pierce was meeting Reggie. Nothing matched.

Two patrol officers had gone to Reggie's house, but the teen's mother had no idea where he'd gone. Wilson tried calling the teen's phone, but Reggie didn't answer. Also, Pierce's neighbors hadn't even seen him leave his house, but confirmed his motorcycle was gone.

Wilson pounded his fist on the desk. He couldn't lose another kid to this psychopath.

"Gary!" Detective Hawkins ran up, huffing. He slapped a printout on Wilson's desk. "Pierce sent a text. It says to meet him 'where the Revolution really started.' Is he talking about Lexington?"

"Too far. Reggie only has a ten-speed."

"Let's call the SWAT team. Maybe they can figure it out."

"Prospect Hill Tower," Special Agent Jefferson said as soon as they'd briefed him on the text message. "It's the most famous Revolutionary War landmark in Somerville. George Washington himself hoisted the flag there to signal the start of the American Revolution."

"Makes sense," Wilson said. "Pierce used to meet Danny Trevino there."

Jefferson promised to send in a team to capture Sack Man and get Reggie somewhere safe. Once they had the suspect, they'd bring the detectives in to question him.

After Wilson hung up, Hawkins asked, "What do we do in the meantime?"

Wilson scratched behind his ear. Even if they caught Sack Man, they needed evidence and a motive to make murder charges stick. Until they questioned him and Reggie, they were grasping at straws. Despite the adrenaline coursing through his body, he shook his head. "Only one thing we can do. We wait."

CHAPTER FIFTY-NINE

Cristina struggled to breathe as she raced back to her office. It all made sense now. Dr. Campbell's cloying remarks about replaced loved ones and mistaken identities. His attempt to throw Wilson off-track. His motorcycle references. And now his being left-handed. Everything added up to one conclusion: Dr. Campbell was Sack Man.

It seemed impossible that one of Quinn's hitmen could be right under her nose, but then Quinn himself had wormed his way into her life and planted spies everywhere. Why wouldn't Zero Dark use the same trick on her again when it worked so well last time?

But she had gone to the Memory Center for a job. It had been her idea. Hadn't it?

As she fumbled with her key to unlock her office door, she remembered Dr. Campbell had tried to recruit her before. How was it he still had the perfect opportunity available a year later, right when she needed it?

She burst into her office. Everything was as she'd left it.

No, not everything. The picture of her parents—*Cristina's* parents—was askew. Again.

Time slowed to a crawl as she reached out and picked up the picture frame. The backing was poorly aligned with the frame. Her pulse boomed in her ears as she removed the backing.

Her blood cooled.

A tiny device was taped inside.

A tiny listening device.

Thoughts swirled in her mind. There was no way to prove it, but she had a strong suspicion Dr. Campbell had placed the device there. She reached for it, preparing to peel it off and crush it under her heel, but stopped herself. If she destroyed it, he would know she was onto him. And then what? Would he expose her? Try to kill her?

She needed to get out of there. As she rushed out the door, she ran into Victoria in the hallway. She told her assistant she was going outside for some air and hopped onto the elevator.

Five minutes later, she ran out of the building onto the sidewalk and crossed the street. Once she was a block away, she fished her cell phone out of her pocket and dialed Special Agent Jefferson, while keeping watch for anyone else suspicious. His phone rang four times and went to voice mail. Frustrated, she hung up and tried Wilson. He answered on the second ring.

"Hey," he said. "I need to leave this line open. I'm waiting to hear—"

"I think Dr. Campbell is Sack Man."

"What?" His voice lowered. "That's impossible. Jefferson took a SWAT team to catch Sack Man right now."

"I found a bug in my office." Cristina swallowed hard, checking over her shoulder for fear a hooded man would sneak up behind her. "And I think he knows about my dual identity."

"Are you sure he planted the bug?"

"Well, no."

"Do you have something else to prove he's Sack Man?"

"No, but—"

"Look, we've got solid evidence to tie the suspect we're pursuing to Sack Man. I'll come by your place tonight and take down information on the illegal listening device in your office. I'd suggest you stay away from there in the meantime."

"Okay, but—"

"I have to go." His voice softened. "Maybe tonight we can also pick up where we left off yesterday?"

She smiled. "That sounds good."

After hanging up with Wilson, Cristina's gaze drifted to the Memory Center building. The detective was right. Her evidence that Dr. Campbell was Sack Man was circumstantial at best, and she didn't even have proof that he'd planted the bug. Before accusing a man who for all she knew was guilty of nothing more than being eccentric, she needed something tangible. Fortunately, she knew someone who could help.

She dialed again. A moment later, a woman's voice answered. "DigiFend Security, this is Devi Patel."

"Hi Devi," Cristina said, keeping her gaze locked on the research building. "It's Cristina. I need your help."

CHAPTER SIXTY

Detective Wilson checked the clock. It had been twenty-five minutes since he called Special Agent Jefferson. He drummed his fingers on his desk as he scrolled through a website on Revolutionary War landmarks.

"Could you cut that out?" Hawkins glared. "You're giving me a headache."

Wilson stopped drumming and started cracking his knuckles. "I thought we'd have gotten an update from Jefferson by now."

"They have to get Reggie safe first, remember? And the knuckles thing is even worse."

"Sorry." Wilson released a nervous chuckle. "I'm, uh, thinking of taking some time off after this case. I'm overdue for a vacation."

"Gary Wilson taking a vacation? The only time that ever happens is . . ." His jaw dropped. "You're back with Cristina, aren't you? Was that who called earlier?"

Scratching the back of his head, Wilson said, "Uh, yeah."

"That's great, buddy. I'm glad, really." Hawkins leaned forward. "But what was that I heard about an illegal listening device?"

The phone rang. Grateful for the interruption, Wilson waved Hawkins off and answered.

"Detective." Special Agent Jefferson's voice was tainted by irritation.

"We're at Prospect Hill. Are you certain you read that text message correctly?"

"They're not there?"

"Would I be calling to ask you if they were? My team has combed the entire area around the monument. No sign of Scott Pierce or Reggie Horne."

"That doesn't make sense. Unless . . ." Wilson grabbed the transcript of Pierce's text message and studied it. *Meet me where the Revolution really started.* The Prospect Hill tower was the oldest in Somerville, so where else . . . ?

His stomach dropped. "Shit."

"What is it?" Hawkins asked.

Wilson scrolled through the website he'd been reading and pointed at an entry near the bottom. "On September 1, 1774, General Thomas Gage led British troops to steal two hundred fifty barrels of gunpowder from the old windmill at the Mallet farm. That triggered the Powder Alarm, a call for the townspeople to rise up against the British, in advance of the Revolution."

"The old Powder House." Jefferson cursed. "That's twenty minutes away from here."

"We're closer," Wilson said. "We'll go."

"You're sure about this? Sack Man is highly dangerous."

"We don't have a choice. Meet us there as soon as you can."

Hawkins was already donning his coat when Wilson hung up. "We should tell the captain," he said. "He could rustle up some backup."

"Call him on the way. We need to catch this guy before he disappears." Wilson grabbed his car keys. "I'll drive."

CHAPTER SIXTY-ONE

After finishing the call, Cristina dashed across the street and then attempted to look casual as she reentered the Memory Center. Several of the afternoon research subjects sat in the waiting area, perusing magazines or browsing on their smart phones. Cristina made a beeline for the elevator. Returning to the building where someone had bugged her office was risky but alerting them to the fact she knew before she had proof of who *they* were seemed worse. And with Devi's help, she would find out soon enough.

When she reached her floor, she found Victoria at her desk, entering data. Her assistant looked up from her computer and gasped. "Are you okay? You ran out so quickly—"

"Just a bug." Cristina pressed on her belly for emphasis. "I'm a little better, but I'm going to stay at my desk for a bit. Could you help Dr. Campbell in the lab in the meantime?"

"Certainly, if it's okay that I leave an hour early today. I promised Maria that I'd take her to the Museum of Science after work."

"That's no problem."

"Thank you." Victoria stood and pushed in her chair. "I hope you recover quickly."

"I'm sure I will."

Cristina returned to her office and shut the door behind her. Her gaze fell on the picture frame. Her tongue felt like cotton. The listening device was still there. Fortunately, she didn't need to say anything for what she was about to do, but the idea of that thing spying on her made her skin crawl. Besides, how did she know there weren't video cameras?

She glanced up at the ceiling. There were no blinking lights or camera lenses she could see, but that didn't mean anything. And for all she knew, there could've been spyware on her computer, though Devi promised to send her software that would eliminate anything that shouldn't be there. The trick now was going to be finding out what information her boss had.

Drawing in a deep breath, she picked up the report Victoria had prepared and left her office. A few minutes later, she reached Dr. Campbell's executive suite. His personal receptionist was on the phone. She flashed Cristina a questioning look.

Cristina lifted the ream of papers a little higher and jerked her chin toward the neurologist's office.

The receptionist pointed at the phone and repeatedly touched her thumb and fingers to indicate a chatterbox.

Smiling, Cristina pointed at her chest and then Dr. Campbell's office.

The receptionist steepled her hands together and then said into the phone, "Yes, ma'am, I know you need those reports, but Dr. Campbell is very busy and . . ."

Without waiting to hear the rest, Cristina ducked inside the office and shut the door behind her. She scanned the room to ensure there wasn't an active security camera and then crossed over to the massive desk. After setting down the report, she searched her boss's workstation, surprised at how disorganized he was. Papers, sticky notes, and paper clips were scattered everywhere.

Following Devi's advice, she went straight for the keyboard tray and slid it out. Sure enough, she found a sticky note stuck to the top of the keyboard with several passwords scribbled on it. She snapped a photo of it with her phone, returned the drawer in place, and then slipped out of the room, waving a thank-you to the receptionist on the way.

As she headed back down the hallway, she sent a text to Devi with the image attached. By the time she reached her office, she'd already received a reply. It would take Devi some time to devise a way for Cristina to access the network undetected, but once she did, she'd have full access to his files. Cristina felt smug satisfaction. By the next morning, she'd be the one doing the spying.

CHAPTER SIXTY-TWO

The sky had turned a dusty gray by the time Wilson and Hawkins arrived at Powderhouse Park. A man tossed a frisbee to his golden retriever on the lawn near the Blue Bikes station. A young couple holding hands strolled along the path toward the detectives. Wilson jogged deeper into the park and motioned for Hawkins to follow.

As they passed the old stone farmhouse, Wilson surveyed the rocks and trees lining the area. There were plenty of places to hide, and with the remaining sunlight fading, it would be harder to find their suspect. He picked up his pace, listening for snippets of conversation, but all he heard was an occasional squirrel chitter and the pounding of his feet on the ground.

They started up the winding path along Quarry Hill, the smell of pine purging Wilson's sinuses. His skin buzzed with anticipation.

Cresting the hill, Wilson spotted the powder mill rising up like a bullet standing on end. He moved his hand near his service pistol as he scanned the top of the hill. No sign of Pierce or Reggie. When they stopped to catch their breath, leaves rustled on the other side of the mill. Wilson held up his hand to Hawkins.

Over the buzzing mosquitoes, a man's voice rose, near the trees. Whoever it was sounded angry.

The two detectives split up and encircled the mill, creeping forward with their pistols drawn and ready, flashlights gripped in their other hands. Wilson peered into the trees. In the gloom, he could make out two moving shadows, one taller than the other.

Wilson moved closer and activated his flashlight. The beam illuminated the clearing where Pierce stood with one arm wrapped around Reggie's throat. Both turned their heads toward him, eyes wide. The light glinted off something in Pierce's hand. Wilson dropped his gaze and spotted a syringe with a long needle.

"Drop the weapon." He trained the gun on Pierce's head. Hawkins came up beside him.

"What are you guys doing here?" Reggie pulled at Pierce's arm. "I had it taken care of."

Wilson spotted a pair of handcuffs on the ground. "Yeah, I can see that. Pierce, let Reggie go."

"I don't think so." Pierce pushed the teen in front of him as a shield. He pressed the needle against the back of Reggie's neck. "You drop your weapons."

Wilson's chest tightened. He shifted his aim, but Pierce moved the teen to block his shot. Reggie grasped at the arm blocking his windpipe, gasping for air as Pierce dragged him back away from the detectives.

"You're not getting away," Wilson said. "We've got a warrant for your arrest for the murders of three teens. If you run, the FBI will find you."

Pierce stopped backing up. He wrinkled his nose. "Look, you've got it wrong. I didn't kill those kids."

"Never heard that one before. You can tell us all about it at the station."

Pierce screwed up his face, eyes darting from one detective to the other.

Reggie swung his fist back, striking Pierce in the groin.

Pierce screamed. With feral viciousness, he plunged the needle into Reggie's neck and suppressed the plunger. Reggie howled in pain.

The detectives rushed forward. Pierce ducked behind Reggie. Wilson shifted his aim.

Pierce flung the teen at the cops, turned, and ran toward the hillcrest.

Wilson fired a warning shot.

Pierce let out a pained grunt and disappeared down the hill.

Wilson charged forward, reaching the hillcrest in time to spot Pierce tumbling into the darkness, scattering rocks and branches behind him. A sickening thud announced his landing. Wilson shined the flashlight onto the bottom of the hill. Pierce lay in a heap, head bent at an impossible angle. His eyes stared up, lifeless.

A quiver started in Wilson's stomach. The hill wasn't steep enough for Pierce to lose control. Had Wilson's warning shot hit him?

"Gary, get over here!"

Wilson trotted back to Hawkins, who was holding Reggie's head off the ground. The syringe was still sticking out of the base of the teen's neck, blood trickling around the needle and dripping onto the grass.

"Pierce?" Hawkins asked.

Wilson shook his head.

"At least Reggie can tell us what happened." Hawkins leaned forward and said to the teen, "We'll get paramedics here to take care of you, okay?"

As Wilson panned his flashlight across the field, something glinted in the grass. He donned a glove and picked it up. His stomach shifted.

It was a pill bottle. The label read MCH-21.

Reggie groaned and said, "What happened?"

"Pierce took you hostage and stabbed you with a syringe," Hawkins said.

"Pierce?" Reggie crinkled his brow. "He's the school security officer."

Hawkins and Wilson exchanged glances.

"You don't remember him attacking you?" Wilson asked.

"I don't remember coming here." Reggie tried to turn his head and yelped. "And why does my neck hurt?"

CHAPTER SIXTY-THREE

Cristina had just finished showering when her phone chimed. Thinking it might be Wilson, she wrapped herself in a towel and ran out to check. There was a text message from Maria. She read a scattered note about a kiss that sent tingles down to Maria's toes and going to get drinks. Cristina chuckled. At least someone was having a good night. Although if Wilson kept his promise, so would she.

She changed into a short black dress and bundled her hair up in a towel turban before checking the lasagna baking in the oven, though she didn't have much appetite. She couldn't stop thinking about Dr. Campbell's creepy questions and the listening device in her office. Wilson would probably think she was crazy for going back there, let alone her plan to hack into her boss's network files. She considered not telling him about it but then remembered her promise to trust him and not make decisions for him.

As she was closing the oven, there was a knock at the door. Grizabella poked her head out from the bedroom and mewled.

Muscles coiled, Cristina crept to the door and looked out through the peephole. She relaxed. It was Bruno Gomes, wearing his leather jacket over a black T-shirt and jeans.

"*Boa noite*," he said when she opened the door. A grin stretched far enough across his face Cristina thought he might damage his facial nerve. "Did I catch you at a bad time?"

Heat flooded her face and neck as she realized she was still wearing the towel on her head.

Managing a nervous chuckle, she cinched the towel tighter. "Maybe a little. I wasn't expecting you at this time of night."

"I wanted to continue our conversation from the other day. I tried calling but you didn't answer." He sniggered. "Now I know why. I can come back another time."

"No, come on in and have a seat." She motioned him inside and shut the door. "Please excuse me. Make yourself comfortable."

As she dried and brushed her hair in the bathroom, she tried to calm her pounding heartbeat. She and Bruno—well, Sabrina and Bruno—had been together in the past. It wasn't like he'd caught a peek at anything he hadn't seen before. So why did she feel so twitchy around him?

When she returned to the living room, she found Bruno stretched out on the sofa, feet up on the ottoman. He really had made himself comfortable.

She sat next to him. "You wanted to continue our conversation?"

"Yes, I mentioned to you how we kept our affair secret from our families." His lips twitched. "What I didn't tell you was why."

"Okay. Why?"

He played with the zipper on his jacket. "After she moved to Rio, your mother and my father became close. This made my mother uncomfortable."

The letters addressed to her mother appeared in Cristina's mind. *FG.* "Were they having an affair?"

"No. I'm certain they were not. But my father took it upon himself to watch out for her. He said it was his duty to protect those in need." He stopped fidgeting and leaned back. "When your mother remarried, they stopped talking. But I overheard my mother telling him no Carvalho was allowed in our house again."

Unease stirred in Cristina's belly. "What about my father? Do you know anything about him?"

"No, my father said he died before Gloria moved with you to Rio."

"From where?"

"I don't know that either."

"Could I speak to your father? Maybe he knows something that would help me find out who my father is."

His face drooped. "He died several years ago. Heart attack."

Cristina's hopes plummeted. Every time she found an opening to her past, it led to a dead end, literally. "I'm sorry. I'm sure that was hard on you."

"A man doesn't dwell on the past." He held up a fist. "We must always remain in control."

"Okay, Mr. Macho." She shifted an inch away, put off by his unexpected arrogance. "You know you can be strong *and* have feelings, right?"

He hid behind his hand. "My father believed we needed to be manly men. I don't realize that sometimes I sound like him. Forgive me."

"I understand." She tried to hide her disappointment. "Well, thank you for telling me what you know."

Without warning, he took her hand. She jumped but didn't pull away. "As you said, I must be true to my feelings. If you ever need anything, I promise I will be there for you."

"How can you say that, after the way I—I mean, *Sabrina*—treated you?"

"That was her, not you." He smiled. "And I believe in second chances."

Cristina felt uncomfortably warm. She withdrew her hand and fought to maintain her composure as she stood. "Thanks. Uh, my dinner's going to burn."

He stood and zipped up his jacket. "Perhaps next time we can dine together."

"Sure, that'd be great." She walked him to the door and opened it. "Well, good night."

Before she could react, he turned, lifted her chin with his finger, and pressed his lips against hers. She gasped and started to pull away, but as his fingers slid along her cheek, she found herself sinking into his embrace.

At last, he pulled away. One corner of his mouth curled upward. "The name may be different, but the kiss is the same."

Before she could respond, someone behind Bruno cleared his throat. Cristina tilted her head to see who it was. Her stomach dropped. It was Wilson.

CHAPTER SIXTY-FOUR

Wilson stood in the hallway outside Cristina's apartment with his hands on his hips, skin mottled, nostrils flared.

"It's not what you think," Cristina said, though she wasn't herself sure what it was.

As Wilson opened his mouth to respond, Bruno turned to face him. The detective's eyes widened. He drew his pistol and aimed it at Bruno's head. "Son of a bitch. You're supposed to be dead."

Bruno's lips thinned. "So I've been told."

"Put that away." Cristina placed a hand on Wilson's arm. "This is *Bruno* Gomes, not Federico. I told you about him, remember?"

Wilson seemed dazed as his gaze shifted between Bruno and Cristina. At last, he holstered his weapon. "Yeah, I remember."

"It's a common mistake." Bruno cast a sideways glance at Cristina and then held out his hand to Wilson. "I promise, I'm nothing like my brother."

Wilson glared at Bruno's hand. He shoved his own hands into his pockets.

Bruno scoffed and turned to Cristina. "Think about my offers." He nodded at Wilson. "Pleasure meeting you, Detective."

Wilson's cheek twitched.

After Bruno swaggered down the hall and disappeared, Wilson glowered at Cristina. "So now you're making out with the brothers of Zero Dark mercenaries?"

"*He* kissed *me*. I . . ." She shook her head. "Can we talk about this inside?"

"Fine."

She ushered him in and shut the door. "Really, it's not how it looks."

"You sure?" He stood with his fists by his sides. "Because from here it looks like you were kissing him."

"That was Sabrina. She—" Cristina threw up her hands. "It's a long story."

Wilson checked his watch. "I've got time."

Cristina explained how Bruno and Sabrina had been in love, but she left him for Quinn. She told Wilson how Bruno had come by to explain about their respective families, and he'd taken advantage of a tender moment. "I swear, I had no idea he would do that."

Wilson's lip twisted. "You might've told me about this before inviting me over."

"I found out a few minutes ago." She understood his being upset, but she didn't like his accusatory tone. "And the reason I invited you over was . . ." She gasped. "The lasagna!"

She ran to the oven and threw open the door. A cloud of black smoke billowed out.

"Damn it!" She tossed the scorched pasta onto the counter. "Well, I can order us a pizza."

"I'm not hungry." Wilson shoved his hands into his pockets. "Wasn't there another reason you invited me here?"

Cristina rubbed her forehead. This night was going worse than she'd expected. "Yes, you said you would help investigate Dr. Campbell for me."

"No, I said I'd investigate who planted a listening device in your office. I can't investigate your boss without suspicion he's done something illegal."

"But if he's Sack Man—"

"Sack Man's dead."

Cristina blinked. "He is?"

"Yeah." He averted his gaze. "We identified him as an ex-cop masquerading as a school security officer. He tried to escape arrest and somehow my warning shot killed him."

"I'm so sorry." Her defensive wall crumbled. No wonder Wilson had gotten so angry at seeing Bruno kissing her. He was already mad at himself. "Did you find out why he killed those teens?"

"No, and now we may never know." His face looked haunted. "And there's something else. This kid got injected with something at the base of his neck. Now he can't remember anything that happened over the last twenty-four hours. The doctors insist he suffered head trauma when he got pushed down, but when I looked into his eyes, it was like part of him was fading away right in front of me."

The hairs on the back of Cristina's neck lifted as she connected the pieces together. An injection in the neck. Memory loss. Sack Man. "Is there anything left of whatever Sack Man gave him?"

He handed her a small test tube. "I had to turn the syringe into evidence but maybe you can get something from this. It's a sample from the kid's neck wound."

"Hopefully it's enough. Sack Man worked for Quinn. My patients, the Zero Dark agents—they all had scars at the bases of their necks. And they . . ." Her cheeks cooled. "Oh, no."

"What?" His eyebrows drew together.

She turned away from him and lifted her hair off the back of her neck. "Do you see anything?"

His voice deep and throaty, he said, "There's a scar."

A wave of nausea ran through her. She turned back to him, barely able to speak. "That's how they did it. When Santos said Quinn stole my memories, he meant it literally. Zero Dark injected people with some kind of memory eraser."

Wilson looked pale. "And then what? Quinn reprogrammed them to work for Zero Dark?"

"Some of them, yes. That's what Recognate was designed to do.

Fabricate false memories, new identities, that he could manipulate." Cristina bit her lower lip. "But why was Sack Man using it on those teens?"

"That's a good question, but right now we need to figure out what he used. I don't think this kid has much time before he forgets everything."

"You're right. Tell his doctors to do a biopsy on the neck wound and run every test possible. I'll take this sample to our lab and have them run it tomorrow."

"Okay." Wilson shook his head. "I should've talked to you about this sooner."

"We're talking now." She swallowed. "And I'm glad we are."

"Yeah." He smiled his lopsided smile. "We work well together, don't we?"

Before she could overthink it, she closed the distance between them and threw her arms around him, pressing her lips against his. He responded by parting his lips. She drank in the smell of his skin. She held back a giggle as his stubble tickled her chin. They held each other until, at last, he pulled his head back.

"There's really nothing between you and Bruno?"

She drew in a deep breath. "No."

"Okay. I believe you." He kissed her again, more softly this time, and then he stepped back, buttoned up his jacket, and started for the door.

"Wait," she said, unable to believe he was going to leave things like that. "Where are you going?"

"I trust you, but Sabrina is another story. You two have some things you need to work out." He swiped his hand through his hair. "Besides, I need to write up a report on what happened tonight. With Sack Man, I mean. I'll talk to you tomorrow, okay?"

Cristina watched Wilson march disappear out the door. Breathless, she managed to whisper, "He's right. What the hell was that with Bruno?"

I couldn't help myself, Sabrina replied. *I do miss those lips.*

"Don't do that again." Cristina shut the door and leaned against it. "My social life is getting way too complicated."

CHAPTER SIXTY-FIVE

The taste of Bruno's and Wilson's lips lingered in Cristina's mouth all night long. Each time her hair moved, she could feel Bruno's fingers grazing her neck and behind her ear. Every time the air conditioner blew, she inhaled Wilson's cologne. When she closed her eyes, she could see their faces, Wilson's features transposing with Bruno's.

By the time she arrived at the Faneuil Hall parking lot early the next morning, her nerves were a jangled mess. Thanks to Wilson's abrupt exit, she'd never had the chance to discuss the listening device with him. Perhaps it was just as well that he didn't know what she and Devi were doing. At least he wouldn't be implicated if something went wrong.

A coupe with tinted windows pulled in next to her, facing the opposite direction. The driver's window rolled down. Devi Patel leaned her head out and flashed an amused grin. "I didn't know parking lot meetings were still a thing."

"It's the best I could come up with," Cristina said. "Anywhere else might be under surveillance."

"I knew there'd be risks when I first agreed to spy on you." Devi clucked her tongue. "And, anyway, I'm a sucker for espionage. Speaking of . . ." She handed Cristina a colorful gift bag. "Happy birthday!"

Inside the bag was a black device with a retractable antenna.

"This will jam the listening device in your office." Devi's dark eyes twinkled. "To anyone listening, it will seem like you're working in silence. And it won't interfere with cell phone signals so you can still make calls. I suggest taking it home at the end of the day in case someone managed to hide a microphone in your apartment."

"Thanks." Cristina placed the device on the passenger seat. "What about the other thing?"

"Did you bring your laptop with you as I suggested?"

Cristina held up her portable computer.

"Good." Devi handed her a small flash drive. "Make sure you disconnect your device from any Wi-Fi or Bluetooth networks when you view the data on this. Don't use your desktop at work. I used multiple backdoors and redirects and immediately air gapped my network after completing the download, so they won't be able to trace it back to me."

Twisting the tiny device between her fingers, Cristina said, "You put all of the company's data on here?"

"No, that would take too long and would expose me for sure. I only copied video and audio files since we're trying to confirm who planted the bug in your office, along with anything that referenced you." Devi puckered her lips. "There was also a hidden folder that I thought might interest you. Everything is in Portuguese."

"Why would Dr. Campbell have files in Portuguese?"

"You'd know better than me. I've only managed to decrypt a few so far, starting with the most recently accessed, and I put those on the flash drive. I'll send you the rest once I've finished." Devi's face grew serious. "But you should check out the Portuguese files as soon as possible."

"Why?"

"Trust me."

Cristina's throat constricted. "You're one of the few people I do trust."

Devi's mouth quirked. "You're playing a dangerous game, Cristina. Please be careful."

Ignoring the growing weight in her chest, Cristina said, "You too."

After Devi drove off, Cristina inserted the flash drive and powered up her laptop. She made sure all connections were turned off before opening the new folder icon that appeared on her desktop. A window appeared and populated with files and subfolders. She spotted an audio file and clicked on it. Reggae music filtered from the laptop's tiny speakers. She quickly stopped playback and tried another file. This time she heard Dr. Campbell's rich, thickly accented voice.

"We are close to identifying the gene encoding for near-photographic memory. Once we have isolated it, we can begin synthesizing the compound to replace proteins and reactivate memories lost to amyloid invasion . . ."

Cristina bit her inner cheek. This sounded like a journal recording of Dr. Campbell's research plan for his top-secret Mnemosyne project. If that information fell into the hands of a competing lab, it could undermine the Memory Center's funding. She clicked onto another file. Again, she heard Dr. Campbell speaking, a bit more excitedly this time.

"I am confident the delusion study will yield vital information to further our understanding of how false memories could be constructed to bury more relevant data with traumatic associations. Once we understand the mechanism, we can learn how to safely restore those true memories without overloading the limbic system and causing further damage or repression. I'm ecstatic that Dr. Cristina Silva has joined our team, as her experience treating patients with similar problems will prove quite valuable . . ."

The tops of Cristina's ears burned. Here she thought he was spying on her, all while he was singing her praise. Maybe she was wrong about him. Besides, Wilson had said Sack Man was dead. That only left the assassin, but from what Special Agent Jefferson had told her, the assassin preferred a direct approach, and they'd moved on to the West Coast in any case. So, did that mean someone else bugged her office?

She tried a few more audio files but heard her voice in none of them. As she was about to give up and put away her laptop, she remembered Devi's warning about the folder she needed to see. Near the bottom of the file list, she found a folder labeled *Jornal de Pesquisa*—Portuguese for *Research Journal*. Curious, she clicked on it.

Several more subfolders appeared, with intriguing names like *Immortalis* and *Tabula Rasa*, but it was the last one that caught her eye: *Renascimento.*

Arteries throbbed in Cristina's temples as she recognized the name of Dr. Jose Kobayashi's research project conducted in the favelas of Rio de Janeiro. The same project in which ReMind tested Recognate.

As she opened the folder and clicked through the files, she realized she was reading Kobayashi's personal journal. Her heart pounded as she read his account of how ReMind manipulated him to help them test the memory drug, of how the drug ultimately failed, and how Quinn and his mercenaries killed dozens of innocent people so ReMind could save face. Then she found an image file labeled *Traidora*—traitor. Her hands shaking, she opened the image.

A now familiar picture appeared of a research team next to the Brazilian flag, Dr. Kobayashi in front. Off to the left, a red circle around her face, stood the woman she once was.

Sabrina Carvalho.

CHAPTER SIXTY-SIX

Throughout the entire morning, Wilson found it impossible to focus on his work. Images of Bruno and Cristina kept popping up in his mind, taunting him, laughing at him. His hand tightened around a pencil. He wanted to punch the guy's face in, and, to make it worse, he didn't have a good reason why. It wasn't like he and Cristina were exclusive. Hell, they'd only been back together for a couple of days. Why shouldn't she see other people?

The pencil snapped in half. He rolled it between his thumb and palm and then tossed it in the trash.

It didn't help that Sack Man's death raised more questions than answers. They'd found Pierce's motorcycle in the bushes near the Powderhouse parking lot, but it was a black Kawasaki, not a Harley-Davidson Fat Boy like Cristina had described. The medical examiner found a bullet lodged in Pierce's heart, but it was a 22-caliber, not the 40-caliber rounds the police used. Wilson dug at his scalp. If the fatal shot hadn't come from his gun, who'd fired it?

His desk phone rang.

"This is Dr. Hanscom at Beth Israel Deaconess," a woman said when he answered. "You're the detective who sent us Reggie Horne?"

"Yes, that's me. How is he?"

"He's medically stable, but his progressive memory loss is accelerating. We're awaiting a neurology consult to get a better handle on what's going on with him."

"I see." His jaw tightened. "Can you ask them to run tests on his neck wound? Imaging, toxins, whatever."

The doctor hesitated. "Is there something we should know?"

"Whatever you can find out will help our case."

"Of course." The doctor cleared her throat. "There's something else. We found his cell phone in a hidden pocket of his jacket. The lock screen showed it was recording audio."

Wilson sat upright. "For how long?"

"At least an hour before he arrived. We gave it to him, but he couldn't remember how to unlock it."

"I'll be there in ten minutes."

Leaping to his feet, Wilson grabbed his jacket and raced to the door. Maybe now he'd get some answers.

CHAPTER SIXTY-SEVEN

Sweat clung to Cristina's forehead as she stepped through the Memory Center's double doors into the lobby. Every gaze seemed to be directed at her, even though she knew that wasn't true. Her footsteps echoed off the walls like cannon blasts as she strolled toward the elevator, lifting her chin defiantly.

Are you sure about this? Sabrina whispered. *Kobayashi's files prove Dr. Campbell knows about me. Even if he didn't know who you were when he hired you, he does now.*

"All the more reason to act like we know nothing," Cristina murmured back once she was safely in the elevator. "We need to find out what else he knows." She stuck her hand in her pocket and wrapped her fingers around the test tube. "And we owe it to Wilson to find out what happened to that teen that got jabbed."

She got off at the third floor and made her way to the diagnostic lab. After speaking to the technician, explaining she needed something analyzed to help a police investigator, she handed over the test tube and then went to her office. When she arrived, she found Victoria Weiss lingering in the hallway.

"Oh, Dr. Silva, there you are," Victoria said breathlessly. "I wasn't sure you were coming in today and was starting to worry. Dr. Campbell is in a mood. He's been asking for you nonstop."

Cristina's tension spiked. Had the neurologist already discovered the breach of network security? Did he know she was involved?

"Why?" she asked.

"Something happened to the research notes. He wouldn't tell me much but said he needed to speak to you as soon as you arrived." The corners of Victoria's mouth turned downward. "I'm sorry I kept Maria out so late last night. We were having such a good time and—"

Waving her off, Cristina said, "Trust me, what you two do together is the last thing I'm worried about. Thanks for the heads-up about Dr. Campbell. Please ensure everything is prepared for the afternoon's cases and I'll meet up with you later."

After Victoria scurried away down the hall, Cristina stuck her key in the door lock and stopped in the middle of turning it. If Dr. Campbell figured out that she'd stolen his network passwords, she should get out of there, go home, call Special Agent Jefferson, and hide until it was safe to come out again. But curiosity threatened to consume her. If he knew who she was, why the ruse? What did he want?

She unlocked her door and entered the office. Everything looked as she'd left it, including the picture frame. Was that because whoever left the listening device knew she'd discovered it? She wanted to check to see if it was still there, but feared showing her hand if they didn't, and she didn't want to spend a second longer there than she had to.

"There you are, Dr. Silva."

She jumped at the sound of Dr. Campbell's baritone. Turning to face him, she said, "Yes, I was preparing to head up to your office."

"No need. We have an urgent matter we need to discuss."

Cristina clenched her jaw. "What is it?"

He swiped a finger across his brow. "This is very difficult. You should know that I value honesty above all else. A business built on lack of trust is destined to fail."

Goosebumps popped up on Cristina's arms. She tensed, preparing to fight if he tried anything. "I understand that."

"Good, then perhaps you'd care to explain this." He held out the sheath of papers Cristina recognized as the ones she'd left on his desk the previous day. "I read through it, and it's very well-organized."

Stammering, she said, "Thank you."

"But you didn't write it, did you?"

She blinked. "Sorry?"

"There are several occasions where you used the British spelling of certain words, like *analyse* with an *s* instead of a *z*, and *flavour* with a *u* added, not to mention reversing the *r* and *e* in *centre* and *fibre*." His lips twisted. "Once or twice, I could see as typographical error, but they were consistent enough they could only have been made by someone from the UK."

She stared back at him, struggling to believe he wasn't going after her for hacking his system, but for taking the credit for Victoria's work.

"I'm guessing this was your assistant covering for you. She's quite talented." He sneered. "As are you, when you're putting forth your best effort. But I feel like your head has been somewhere else. Are you still dedicated to the work we're doing here?"

Like a child who'd been caught scribbling on the walls, she nodded.

"I certainly hope so. I think you'd be a great asset to the Mnemo-syne project, but I need you to demonstrate your commitment." Dr. Campbell's features softened. "And I want to apologize for my temper as of late. I'm under quite a bit of pressure. Some of our more influential investors want us to deliver a product now, but it's not yet ready and I refuse to release an untested memory drug on an unsuspecting public. We don't want a repeat of the ReMind disaster, do we?"

Cristina searched his face for signs of deception. Of course, he knew all about ReMind. "No, we don't."

"Oh, and I understand you asked our lab to analyze a wound sample?"

Damn, she thought she could trust the tech to keep her mouth shut. She scrambled to think up a lie that sounded believable and abandoned the idea. If Dr. Campbell was dirty, he might let something slip that would help prove his deception, and if not, he was a brilliant neurologist who understood memory loss better than anyone she knew. "Detective

Wilson asked me for help with his case. One of his witnesses was injected with something that appears to be causing rapid memory loss."

"Really? Some sort of neurotoxin?"

"Your guess is as good as mine. I thought our lab might be able to identify it."

"Well, any opportunity to assist law enforcement is good for us. But in the future, please, run this sort of thing by me first."

Abashed, she said, "Yes, I will."

After he left, Cristina slumped into her chair. If Dr. Campbell knew she'd seen Kobayashi's files in his system, he'd shown no sign of it. But his mention of ReMind left a feeling of cold dread inside her. She'd learned from dealing with Quinn that some people took manipulation to new heights. If he was toying with her, she'd need help to fight back.

She quickly closed and locked her office door, then removed the jamming device Devi had given her from her backpack. A flip of the switch made a small green light activate, but that was it. She wasn't sure what she'd expected—maybe the sound of feedback or a robotic voice telling her she was now secure, but instead the room seemed as quiet as it had been before. Praying it worked the way Devi claimed, she pulled her cell phone out of her pocket and dialed.

Special Agent Jefferson answered on the first ring. "Dr. Silva, is everything okay?"

"No, I need to come talk to you." She swallowed, wondering how much she should say over the phone. "I think my boss is working with Zero Dark."

There was a long enough pause Cristina wondered if the jammer had blocked their call. But then Jefferson said, "Not here. Meet me at the Chestnut Hill Reservoir at six thirty tonight, by the gatehouse across from the Waterworks."

"But don't you want to know—"

"We'll talk tonight."

The line went dead.

Cristina lowered the phone and deactivated the jammer. Now what?

She considered calling Wilson and thought better of it. He already had enough going on with his case. She could call him once the lab finished analyzing the sample that he'd given her. She made sure the Glock in her backpack was loaded. In the meantime, she needed to prepare for her meeting with Jefferson.

CHAPTER SIXTY-EIGHT

"*. . . I know what you did. You killed Caleb, didn't you?*"

Reggie Horne's recorded voice sent a shiver down Wilson's back as he paused the phone playback. It had taken the tech team a few minutes to unlock the teen's phone after Wilson returned from the hospital. The kid had been in bad shape when Wilson saw him, barely able to remember anything from the past two months. To every question Wilson asked about Sack Man and the other teens, Reggie gave the same answer in a progressively weaker voice: *I don't know what you're talking about. When can I go home?* Listening to him now, speaking confidently and defiantly, made it clear how much he'd lost.

From what Wilson had heard so far, Reggie had convinced Pierce he wanted to take over distributing RAM Boost to other teens, claiming he needed the money to help his mom. But only two minutes into the meeting, Reggie admitted he'd lied so he could accuse Pierce of murder to his face and then demanded Pierce turn himself in. Setting his jaw, Wilson hit play.

"*You got it wrong, kid.*" Pierce's voice hissed through the tiny speaker. "*I didn't kill anyone.*"

"*Don't bullshit me. I heard the detective talking to Dr. Wakefield. I know Danny got that RAM Boost shit from you, and he gave it to Eddie and Caleb. Now they're all dead. I won't let you hurt anyone else.*"

Wilson stopped the playback and gripped the table as a blast of nausea struck him. Reggie had followed him to NatureBoost and overheard his conversation with Wakefield, and Wilson had no clue. How disconnected from things had he become? Now, because of his mistake, the teen was in danger of losing his mind.

Swallowing hard, Wilson resumed playback.

"*Yeah, I sold them the drugs, but I didn't kill anyone. That was out of my control.*"

"*Then who did?*"

"*Look, get out of here. Don't stick your nose where it might get cut off.*"

"*You threatening me?*"

"*No, I'm warning you. This guy's dangerous. If he knew we were having this conversation, he'd kill us both.*"

Wilson's chest tightened. What guy?

"*Why did he kill them?*" Reggie's voice rose in pitch, broken by sobs. "*Over some stupid drug?*"

"*It's bigger than that. I had no idea how bad it was. That's why you should walk away. Forget about all of this.*"

There was a pause, then the sound of metal clinking as Reggie said, "*I can't do that.*"

"*Handcuffs? You didn't think this through kid.*"

There was the sound of a scuffle. Reggie yelped.

Pierce spoke again, panting with exertion. "*I didn't want to have to use this, but I can't let you tell anyone what you—*"

"*Drop the weapon.*"

Wilson cringed at the sound of his own voice on the recording. That had been when he and Hawkins arrived. He stopped the playback. Removing the earbuds, he leaned back in his chair and pressed his knuckles against his forehead. If Pierce was telling the truth, the trail didn't end with him. Now he was dead, and there were no more breadcrumbs to guide the way.

Detective Malone's voice carried from the break area on the other side of the detective's pen: "I heard that slimebag they caught was an ex-cop." He was chatting with two junior detectives over coffee. "I think my old man worked with him."

One of the other detectives said something Wilson couldn't hear. After a moment, Malone made a face. "Reggie Horne? Why's that name sound familiar?"

Wilson clenched his fist. Break room gossip was common around the station, but not about his case. Not today.

"Oh, yeah, now I remember." Malone guffawed. "That punk I booked for breaking into a nutrition store. I knew he was trouble from the moment I laid eyes on him. He got a lucky break that the ADA took pity on him. Hell, she's probably his cousin."

Wilson stood and started walking toward the break area.

"Those people are always causing problems." Acid laced Malone's words. "If it had been my case, I would've made sure he got pinned with accessory charges, you know? And then, if he resisted arrest, he'd end up at the hospital anyway."

Wilson cleared his throat.

Malone turned around. "Oh, hey, Gary, what's—"

Wilson's fist crashed into Malone's nose.

"What the fuck?" Malone covered his face with his hands. "Jesus!"

"That kid has twice the balls as you." Wilson jabbed a finger at Malone. "You're a disgrace to the uniform."

"At least I don't sleep with my witnesses."

"You son of a bitch."

Wilson lunged at him. Strong hands grabbed his arms and held him back.

"Ease up, Gary," Hawkins whispered in his ear. "He's not worth it."

"What's going on out here?" Captain Harris appeared in the hallway, hands on his hips. He squinted at the blood dripping from Malone's nose and then snapped his gaze toward Wilson. "Someone better have an explanation."

"Just a misunderstanding," Hawkins said before Wilson could speak. He gave Malone a pointed look. "Right?"

Malone dabbed at his nose, glared at Wilson, and then nodded.

Harris turned back to Wilson, nostrils flared. "Any more *misunderstandings* and you're suspended. Got it?"

Wilson's cheeks cooled. He gave a slight nod.

"The rest of you, get back to work." Harris pointed at Malone. "And go clean that up."

As Hawkins dragged Wilson away, he said, "What the hell was that about?"

"I wanted to wipe the smirk off that racist asshole's face." Anger continued to bubble under Wilson's skin. "We're supposed to be better than that."

"Yeah, we are. But Malone is a third-generation cop. Hell, his grandfather was one of the first at this station. There are lot more who'd defend him than criticize him. You're lucky Harris let you off with a warning."

"So what? We lie down and do nothing?"

"No, we play the long game. Scum always turns up in the dirtiest of spots. We make sure to shine the light on him when he does." Hawkins narrowed his gaze. "But right now, I'm more worried about you. I've never seen you this worked up."

"I didn't get much sleep, thinking about how things went down last night."

"Yeah, that wasn't what I'd expected either." Hawkins clapped Wilson on the shoulder. "Maybe now you can take that vacation you wanted."

Wilson forced a smile. "Yeah. I need it."

As Hawkins wandered off, Wilson scrubbed his hands over his face and then picked up the phone to dial the DEA. They should've finished their full analysis of the MCH-21 sample by then. Maybe there was something Agent Delaney's preliminary had missed.

"This is Detective Gary Wilson, Somerville PD," he said when a receptionist answered. "Transfer me to Special Agent Connor Delaney."

"Hold, please."

While he waited, Wilson's thoughts drifted to Cristina. He knew he should believe her when she said she wasn't interested in Bruno. He *wanted* to believe her. But this dual identity deal of hers was tougher to handle than he'd thought. Not only did she have baggage—she had an extra passenger. If he wanted to be with her, he was going to have to accept all of it.

"Detective, are you still there?"

"Yes."

"You said you wanted to speak to Connor Delaney?"

Wilson's jaw tightened. "Yes, that's what I said."

"There's no agent here by that name."

The floor fell away from under Wilson's chair. "Are you sure? Maybe he was visiting from another field office?"

"I double-checked our personnel files. There was a telecommunications specialist named Connor Delaney, but he was terminated last week."

"Then who did you send to investigate the NatureBoost Vitamin Shoppe at Assembly Row?"

"We never received a call to that location, Detective. Would you like me to transfer you to an administrative officer?"

"Uh, no, but could you tell me why Delaney was terminated?"

"I don't have access to that information, sir."

"All right. Thanks, anyway."

After hanging up, Wilson locked his computer, grabbed his car keys, and headed for the door.

CHAPTER SIXTY-NINE

Although she'd finished her work an hour earlier, Cristina remained at her office until the clock read 6:10, then gathered up her things. It took her twenty minutes to drive to the Chestnut Hill Reservoir. She parked in the shadow of the Metropolitan Waterworks Museum, where a handful of cars remained.

The lights from the Prudential Tower mirrored off the smooth, black waters of the reservoir. Across the street, the boxy gatehouse hunkered on the edge of the walking path. A pair of joggers plodded along the trail, reflective stickers blinking in and out.

A silhouetted figure stood behind the gatehouse, peering out over the water. As Cristina shielded her eyes against the lamplights, she could make out Special Agent Jefferson's bald pate and black suit. She crossed Beacon Street, fiddling with the straps on her backpack, eyes darting side to side, fingers tingling.

When she reached the gatehouse, Jefferson turned to face her. His eyes were sunken with lack of sleep and his face was far more serious than she was used to seeing.

"Thank you for meeting me, Dr. Silva," he said in a low voice.

"The last time I met someone in a park like this," Cristina said, "they got killed."

A muscle in his cheek twitched. "I understand this seems risky, but I believe my office is compromised so we're left with limited options."

"You found the mole in the Bureau?"

"I told you those agents were the tip of the iceberg. I've gained access to intel that Zero Dark is much bigger than we thought. They have operatives in play not only in the Bureau, but in intelligence, military, healthcare, and criminal organizations across the globe." He hunched his shoulders. "Quinn staged a coup to promote his own agendas. Now that he's dead, the new leaders want to erase his pet projects, and everyone associated with him."

Cristina's chest tightened. "Including me?"

"No, as I said, they want information locked away in your brain." He glanced over his shoulder and then leaned close. "It has to do with your father."

"Jorge Silva?"

"No." He narrowed his gaze. "Your *real* father."

CHAPTER SEVENTY

When Wilson arrived at Assembly Row, he spotted Allison Wakefield locking up her storefront. He flashed his blue light and pulled in alongside her SUV. Wakefield's brow crinkled.

"If I didn't know better, Detective—" her mouth twisted coyly as he walked up to her "—I'd think you missed being near me."

Wilson wrinkled his nose. "What are you hiding?"

"I'm not hiding anything."

"How well do you know Connor Delaney?"

Her posture perked up. "Like he said, he ran an audit on me last year. That's it."

"You hadn't spoken to him again until the other day?"

"No, I hadn't."

His jaw clenched. "And if I run your phone records, I won't find any calls between the two of you?"

The color drained from her face. "What are you getting at?"

"Connor Delaney isn't a DEA agent."

"He's not?" Her eyes widened. "Then why did he say he was?"

"Cut the crap. I know you hired him to lie about your supplements."

She chewed on her lower lip, avoiding his gaze, but then she folded her arms across her chest. "If you *knew* that, you'd be reading me my rights, not casting unfounded accusations. You don't have anything against me because there's nothing to be had. Whether or not Delaney was a fraud, my supplements are safe."

A storm raged inside that Wilson was barely able to contain. He steeled himself. "Then why was Scott Pierce selling them to high school students? Supplements with no narcotic potential have low street value."

"He must have modified them somehow, mixed them with a narcotic and then repackaged them. He could've learned how to do that on the internet."

Wilson struggled to restrain his frustration. What she'd said was plausible. He showed her a picture of the pill bottle he'd found at Powderhouse Park. "So if I ask our lab to run their own analysis, you'll have nothing to worry about, right?"

"Certainly not." She leveled her gaze. "But I hope you have a good explanation for how you got those pills."

"How about that I took them off Pierce's corpse?"

She blinked rapidly, jaw dropping. "Pierce is dead?"

"Last night."

Wakefield picked at her cuticles as she gazed at her storefront.

"Something the matter?" Wilson asked.

Her eyes, at first blank, slowly sharpened. Her lip curled. "Do you have one shred of evidence that ties me to Scott Pierce or those teens?"

His chest tightened.

"I didn't think so." She stepped closer and jabbed her finger in his face. "If you ever come around here again, casting empty threats, I'll make sure your boss knows how much you're willing to bend the rules to save your own skin."

Before Wilson could recover enough to respond, she got into her SUV and drove off.

CHAPTER SEVENTY-ONE

Cristina could barely breathe as she stared at Special Agent Jefferson. Her body tingled all over. "You—you know who my father is?"

Jefferson's mouth twisted grimly. "No. But I've found intel suggesting he's someone very important to Zero Dark. It looks like he was once high up the food chain. In fact, he's the reason Quinn usurped power."

Her heart sank. "My father put Quinn charge of Zero Dark?"

"I don't know the details, but it seems your father left the organization around the same time Quinn took control. Now that Quinn is gone, the new leaders have targeted your father."

"Why?"

"He has information that could ruin Zero Dark's master plan to gain control over the world's healthcare, military, and governments, and so they're desperate to get to him first." The skin over his temples tightened. "That's why they're so interested in your memories. You have information locked away in your brain they can use against him."

"So if I regain my memories, Zero Dark could destroy my father?" Jefferson nodded.

The ground seemed to tilt and shift beneath Cristina's feet. Now she understood why it had been so difficult to integrate her memories with Sabrina's, and why there were memories they still couldn't access.

Those memories were dangerous if they could destroy their father—whoever he was.

"How do you know all this?" she asked.

"They have their moles. I have mine." Jefferson squared his jaw. "I can't tell you more than that, but I felt it imperative you knew why you're being targeted."

"My boss, Dr. Winston Campbell, invited me to join his research study to create a drug that can access suppressed memories. But he has Jose Kobayashi's notes about Recognate, which means he probably knows who I really am." She swallowed hard. "Do you think he plans to use his new drug to access my memories for Zero Dark?"

Jefferson rubbed his chin. "It's possible. Like I told you, you can't trust anyone."

"Not even you?"

His lips twitched. "Except me, of course. Here's what I want you to do. Tomorrow, go back to the Memory Center and tell Dr. Campbell you want to join his project as soon as possible."

"You want me to go back to work for him?"

"I need you to get closer to him. Find out what he knows. You said he has Kobayashi's notes. Were they only about Recognate?"

"No, there were some other projects I didn't look at yet. And I have a friend decrypting the rest of Dr. Campbell's files."

He hooded his eyes. "Bad plan. Get those files to me and I'll decrypt them myself."

"My friend is very talented."

"Then that makes them a bigger target. If Sack Man were to find them—"

"Sack Man?" Cristina recoiled. "I thought he was dead."

"No, your detective friend had the wrong man. Pierce was a stooge Sack Man was using to get close to the teens he was using as guinea pigs." Jefferson's chest rose and fell. "The real Sack Man is—"

A gunshot rang out.

Jefferson made a choking sound and staggered backward.

Cristina ducked behind the gatehouse wall and dug through her backpack for her gun.

Two more gunshots in rapid succession, coming from somewhere above.

Finding her pistol, Cristina squatted as low as she could, creating as small a target as possible. She edged around the corner and looked up.

There, on the roof of the Waterworks Museum was the silhouette of someone wearing a hood and holding a rifle.

Cristina aimed and fired.

Her shot went wide. The shooter spooked, turned, and jumped off the roof.

Cristina jumped out of her hiding spot, preparing to give chase.

A groan from the side of the gatehouse made her stop. She sprinted over to the source of the sound.

Jefferson was lying on the ground, hand over his belly. Blood pooled around him. His breath came in short gasps.

"Shit."

Cristina tucked her gun into her waistband. Crimson fluid trickled from a spot on his left forehead. The bullet must've grazed him. More blood seeped through his shirt over his left lower abdomen.

"Hold on." She ripped open his shirt, exposing his abdomen. No way of knowing if the bullet had gone through unless she rolled him. "I need help!"

Jefferson grabbed her shoulder and lifted his head and back off the ground. His mouth opened but no sound came out except for a weak groan. His eyes rolled back, and he collapsed into her arms.

Cristina pulled out her cell phone with one hand and dialed 911. "This is Dr. Cristina Silva. Please send an ambulance to the south gatehouse at the Chestnut Hill Reservoir. A man's been shot."

As she lay the agent on the ground to start CPR, her fingers grazed a rough spot on the back of his neck.

A sinking feeling worked its way through her stomach. She knew Jefferson needed resuscitation, but her hands had their own idea. She rolled the agent on his side, bent his chin down, and leaned forward to inspect his neck. Bile rose in her gullet.

There was an annular scar at the base of his neck.

From her vantage point atop the low service pumping station across the street, DB watched Cristina and the dying FBI agent through her binoculars. Respect glimmered in her chest. Not only could the impostor play doctor, but she knew how to handle herself in a fistfight and was pretty good with a gun too. DB knew of one and only one organization who could've taught the pretender those skills, the same one that had trained DB.

Zero Dark.

Now DB at last understood why her employers were so interested in her doppelgänger, and why they'd chosen her as a replacement. But why had they kept DB alive, turning her into a professional killer?

She scanned the reservoir for any sign of Sack Man, but he appeared to be long gone. Gritting her teeth, she lowered the binoculars. So not only was he still alive; he'd violated their truce by interfering with her plans.

DB stowed the binoculars inside her jacket, climbed off the roof, and slunk toward the parking lot. Now Silva would be on high alert. DB would have to ramp up her timeline.

And she knew how to get what she wanted.

CHAPTER SEVENTY-TWO

Cristina waited with Special Agent Jefferson until the paramedics arrived. She rode in the back of the ambulance on the way to Beth Israel Deaconess, answering questions while the EMTs pushed fluids through two large-bore needles, one in each arm, lines wide open. His skin was ashen and his heart danced a fast rhythm on the monitor. Her own heartbeat raced uncontrollably as she called Wilson during the ride and asked him to meet her at the hospital.

Once they arrived at the hospital, emergency room physicians whisked the FBI agent away to a trauma room, leaving Cristina in the waiting area. In her mind's eye she kept seeing the scar at the base of his neck. What did it mean? Had he been mind-wiped by Zero Dark? Was he a mole who had been manipulating her all along?

Two Brookline PD detectives arrived and took her to a private room to question her. She explained Jefferson had contracted her as a consultant and asked her to meet him at the reservoir. She arrived right when a hooded man shot him. She'd fired against the assailant in self-defense, but she didn't know why he shot Jefferson. They pressed her for more details, but she held fast to her stance that she had no idea who the gunman was. And that part was true. Jefferson had said the man Wilson captured was only an accomplice. She was certain the hooded man who shot Jefferson was the real Sack Man, but she still had no clue as to his real identity.

After another ten minutes of questioning, they allowed her a bathroom break. The moment her body touched the toilet seat, her muscles turned to Jell-O. She braced herself, bent her head, and took slow breaths. She didn't even notice she'd voided until after she'd already finished.

It took all her strength to stumble to the sink. As she washed up, her legs gave out. She leaned on the sink for support and stared at herself in the mirror. Jefferson's blood stained her forehead. She scrubbed it off and splashed more water on her face.

We can't trust anything he told you. Sabrina's voice sounded distorted, as if she was exerting great effort to communicate with Cristina. *If he worked for Zero Dark, then everything he said was a lie.*

"Everything?" Cristina stopped patting her face with a paper towel and glared at her reflection. "You mean like what he said about our father? Or are you afraid to admit that our father was the reason you fell into Quinn's clutches?"

Storm clouds swirled in her head. Growling, Sabrina said: *If that's true, then he owes us an explanation.*

"We don't even know who our father is, or where he is." Cristina leaned against the sink to support herself against the sinking weight on her shoulders. "In order to find him, we need to access your buried memories . . ."

. . . But if we're able to find him, so can Zero Dark.

Heaving slow breaths, Cristina balled up the paper towel and tossed it in the trash before adjusting her blouse and leaving the restroom.

When she returned to the detectives, there was a doctor in blue scrubs standing next to them. He gave her a hangdog look as she approached.

"What happened?" she asked.

"We did all we could," the doctor said. "When they transported him, the bullet dislodged and nicked the aorta. Agent Jefferson lost too much blood. I'm sorry, but he's dead."

Maybe it was the crash as the adrenaline wore off, or the reality that the life she'd finally thought had been coming together was now falling apart. Either way, Cristina had to lean on the wall to keep from crumbling to the ground. One of the detectives said something to her but she couldn't make it out over the barrage of thoughts. Jefferson had been the only law enforcement officer besides Wilson she had trusted, and now she wasn't even sure he ever deserved that trust. Now that he was dead, she was left with nowhere to turn.

Shadowy faces surrounded her, mocked her. Rising above them all, Quinn spread his arms, beckoning her, laughing at her. She jammed her fists against her temples, shut her eyes, and sank to her knees. A hand touched her wrist, gentle as a light breeze. She opened her eyes and looked up.

Wilson.

For several beats, they stared at each other, neither speaking. Cristina's heart thumped as she studied the grim lines of his face, the oceanic depths of his eyes, wondering if he was really there, or if he was another illusion created by her tormented mind.

At last, his stony countenance cracked. "Sorry for being an ass the other night."

She threw her arms around him, her fingers seeking confirmation in the solidness of his body. The familiar musky scent of his skin snapped her back to reality. A tremor started in her stomach and radiated outward until her body quaked. Tears streamed down her cheeks. She squeezed Wilson close as the grief poured out of her.

When she had no tears left, he sat back and wiped her face with his fingertips. He stood to talk to the Brookline detectives. They glanced at her and murmured something Cristina couldn't hear. Wilson spoke again. The detectives nodded, shook hands with Wilson, and left.

"What did you say to them?" she asked when he returned to her.

"That you'd go to their station tomorrow to review your statement with the feds. They're going back to search the crime scene for leads before the trail gets cold. I said you'd remain under my watch in the meantime." He smiled sheepishly. "If that's okay with you."

"Of course, it's okay." She entwined her fingers with his, grounded by the touch of his skin. "But there's a lot I have to tell you. Sack Man's not dead."

"I know. Let's go somewhere more private." As they started walking, he whispered in her ear, "Sack Man's not our only problem."

CHAPTER SEVENTY-THREE

On the drive to Cristina's apartment, Wilson told her about the bullet the medical examiner found in Pierce's back and surmised that the real Sack Man had killed Pierce to cover his tracks before going after Special Agent Jefferson. He summarized what he'd learned from Reggie's audio recording, that Pierce admitted to selling a memory supplement to the teens but denied killing them.

"You said this supplement affects melanin-inhibiting neurons?" Cristina asked as Wilson veered off the highway.

"Yeah, I guess so."

"Over-the-counter nootropics have limited effect on cognitive processes like memory. If it was strong enough to have any real impact, it would have to be prescription, and anyone taking it would be at risk for a number of toxic effects."

"Yeah, that's why I contacted the DEA." He glowered as he turned toward Davis Square. "The storeowner, Dr. Wakefield, insists her supplement is safe, but I think she's lying."

"Why?"

"Because she paid someone off to pose as a DEA agent and claim it was safe."

She touched her lips. "Do you think Sack Man is working with this Dr. Wakefield? We know Zero Dark is obsessed with memory."

"It's possible." Wilson's jaw clenched. "I asked the medical examiners to review the autopsies on the three dead teens. All of them had annular wounds at the bases of their necks."

"So Sack Man used this memory eraser on them, and then killed them? Why?"

"I don't know." Wilson thumped his fist against the steering wheel. "Did Jefferson tell you anything before he died?"

Fighting against the nausea that threatened again to overpower her, Cristina recapped her encounter with Jefferson, from his revelation about her father to her discovering the scar on his neck. Wilson's eyes bugged out in a way that would've been comical in different circumstances.

When she finished, he wiped his hand across his mouth and said, "No wonder you were a wreck when I got to the hospital. But why would Sack Man kill Jefferson if they both worked for Zero Dark?"

"Maybe for the same reason that assassin killed those other agents. Jefferson told me Sack Man worked directly for Quinn. If Zero Dark is cutting off loose ends by killing anyone connected with Quinn—"

"Then Jefferson was hunting Sack Man for Zero Dark." Wilson groaned. "This is way above my pay grade. We need to take this to someone with more authority."

"Who? According to Jefferson, Zero Dark has moles everywhere, in every federal agency and major corporation." Cristina wrapped one hand around the other and pressed her knuckles against her chin, as if the pressure would chase away the madness. "He probably told me all that so I would trust only him, but I would've noticed if he was outright lying. It's easier to deceive someone if you tell them the truth."

"Do you think Dr. Campbell is Sack Man? It would've been easy for him to follow you to the reservoir from your office, he knew Dr. Wakefield, and Jefferson wanted you to spy on him."

Cristina considered that and then shook her head. "No, Jefferson was worried Sack Man would get his hands on Dr. Campbell's files.

That wouldn't make sense if they were the same person. There had to be another reason Jefferson wanted me to get close to Dr. Campbell."

After Wilson pulled into the parking lot at Cristina's apartment building and set the emergency brake, he turned to her, his face ashen. "So what do we do now?"

"The only thing we can do." Cristina set her jaw. "You catch Sack Man, and I find out why Jefferson so badly wanted my boss's files."

CHAPTER SEVENTY-FOUR

Cristina woke from sleep to the sound of her cell phone ringing. She'd been up late talking to Maria, updating her on everything that had happened, and warning her about Sack Man and other Zero Dark operatives possibly going after them. Maria had tried to convince Cristina to stay home from work, but Cristina remained firm that she had to find out what else Dr. Campbell knew, at least until Devi got back to her with the rest of the decrypted files. At the thought of Devi, Cristina remembered to activate the jammer in case anyone was listening, and then told Maria about the memory eraser and what Jefferson had told her about her father. They ultimately agreed that Maria would avoid leaving the apartment until things cooled down.

As she rubbed the sleep from her eyes, Cristina checked the caller ID. It was a 508 area code, and a number she didn't recognize. She checked the time. Six-thirty. Who the hell was calling so early?

Bracing herself, she answered and said, "Hello?"

"Is this Cristina Silva?"

"Yes."

"This is Detective Tannhauser, Framingham PD. Do you know Mr. and Mrs. Manny Feldman?"

Cristina bolted upright. "Did something happen to them?"

"They're okay now, but they've been through quite an ordeal. We got a call from a neighbor about a suspicious noise coming from the house. The Feldmans' car was gone, so the neighbor assumed they were away. A first responder heard someone yelling from inside, and when they broke into the house, they found the Feldmans tied up in the basement."

Cristina's hand flew to her mouth. "Oh, my God."

"They said they'd been there for several days. Whoever kidnapped them left enough food and drink to keep them alive. Mrs. Feldman was finally able to wriggle free enough to remove the gag from her mouth." The detective cleared his throat. "We're still searching for trace evidence that might lead to a suspect, but Mr. Feldman insisted I call you."

"Why?"

"Because he said to tell you they were kidnapped by Cristina Silva."

"He said *I* kidnapped them?"

"No, ma'am. He made it quite clear you had nothing to do with it. But he said their kidnapper *was* Cristina Silva, and that you would know what that meant."

Cristina reeled with confusion. Why would Manny say he was kidnapped by Cristina Silva, but not her? What else could he mean?

Her mouth went dry.

"Did he give you a description?" she asked.

"We're working on getting a forensic artist to get more details, but Feldman told us the suspect has blond hair, brown eyes, and white skin, though he thinks she used some kind of powder to lighten it. Do you know who he's talking about?"

Cristina wet her lips. "No, Detective. I'm sorry but I don't."

"Are you sure? Mr. Feldman seemed certain you could help us out."

"Maybe he meant someone is pretending to be me, but if so, I'm afraid I don't know anything about it. If I think of something, I'll give you a call. I'm glad Manny and his wife are okay."

As she hung up, Cristina took slow breaths to calm her racing heart. Manny could only have meant one thing.

The real Cristina Silva was alive.

CHAPTER SEVENTY-FIVE

Reggie Horne's chest rose and fell, rose and fell, keeping time to a beat only he could hear. Every so often, he twitched and moaned. His nurse told Wilson he'd been asleep for over an hour following a fifteen-minute rant that a hooded man had stolen his mind. Doctors had to sedate and restrain him.

An acrid taste filled Wilson's mouth. He'd woken early and searched through every database he could access for anything that might give him a clue to Sack Man's identity. The markings on the bullets they'd pulled from Jefferson were from a commonly sold hunting rifle and matched the slugs they'd found in Pierce. While the shell casings found on the water tower roof confirmed the killer's location, they didn't help to identify him.

Wilson clenched and unclenched his fingers. The teen was deteriorating. Reggie's memories were crumbling away in a landslide. His mother, who had remained awake and by his bedside all night, had finally gone home to rest, broken when Reggie had stared at her and asked who she was. The doctors didn't have the slightest clue how to treat him, and at the rate he was declining, they estimated within two days he'd no longer know his own name.

A knot formed in Wilson's stomach and twisted. This was his fault.

If he'd been paying more attention, Reggie wouldn't have been able to spy on Wilson's conversation with Wakefield. He wouldn't have discovered Pierce was a suspect or tried to be a hero.

"I'm sorry," he whispered, wondering if Reggie could hear him. "You're a brave kid and you deserve a future. I promise I'm going to catch Sack Man and find out what he did to you. If there's a cure, I'll make sure you're the first one to get it."

Wilson's phone vibrated.

"Where are you?" Hawkins asked.

"Visiting Reggie at Deaconess before our shift starts. Why?"

"A silent alarm triggered at NatureBoost. Security cameras picked up a man wearing a black hood going inside."

"I'm on my way."

CHAPTER SEVENTY-SIX

On the drive to work, Cristina's mind buzzed with the realization that the woman she'd replaced was not only still alive, but she was a kidnapper. Did this woman blame the Feldmans for what had happened to her? And why hadn't she contacted Cristina?

A horrible thought struck Cristina as she pulled into the Memory Center's parking lot. Maybe the kidnapping *was* a message to Cristina, a warning.

She's probably mad that you took her place, Sabrina said. *I was pretty pissed at you too.*

"But how do we find her?" Cristina asked as she shut off the engine. "There are no photos of her anywhere, and Manny's description is useless."

We'll have to wait for her to make a move.

With a bad taste in her mouth, Cristina entered the Memory Center and rode the elevator up to her office. When she reached her floor, she stopped by Victoria's desk, but her assistant's chair was empty. Cristina asked the other technicians but none of them had seen her yet that morning. As she walked to her office, Cristina recalled Victoria's doctor visit the other day. Maybe she had health issues she didn't want to disclose.

As she reached her office, Dr. Campbell appeared around the corner.

"Ah, there you are, Dr. Silva," he said, his voice bright and cheerful. "I was hoping I would run into you."

Cristina tensed. Maybe he wasn't Sack Man, but she didn't trust him, not when she knew he was keeping secrets from her. She rearranged her expression into one that appeared more innocent and said, "I'm nearly done with the analysis of yesterday's data. I'll get you the report by this afternoon."

Blowing out his lips, he said, "Take your time. We received an extension on the deadline for the delusion project."

"Oh." Cristina blinked. "That's good to hear."

"Besides, you've helped uncover something far more important. Something that will move the Mnemosyne project light-years ahead."

"I did?"

"Yes, you brought in that sample Detective Wilson gave you to analyze. It's quite sublime, really." He pushed his glasses up on the bridge of his nose and leaned forward to whisper, "PCR shows a mixture of anti-neurexin antibodies, polyamines, and disulfide peptides."

The names muddied in Cristina's head. "What does that mean?"

"Those are the components of spider venom."

"You're joking."

"Not at all. The neuroactive polyamines in spider venom have been studied as potential treatments for PTSD. They can turn off the AMPA switches involved in memory function. The ability to access stored data would be gradually blocked, allowing one to recover by effectively forgetting those traumatic experiences." He made a dour expression. "I now regret so quickly brushing off the detective's story about the teens losing chunks of memory. If they were injected with this compound, it's certainly plausible."

"But wouldn't that do incredible damage to their brains?"

"If it were administered selectively, using the antibodies to deliver the toxic payload to specific hippocampal astrocytes and cortical neurons like a smart missile, only existing memories would be affected. The ability to consolidate new memories would remain intact."

Despite her horror that Zero Dark had created such a terrible weapon, Cristina was excited that now they knew how it worked. "So we need to administer an antivenin, right?"

"I'm afraid it's not that simple. There is currently one approved antivenin, and that's for the black widow spider. The peptides in the sample you provided are only found in one species: *Phoneutria nigriventer*, the Brazilian wandering spider."

Cristina's scalp prickled. "Brazilian?"

"Yes. So I'm afraid antivenin is not an option. We might be able to neutralize the delivery system, effectively reactivating those AMPA switches, but we simply don't have that information." Dr. Campbell tilted his head. "Judging by the look on your face, I surmise that sample wasn't ex vivo, was it?"

She shook her head. "A teenager was injected with it. That sample is from his wound."

"That's a shame. Anyone affected by that toxin would likely lose all personal memories within a week's time. Their mind would be wiped clean, like a blank slate."

Her mind jumped at Campbell's last words. She recalled scrolling through Jose Kobayashi's files. Her mind zeroed in on one of the other folders, one she hadn't opened, though the name stuck in her mind: Tabula Rasa.

Latin for 'blank slate.'

"Thank you, Dr. Campbell," she said quickly and ushered him toward the elevator. "I'll let Detective Wilson know what you've found. I know you're very busy and I have to finish that analysis."

"Yes, well, I'd like to analyze that sample some more. As I said, understanding how the venom turns off those switches could be the key to learning how we can turn them back on." Dr. Campbell stopped at the elevator and turned to Cristina. "I could use your help. Have you considered my offer to join the Mnemosyne project?"

Cristina hesitated. Joining the top-secret project would be a way into his inner circle, like Jefferson had wanted. But if Dr. Campbell knew more about Cristina than he let on, would joining the project put her at an even greater risk? If he was working for Zero Dark, was that how they planned to access the information locked away in her memories about her father?

"I need a little more time to think about it," she said at last, holding the elevator door open for him. "I imagine it will require longer hours, and right now I'd like to spend time with my sister before she returns home."

"Family is important." He nodded and stepped into the elevator. "But please decide soon. In the meantime, I need you and your assistant in the EEG lab in an hour. I want to make adjustments to the study protocol now that we have extra time to do so."

"Yes, sir."

The moment the elevator doors closed, Cristina ran back to her office and shut the door behind her. She slipped Devi's jamming device out of her backpack and activated it, then pulled out her laptop and inserted the flash drive with the files Devi had sent her. She searched for Dr. Kobayashi's files and then clicked on the folder marked Tabula Rasa.

A window popped up asking for a passkey.

She frowned. This must have been one of the folders Devi hadn't yet decrypted. She tried typing *Kobayashi*. A message appeared in red: *Invalid entry. Two tries remaining.*

Mentally crossing her fingers, she tried *Mnemosyne*.

Another pop-up: *Invalid entry. One try remaining.*

Cristina gave up. She didn't know if it had been Dr. Campbell or Dr. Kobayashi who encrypted the files and had no idea what the passkey could be in either case. But there was someone who might know. She dialed Devi.

"Cristina, I was about to call you," her friend said. "Where are you?"

"In my office, but I'm using the jammer you gave me. What about you?"

"At home. I told my boss I was telecommuting today so I could decrypt those files on an air-gapped system."

"Did you finish?" Cristina asked.

"Yes, and you're not going to believe what I found."

"I need to know what's in the folder labeled Tabula Rasa," Cristina said, knowing if she didn't cut Devi off her friend would launch into a detailed description of her hacking technique.

"That one had a lot of information I didn't understand." Devi clucked her tongue. "Something about spider venom and a way to erase memories."

Cristina's adrenaline spiked. "Did it say anything about an antidote?"

"No, but it looks like Kobayashi found evidence that ReMind was trying to create one."

"ReMind?" Cristina connected the dots. "That's what they intended for Recognate. They wanted it as a way to reverse the memory eraser, but it didn't work the way they expected."

"It's worse than that, Cristina." Devi's voice deepened, becoming more serious. "Dr. Kobayashi learned from Jorge Silva that Quinn was using human brains as biologic hard drives, ones he could deactivate to protect his secrets, completely unable to be hacked."

"And then once he had a workable antidote, he could reactivate them and access those secrets." Cristina marveled at Quinn's cruel but elaborate plan. "That's why he killed the Silvas, because Jorge had discovered his plan."

"That's not all of it. I found a partial list of names. People Quinn planned to use as his personal data systems. Sabrina Carvalho was on the list." Devi paused. "And so was Cristina Silva."

Cristina's face went numb. "What?"

"According to Kobayashi, Quinn was obsessed with Jorge Silva's family—especially his daughter. He knew she had information about Jorge, secrets he would only have shared with her. It turns out Jorge and Quinn had once been friends in the CIA until he thought Jorge betrayed him. After Quinn ran off to join Zero Dark, he saw using Jorge's daughter for his own purposes as a final revenge against his old friend."

"So his plan had always been to keep Cristina alive, and he replaced her with me as an afterthought?" Cristina rubbed her forehead. "I thought I knew the extent of how twisted Quinn was, but I was wrong."

"There's more, Cristina."

"I don't think I can take anymore."

"There's a video file of the team that created Tabula Rasa."

Cristina brightened. "That's good. If we can find them, they may already be working on the antidote."

"The video didn't include any names, and I didn't recognize their faces. Except for one." Devi sighed. "Yours."

CHAPTER SEVENTY-SEVEN

Wilson pulled into the NatureBoost parking lot next to Wakefield's SUV. The shop door was ajar. As Wilson approached, he glanced through the window. Inside, the store appeared empty.

A tingling started at the back of Wilson's neck. Something was off. He should wait for Hawkins.

From inside the store came a petrifying scream.

Wilson drew his service pistol with one hand and said into his radio with the other, "Detective Wilson answering the call to Assembly Row. Someone's in distress inside the NatureBoost shop. Proceeding to investigate. Send additional backup."

"Copy, Detective," said the dispatcher.

Nudging the door open with his foot, Wilson shouted inside, "Detective Wilson, Somerville PD! Do you need help?"

A radiator rattled near the back of the store.

Wilson crept inside and scurried to the far corner of the room before performing a *slicing the pie* sweep. A few of the bottle displays had been knocked over. The translucent tables afforded little cover for someone to lie in wait. He held still and listened.

The sound of ragged breathing came from the back room.

Keeping his gun at eye level, Wilson crossed the room and ducked behind the register. He pulled out his phone and turned on the front-facing camera. Angling it carefully, he used it to peer inside the dimly lit back room.

A woman's body lay on the floor, unmoving.

Clenching his jaw, Wilson tilted the camera another fifteen degrees. At the back of the small room, next to a framed photograph of Boston Harbor, a thick beam of sunlight streamed in through an open door.

"Damn it," he said under his breath. He pulled out his radio again as he entered the storage room. Now he could see blood pooling around the body. Allison Wakefield was staring at the ceiling, gasping.

"This is Detective Wilson. I need an ambulance to Assembly Row. Suspect escaped out the back. He may be wearing a black hood but—"

The door crashed into Wilson's shoulder. He fell. His knee struck the concrete floor. Pain shot up his leg.

A dark figure stepped out from behind the door, silhouetted against the sunlight. One of the man's gloved hands held a bloody knife. The other clutched a syringe filled with crimson fluid. A black hood covered his face.

Wilson's chest tightened.

Sack Man.

CHAPTER SEVENTY-EIGHT

The clock on Cristina's office wall ticked as she processed Devi's last words, that somehow she'd been involved in creating Tabula Rasa. It took a great deal of effort to say, "That couldn't have been me."

"It looked a lot like you. Or at least how you looked in those photos from Brazil."

"You mean Sabrina," Cristina said, directing the question not only to Devi.

If I was involved, Sabrina answered, *it must have happened during that missing year. I have no memory of it.*

"Whichever one of you, it doesn't matter," Devi said. "I don't think I should risk sending it to you electronically. If someone got their hands on this, it could incriminate you."

"I understand. Can you copy everything onto another flash drive? I can pick it up from you after work."

"Sure. But I'm turning on a high-level jammer after we hang up. You won't be able to reach me by phone. Buzz the intercom when you arrive."

"Thanks, Devi. You're a lifesaver."

After hanging up, Cristina stared at her laptop. If she'd been involved in Tabula Rasa's creation, could her father have been one of the other researchers? When she got her hands on the video, she'd study it carefully. But another matter weighed on her shoulders. The real Cristina Silva was alive, and Quinn had planned to erase her memories the way he had Sabrina's. Where had she been all this time, and who did she believe she was?

An alarm beeped on her desktop. She turned on her monitor and found a pop-up message from Dr. Campbell, reminding her to join him in the EEG lab. Biting her cheek, she cleared the message. How familiar was he with Kobayashi's files? Was it a coincidence that he'd used the term *blank slate*, or had he seen the video showing her helping to create Tabula Rasa? There was only one way to find out. She'd have to confront him directly.

Summoning her courage, she packed her laptop and the jammer into her messenger bag and locked her office. On the way to the elevator, she swung by Victoria's desk, but her assistant still wasn't there. She called Victoria's cell phone, but she didn't answer. A thought crossed her mind as she rode the elevator down to the sublevels: if the real Cristina Silva wanted to get back at her, might she go after her assistant?

At the EEG lab, she found Dr. Campbell fiddling with one of the sensor nets. He fumbled with it for another few seconds, then tossed it on the bench. "Blast it! Someone monkeyed with the probes. I'll need to recalibrate them." He viewed Cristina over his shoulder. "Where's your assistant?"

Cristina hated to throw Victoria under the bus, but she hoped Dr. Campbell might know something she didn't. "She hasn't come in yet. Did she say anything to you yesterday?"

"No, she didn't. Anyway, she's your responsibility." He smoothed out his eyebrows and puckered his lip. "If she doesn't show up today, you'll have to let her go. I know she idolizes you, but I already made one exception for her."

Cristina narrowed her gaze. "What are you talking about?"

"She was originally supposed to work on the neuroimaging study, but when she found out you were working on the EEG project, she specifically asked me to transfer her to your supervision."

"She did? Why?"

"She said something about speaking to your old friends at ReMind and falling in love with your work." Dr. Campbell shrugged and held up the sensory net. "Would you mind helping me with this?"

Cristina didn't move. She was frozen in place as thoughts tossed and turned in her head. Victoria had done everything she could to learn about Cristina, going out of her way to earn her trust while avoiding talking about her own background. Each time Cristina had been followed or attacked, it had been after she'd left the Memory Center. And Victoria had access to Cristina's office, where she could've easily planted a bug.

On the photo of Jorge and Claudia Silva.

One explanation made perfect sense: Victoria was the real Cristina Silva.

CHAPTER SEVENTY-NINE

Wilson and Sack Man faced off in the small back room of the Nature-Boost Vitamin Shoppe. A low wheeze came from Allison Wakefield's lips as she lay unmoving on the floor. Sack Man clutched a syringe, red fluid dripping from the tip.

Wilson swung his pistol toward Sack Man and said, "Don't move, asshole."

Sack Man kicked the gun from Wilson's hand. He lunged at the detective, knife-first.

Wilson dodged and chopped his hand against the attacker's elbow. Sack Man grunted, and the knife clattered against the floor.

Sack Man charged the detective, head down. He crashed into Wilson's chest, knocking him off his feet. The back of the detective's head crashed against a metal storage rack.

Sack Man pressed a gloved hand against Wilson's face. The tang of leather assaulted Wilson's nostrils. Between the fingers, he could make out Sack Man's dark eyes glinting.

Wilson closed his hand into a fist. He swung. His knuckles cracked against jawbone.

Sack Man released him and stumbled backward. Wilson lunged.

He used his attacker's technique against him, striking Sack Man square in the abdomen.

Something bit into Wilson's neck.

A burning sensation ran through him. He staggered two steps back.

Sack Man held up the empty syringe. His eyes gleamed.

"What—?" Wilson touched the back of his neck. His fingertips grazed a sticky liquid. He withdrew his hand. Blood clung to his fingertip. "What did you do to me?"

Without answering, Sack Man bent and reclaimed his knife.

Anger bubbled up Wilson's gullet. He spotted his pistol under a storage rack. He scrambled over to it. He snatched up the gun, turned, and aimed.

But Sack Man was gone.

CHAPTER EIGHTY

DB waited outside the apartment building until the front door buzzed and she heard a clunk, indicating it was unlocked. She adjusted her gray sweats and ruffled her hair to make herself look just the right amount of harried before swinging open the door and stepping inside.

When she reached the end of the hall, she heard through the apartment door the melodramatic music of a Brazilian *novela*. She might've found it charming under different circumstances. After slapping her cheeks to bring out the color, she pounded on the door.

The door flew open. Maria, wearing skinny jeans and a cream-colored blouse, looked her up and down and said, "Victoria, are you okay? What happened?"

"I'll explain inside." DB pushed past her. "It's not safe out in the open."

"That's what you said in your text messages." Maria shut and locked the door before turning to face DB. "What did—"

DB fell into Maria's arms and hugged her tight.

"I'm sorry," she said, allowing her voice to crack. "I didn't know where else to go."

"*Shush*," Maria murmured, lightly stroking DB's back and nuzzling her hair. "You're safe now."

"No, I'm not." DB raised the pitch of her voice. "Someone followed me on my way to work. A man wearing a hood over his face."

"*Meu Deus*," Maria said, pulling her head back to inspect DB again. "Are you okay?"

"My leg's a little gammy after falling arse over tit to get away from him, but I'll be okay." Tears streamed from DB's eyes. "Why would someone try to hurt me? What does he want?"

Maria planted her feet. "It's not you he wants. It's my sister."

"Cristina? Why?"

"Years ago, she fell in with some bad men, and they did things to her. She managed to break free of their grip, but they are still after her." Maria turned away. "I'm sorry you were dragged into this. I should've warned you."

Before DB could ask what the bad men wanted, to finally know the whole story, Maria's cell phone rang.

Maria looked down at it and cocked her head. "It's Cristina."

The muscles in DB's shoulders tensed. "Call her back later. We need to get somewhere safe."

"We're safe here."

"No, we're not." DB grabbed Maria's hand. "If these bad men are after her, they might try to hurt you to get to her. I need to know everything about who these men are."

Maria's phone chirped again. As she studied the screen, her face paled. "*Misericórdia.*"

There was no need to ask what the text said. DB could tell from Maria's face that she knew the truth. Calmly, she said, "I can explain."

Maria turned to run.

Cursing, DB tackled her. Holding her down with one hand and her body weight, she reached under her sweatshirt to slip a white tablet out of a pouch on the leather bodysuit she wore underneath. She shoved the sedative into Maria's mouth. Maria tried to spit it out, but DB pushed it back in and clamped her jaws shut. The more Maria struggled, the more tightly DB held her. Eventually, Maria stopped thrashing, her eyes rolled back, and she slumped to the ground.

"I'm sorry it had to go this way," DB whispered in Maria's ear, though she wasn't sure how much her would-be lover could hear. "But soon this will all be over."

CHAPTER EIGHTY-ONE

"Gary?" Hawkins's voice carried from the main room of the Nature-Boost store. "Talk to me."

"Back here," Wilson called out. He crouched next to Allison Wakefield. Her breathing was more ragged. A red stain blossomed on her white lab coat. He ripped it open. Her blouse was doused in blood. A jagged wound peeked out between the torn edges of the fabric. "Stab wound to the abdomen. Paramedics are already on their way."

Hawkins appeared in the doorway. "What happened?"

"Sack Man." Wilson applied pressure to the wound, but he didn't know what good it would do. "He caught me by surprise and escaped out the back."

Hawkins scanned the room. "What did he want?"

Wakefield coughed and wet her lips. A low groan escaped her lips.

"Don't try to talk," Wilson said to her.

Her arm lifted off the ground and she pointed at the picture of the Boston Harbor. Her voice was barely a whisper. "Two . . . five . . . six . . . one."

Adrenaline coursed through Wilson's body. He rushed over and tossed the picture to the ground, revealing a wall safe. He punched in the code and opened the door. Inside were stacks of hundred-dollar bills and a sheaf of papers. He removed the papers and flipped through them.

"What is it?" Hawkins asked.

"Notes on their attempts to make an antidote for something called Tabula Rasa."

"Tabula what?"

"It's the memory eraser Pierce used on Reggie." Wilson's fingers tingled with electricity as he kept reading. "After Pierce hooked kids on RAM Boost, Sack Man went after them and injected them with Tabula Rasa. Then he would test the modified MCH-21 on them. Son of a bitch! That's why Caleb was so afraid of Sack Man biting his neck."

"He was talking about the injections," Hawkins said.

Wilson nodded and kept reading. "But Wakefield discovered the supplement blocks the breakdown of narcotics."

Hawkins's eyes widened. "Like amphetamines?"

"That's why they were so amped up. Sack Man killed them to cover it up." Wilson squeezed the paper, feeling it crumple. He'd had the asshole and let him get away! Acid burned its way up his gullet. Crouching next to Wakefield, he grabbed her lab coat by the lapels. "Sack Man— who is he?"

Sirens blared outside.

"Answer!" Wilson leaned over Wakefield, panic rising in his chest. "Who is Sack Man?"

A murmur escaped her lips. Wilson leaned his head closer but couldn't make out her words. He heard footsteps behind them.

"Gary." Hawkins laid a hand on Wilson's shoulder. "Paramedics are here. Let them do their job. We'll get answers when she wakes up."

Wilson stood and allowed the emergency responders to work. He turned to Hawkins. "Put out an APB on Sack Man."

"But we don't have a description—"

"I want anyone wearing all black stopped and questioned."

"You know we can't do that." Hawkins squinted at Wilson. "Wait, what's going on with your neck? Is that blood?"

Wilson squeezed his hands into fists, aware of his racing heartbeat, the sweat rolling down his cheeks. The paramedics finished strapping Wakefield to a backboard and lifted her up. One of them turned to the detectives and said, "She's in critical condition. We need to move."

"We'll give you an escort," Wilson said. To Hawkins: "Ride with me. I'll explain everything on the way."

CHAPTER EIGHTY-TWO

"Maria, where are you?" Cristina said into her phone while running to her office parking lot. She'd tried calling her sister's phone three times, but it kept going straight to voice mail. Dr. Campbell's face had been a mixture of confusion and anger when Cristina fumbled an excuse about having left the gas stove on at home before fleeing the EEG lab. She'd apologize to him later, once she made sure Maria was safe. "Please call me back, and don't answer the door to anyone, especially Victoria."

On the drive home, she tried calling Wilson, but he didn't answer either. Her anxiety skyrocketed. She drove even faster.

She burst into her apartment, shouting, "Maria!"

Silence answered her.

Pulling the Glock out of her backpack, she searched the bedroom and bathroom. Both empty. She called Maria again.

She froze. Maria's ringtone was coming from the living room.

Cristina returned to the living room and dialed Maria's number once more. The ringing was coming from under the couch.

Holding her breath, she bent down and found Maria's phone, but not Maria. The last text message Cristina had sent appeared on the lock screen, along with several missed calls.

Frantic, Cristina called Victoria's cell phone. She heard a *number not in service* message.

She called Wilson again, but again reached his voice mail. Holding back a scream, she said into the phone, "Maria's missing. Someone took her. Call me back."

As a last-ditch effort, she tried calling Devi. No answer. Cristina cursed as she recalled Devi saying she'd be using a jammer while she worked on Dr. Campbell's files.

Cristina paced the room, trying to come up with a plan. She had no idea where Victoria would've taken Maria, or even if it was Victoria. The longer she waited for Wilson to call back, the greater the chance something bad might happen to her.

Someone coughed behind her.

She drew her Glock and spun around.

Bruno raised his hands next to his head. His hair was tousled, like he'd been taking a nap. The corner of his mouth twisted wryly. "Is this how you greet all your old friends?"

"How did you get in here?" she demanded, keeping the gun trained on his chest.

He jerked his thumb. "You left the door open."

Damn it, he was right. "What are you doing here?"

"I had something to discuss with Maria. I tried calling but she didn't answer, so I decided to stop by." His brow furrowed. "Where is she?"

Cristina lowered the pistol. Her hands had started to shake too much to hold it steady anyway. "Someone's kidnapped her."

"Why would anyone do that?"

She sighed. "It's a long story."

"If Maria is in trouble, we only have time for short stories." He gave her a stern look. "Do you know who took her?"

"It could be one of two people. Either a criminal who goes by the name Sack Man . . ." She swallowed. "Or a woman who used to be called Cristina Silva."

The creases in his forehead deepened. "I don't understand."

"She calls herself Victoria Weiss, but I think her memories were stolen by the men who worked with your brother and given to me. Somehow she's realized I took her place, and now I'm afraid she's trying to get revenge."

His eyebrows drifted upward, and his jaw dropped slightly.

"I know it's confusing," she said, and then a thought dawned on her. "Did your brother ever mention Sack Man? They both worked for the same man."

"*Hmm?*" Bruno blinked rapidly. "Oh, no. He never mentioned him."

"Are you okay?" Her gaze fell on the black shirt he wore under his leather jacket. "Oh, you're bleeding!"

He glanced at his shirt in surprise, then shrugged. "I cut myself shaving this morning. I didn't have time to change."

"But your face isn't—"

Her cell phone rang. Thinking it might be Maria, she sprang to answer it.

"Cristina, I just got your message." It was Wilson, and the tension was obvious in his voice. "Did you find Maria?"

"No." She was about to tell him Bruno was there to help and thought better of it. The way he'd reacted the other night, she needed Wilson focused, not jealous. "I believe either Sack Man or Victoria has her."

"Who's Victoria?"

"The real Cristina Silva."

"When did that happen? Never mind, it couldn't have been Sack Man. I just faced off with him. He stabbed Allison Wakefield. She's lost a lot of blood."

Cristina pressed her palm against her cheek. "Oh, my God. Are you okay?"

"I hurt him, but he jabbed me with something. I'll be okay. But, Cristina, Sack Man has a working antidote for the memory eraser. It's called—"

"Tabula Rasa." She caught Bruno's puzzled look and waved him off. "I know. How did he get it?"

"It looks like he initially cut a deal with Wakefield and gave her samples of Recognate as a base for her MCH-21 supplement," Wilson said. "She knew he was testing it on teens that he met through Pierce, but when she found out Sack Man was killing them if the antidote failed, she tried to get out. That's when he threatened to kill her family if she didn't cooperate. Once he got a working antidote, he didn't need her anymore."

"Zero Dark wants to eliminate Sack Man. That's why Jefferson was after him. He must want the antidote as protection in case they try to use Tabula Rasa on him." A chilling thought struck Cristina. "Or he's trying to continue Quinn's work."

"What do you mean?"

"Quinn was using human brains as secure data storage drives," said Cristina. "If someone had secrets, he would wipe their brains with Tabula Rasa. That's what Quinn did to me, and to the real Cristina Silva. When he was killed, he was working to create an antidote so he could later access that data."

"How do you know all that?"

She swallowed. "I asked Devi Patel to help me hack Dr. Campbell's files."

"That was incredibly dangerous, Cristina. And illegal."

"I know, but I thought Dr. Campbell might be Sack Man. I should've told you, but I didn't want to screw things up again between us."

She caught Bruno's breath hitch. Well, she didn't have time for jealousy. "I'll explain the rest to you later, but right now we have to find Maria."

"So if Sack Man didn't take her, you think she's with this Victoria?"

"Yes, Victoria Weiss. I'm certain. She's blond with brown eyes, my height."

"I'll put out a BOLO. As soon as I'm done here, I'll join the search. We'll find her."

After hanging up, Cristina turned back to Bruno. "I'm sorry to drag you into this. It seems everyone close to me ends up in danger. It's like I'm cursed."

"You are not cursed." He held her gaze. "You are a very special woman. There is so much inside your head that could change the world."

"Thanks." She felt a blush coming on and shook her head. "But we need to find Maria."

"I promise I will do everything in my power to help you," he said and crossed his heart.

The room spun out of control around Cristina.

He'd used his left hand to sign the cross right to left.

CHAPTER EIGHTY-THREE

Bruno met Cristina's gaze. The air hung heavy around them.

The blood on Bruno's black shirt—it had to be Dr. Wakefield's. Bruno knew where she lived, what route she took to work. She'd never seen what he drove but judging from his gear a motorcycle wouldn't be out of the question. If she searched him, would she find a black hood?

Cristina tried to keep the shock from showing on her face but knew she'd failed when his mouth pressed into a thin line and his eyes turned cold and menacing. His hand crept toward his belt.

She drew the Glock and aimed it at him.

"Why, Bruno?" Her voice threatened to break, but she kept it and the gun steady. "Why are you doing this?"

"It's just like you told your boyfriend; I want my freedom from Zero Dark. I need the antidote as protection, in case they come after me with Tabula Rasa. No one's erasing my brain!" His mouth twitched. "But I'm giving you my offer to join me once more, in deference to the mistake I made trusting Sabrina and Quinn."

A wave of nausea passed over her as a memory burst forth of the first time Sabrina met Quinn and other Zero Dark mercenaries at a café in Copacabana. Quinn's attraction to her had been immediate and obvious. And, sitting next to her, squeezing her hand, eyes glittering with jealousy, had been Bruno Gomes.

She was barely able to form the words. "It was you—not Federico—who introduced Sabrina to Quinn."

"And in gratitude, he ordered me here, deep undercover." Bruno's eyes glittered like obsidian crystals. "All so he could keep me out of the way while he moved in on Sabrina. But now he's dead, and we can both be free."

The gun grew heavy in Cristina's hand. She studied the smooth contours of his cheeks, recalled the taste of his lips.

Not now, Sabrina, she thought. *We can't trust him.*

I loved him once, Sabrina replied, her voice cold and distant. *And he has the antidote. He can put me back in control.*

"By erasing me!" Cristina said aloud.

Bruno cocked his head.

Cristina steadied her aim on his forehead. "I'm not going anywhere with you."

"That's too bad. I guess you don't want to know the truth about your *papai*."

She nearly dropped the gun. "What?"

"I know where to find him. Quinn told me." His lip curled. "You can finally have that sweet daddy-daughter reunion you've been wanting for so long."

That's what's been keeping us apart, Sabrina said. *If we find him, he can help us recover those memories and Zero Dark won't be able to use them against him. We can finally end this.*

"I don't trust you," Cristina said. "Everything you say is a lie."

"You have little choice but to trust me," he said, dropping his hands an inch. "First, we'll go save Maria—I have an idea where she is—and then I'll take you to him."

"Don't move!" Cristina's finger tightened on the trigger.

No!

Cristina felt her thoughts being shoved aside. Sabrina was wrestling for dominance over their body.

Not this time, Cristina thought and fought back, exerting sheer will to stay in control. But it wasn't enough. The gun lowered an inch.

Bruno quickly pulled a gun from his belt, a suppressor attached to its barrel. He aimed it at her and fired.

Cristina dove behind the couch. Bullets thudded into the cushions. She heard footsteps retreating.

Rolling to the side, she aimed the Glock around the couch.

Bruno was gone.

CHAPTER EIGHTY-FOUR

Even the vibrations from Grizabella's soft purring couldn't soothe Cristina's jangled nerves as she dialed Wilson. She'd run down the hallway after Bruno, but there was no sign of him. She went back to her apartment, tried to calm her mewling cat, and considered her next move. She still had no idea where Maria and Victoria were, but now she had a more pressing problem.

Wilson answered after the second ring. "Did you find Maria?"

"No. Bruno Gomes is Sack Man."

"I think you cut out for a moment. It sounded like you said Bruno was Sack Man."

"He is. He just shot at me."

"*What?*" Wilson's vocal tone spiked. "Are you okay?"

"I'm fine. He wasn't shooting to kill. He wanted to escape." Cristina brushed loose hair out of her eyes. "But he heard us talking about Devi and the information in Dr. Campbell's files. I'm afraid he might try to go after Devi."

"Where does she live?"

Cristina gave him the address.

"That's only four blocks from where I am now. I'll go check on her. You keep looking for Maria."

"Okay. And Gary?"

"Yeah?"

She wet her lips. "Thank you. I'd be lost without you."

His voice sounded strained as he said, "We'll find them. You have my word."

After hanging up, Cristina turned her thoughts inward. "We need to talk about what happened. It's because of you that Devi is in danger."

I know, Sabrina replied, her inner voice small and meek. *But if Bruno knows who my father is, I couldn't let you kill him.*

"I wasn't going to kill him. You share my thoughts. You should know that." Cristina spat in disgust. "You're so impulsive. You don't think before acting. And you've got terrible taste in men. Maybe that's why I'm the dominant one."

You're right.

"This needs to stop. We can't be at odds with each other when we're dealing with . . . Wait. What?"

This is my fault. All of it. We're too different from each other. That's why we haven't been able to integrate. Because I need to be in control. But I don't deserve to be.

The hairs on Cristina's neck lifted. "What are you saying?"

Once we find Maria, you need to find a way to erase me—for good, this time. Gary Wilson is a good man, and you deserve to be together. If I'm still inside your head, I'll mess it up.

"I can't erase you. You're part of me." Cristina's words caught in her throat. "But I think we need to resolve our differences."

We're beyond that. And if I remember everything, our life and our father's life are in danger. It's better if you go on being Cristina Silva.

Cristina swallowed hard. "If Victoria is trying to reclaim her identity, that may not be an option. For now, let's focus on finding Maria. We can deal with each other later."

When her phone rang, she answered without checking the caller ID. "Is Devi okay? Did you find Maria?"

"Oh, I found her all right, *Cristina.*"

Cristina's blood froze. "Victoria."

"You want to see your sister? Come on over. Alone. No calling 911 or I'll know."

Gears turned in Cristina's mind. She'd forgotten to activate the jamming device when returning home. Victoria had probably been listening to her every word. Since listening devices had short range, she was likely nearby. "Where are you?"

"Around the corner on Winslow, in the apartment building next to the barber shop. Go to the fifth floor. But I won't wait long. *Ticktock. Ticktock.*"

The line went dead.

Sucking in deep breaths, Cristina bent down and kissed Grizabella on the back. "Mommy has to go, but I'll be back to take care of you."

Cristina tucked the Glock into her purse and raced down the stairs. She didn't have time to call Wilson or anyone else. If she wanted to save Maria, she had to do this herself.

Ticktock. Ticktock.

CHAPTER EIGHTY-FIVE

As Wilson ran up the stairs to Devi's walk-up apartment, he tried to ignore the way his thoughts stretched and wriggled away each time he tried to grab hold of them. He needed to get a hold of that antidote before all his memories dissolved into gelatinous mush. It had probably been a mistake to sneak out of the hospital, leaving Hawkins behind to wait for news on Dr. Wakefield's condition, but he couldn't let Cristina down.

He reached Devi's floor, drew his gun, and crept down the hall. He stopped at her door, which was ajar, and listened.

A woman groaned inside the apartment.

Muscles spasmed in Wilson's neck as he fought to come up with an action plan. Procedure dictated he should call it in . . . he thought. Maybe he was supposed to secure the area first. He wasn't sure.

A childhood memory of playing basketball with his father flitted through Wilson's mind. He swiped at his forehead and stared at the sweat covering his hand. Steeling himself, he crept into the apartment, gun first.

He found Devi sprawled on the linoleum floor. A massive bruise blossomed on her forehead. "Devi, can you hear me?"

She groaned and lifted her head. Her eyes wobbled. "Wilson?"

"Don't move. I'm going to call for help." Wilson dialed 911. A series of rapid beeps answered him. "What the hell?"

"Cell phone jammer."

"Damn it." He pulled out his police radio. "This is Detective Wilson. I need paramedics for an A-and-B." He rattled off the address.

Wilson put away the radio and checked Devi for signs of more serious injury. "Is Gomes still here?"

"Who?"

"Bruno Gomes. Cristina said he's Sack Man."

"This wasn't Sack Man." Devi touched her forehead and winced. "It was a woman. She had blond hair and was wearing black leather."

"Blond hair?" A scrap of something Cristina had said flittered in the back of his mind. He pounced on it. "Was her name Victoria?"

"I don't know her name. She didn't say anything, just took the flash drive I made for Cristina and smashed my computer before knocking me out." Devi's eyelids fluttered. "You need to get to Cristina. The information on that flash drive could destroy her."

CHAPTER EIGHTY-SIX

The elevator walls closed around Cristina, making her struggle to breathe. As she rode up to the fifth floor, she kept her hand on the Glock, praying she wouldn't need to use it.

When the elevator doors opened, she slunk to the last apartment. She aimed the Glock at the door and knocked.

The door opened. Victoria stood inside, dressed all in black except for her head, holding a semiautomatic pistol with the barrel trained on Cristina's chest. Her lips stretched into a vicious smile. "Great minds think alike."

The smell of leather assaulted Cristina's nostrils, as realization struck her. "You're the one who attacked me by the children's hospital. You've known about me all along."

"Well, *duh*." Victoria rolled her eyes.

"You better not have hurt my sister."

"*Ooh*, touchy." Victoria stepped back and made a sweeping motion with the gun before retargeting Cristina's chest. "Come inside."

Cristina entered the room, keeping her Glock trained on Victoria, while the other woman circled around and shut the door with her foot. A whimper caught Cristina's attention. Her heart sank as she saw Maria tied to a wooden chair, mouth gagged, head lolled forward like she'd been drugged. Cristina started toward her sister.

"*Uh-uh.*" Victoria shifted her aim to Maria. "Stay where you are if you want her to keep breathing."

Cristina froze in place. "What do you want?"

"That's the million-dollar question, isn't it?" Victoria toyed with the trigger. "What can you possibly give that you haven't permanently stripped away from me, *Sabrina*?"

The words filtered through Cristina's mind until she understood. "I was right. You are Cristina Silva."

"Bravo for figuring that out. Better late than never, I suppose." Victoria's lip curled. "I know you weren't responsible for what happened to me, so I'm giving you and your sister the chance to live. First, tell me why Quinn stole my memories."

"I don't know. I didn't even know you were still alive."

She held up a flash drive. "This has the information your friend Devi stole from Dr. Campbell. If I share it with you, can you fix me?"

"You want me to restore your memories? I don't know if I can do that."

"Not that." Victoria's eyebrows met. "I want to get rid of these memories, these feelings, this . . . *regret* over the things I've done. The things they programmed me to do."

More pieces clicked into place. "You're an assassin, killing ReMind employees. That's how you found out about me."

Victoria nodded. A teardrop clung to her eyelash.

A wave of both horror and sympathy washed over Cristina. She understood better than anyone the conflict Victoria felt, but at the same time, Victoria *had* done horrible things. And now she was threatening Maria's life. Although she felt the urge to help her, it wasn't within Cristina to forgive her.

"You can't undo what you've done," she said, choosing her words carefully. "And even if I could again erase that part of you that was Cristina Silva, it won't undo the changes that have happened to you since. Those feelings you're experiencing, that regret and grief—those aren't *her* feelings. They're *yours*."

Victoria's expression softened, but the effect was fleeting. She turned her gun to aim at Maria's head. "That's bullshit."

"That is the truth." Cristina's stomach flip-flopped as she searched for a way to either talk Victoria down or wrestle the gun away from her. "I know because that's what happened to me. Zero Dark recreated you as someone else. Cristina Silva is still there, trying to claw her way to the surface, but Victoria Weiss—"

"Dama Branca. Victoria Weiss is who they told me I was, but she doesn't exist."

Cristina swallowed. "Dama Branca is real. She's as much a part of you as Cristina is."

Victoria stood still, squinting. "So I'm fucked, is what you're saying."

Forcing herself to hold Victoria's gaze instead of staring at her gun, Cristina recalled her earlier argument with Sabrina and their battle for control. If they couldn't resolve their differences, how could she expect Victoria and her alter ego to do so, especially when one was a professional killer?

"I think you need to decide what kind of person you want to be. Not what Zero Dark created you to be. Not even what your parents wanted for you." Cristina wet her lips and inched forward, holding out her hand. "Forget about what you've done. Ask yourself who you *are*. If you want, I'm here to help."

Victoria's scowl wavered. For the briefest second, she seemed about to do as Cristina asked. But then her face darkened, and she stroked the trigger. "Don't move any closer."

Cristina froze.

"You almost had me." Victoria's cheeks reddened. "But you're full of psychobabble bullshit. I heard you arguing with yourself. You don't even know who you are. How are you supposed to help me?"

Nice try, Sabrina said. *But she's right. You're going to have to stop her another way.*

Clenching her jaw, Cristina trained her Glock back on Victoria's forehead. "I will kill you if you hurt Maria. You know I will."

Victoria gazed down at Maria.

And that's when Cristina saw it: Victoria felt something for Maria.

Hope blossomed in Cristina's chest. Finally, something she could use.

"You want your life back," Cristina said carefully. "Or, at least, *a* life. I get it. You want to love. You want to dream. The part of you that's Cristina Silva can still have that."

Victoria's eyes widened. Her pressure on the gun relaxed, ever so slightly. "How?"

"Turn yourself in. You'll get help. Treatment."

"No way. If I turn myself in, the only treatment I'll get is a lethal injection."

Maria let out a low moan.

Victoria turned toward her.

Cristina dropped her aim and shot at her leg.

Victoria flipped out of the way, the bullet whizzing past her knee, and ducked behind Maria's chair.

"Shit." Cristina ran to get a better angle. Bullets whizzed past her head. She rolled under the dining room table.

She heard a *click*. Victoria was reloading her gun.

Cristina searched for her target. *Damn it.* Victoria was still shielded by Maria.

"You're the good one, right?" said Victoria. "You always try to do the right thing, even when others around you get hurt. You almost had me convinced you cared about what happened to me." Victoria slid the cartridge into place. "That was my mistake, and I won't make it again."

CHAPTER EIGHTY-SEVEN

DB's—or, rather, Cristina Silva's—life flashed before her eyes. Riding her tricycle down the driveway, proud parents Jorge and Claudia Silva cheering behind her. Marching across the gymnasium podium to claim her high school diploma, thrusting it in the air to the cheers of her classmates. Going to the bowling alley for her first date with a cute boy from her college Organic Chemistry class and spilling soda all over the shiny pleather pants she'd worn. Crying on her father's shoulder as he stroked her back, whispering that everything would be okay because he'd always be there for her.

DB's throat constricted. Her chest grew heavy. Feelings of joy and sorrow and anxiety tumbled inside her. DB drew in breath. She knew what she had to do.

The fake doctor did have one good point. The only way out of this is to accept who I am. DB aimed the Sig Sauer at the table. *But to do that, I have to erase everything Zero Dark took from me.*

From under the table, Cristina struggled to come up with a plan over the pounding pulse in her temples. Trying to wound her opponent had been a mistake. The only way she was getting out of this alive was to do what had to be done: go for the kill.

You're not a killer. And neither is she.

A bullet crashed into the table, sending splinters flying. Cristina huddled to one side. *Tell that to her.*

Convince her *who the real enemy is.*

Understanding crept in. Sighting her Glock at the sofa, Cristina called out, "Think about it. Why did Zero Dark keep you alive and turn you into their assassin when there was always the chance you might learn the truth? They're using you."

"Of course they're using me. They've always used me. That's why I'm going to claim payback once I'm done with you."

Cristina tensed, gripping the Glock close to her cheek. Victoria's voice was growing closer. She had to keep Victoria talking. "Payback? How?"

"Don't worry." Soft, padding footsteps approached. "Zero Dark won't be a problem for you anymore. Nothing will."

Cristina fired twice. Bullets tore through the underside of the table.

She rolled out into the open and sprang to her feet. Her aim swung to target her opponent. Her gut twisted.

Victoria's aim was locked onto Cristina.

"Only one of us can leave here alive."

The apartment door burst open. Both women shifted aim.

"Then it must be up to me to resolve this stalemate." Bruno Gomes swept a submachine rifle from Cristina to Victoria. "Let's talk."

CHAPTER EIGHTY-EIGHT

Cristina's heart thumped as she kept her Glock trained on Bruno's forehead. He gazed back at her silently, his handsome face marred by desperation and deception. She glanced at Victoria, who remained motionless, her pistol aimed at Bruno's chest, her jaw locked.

"My two favorite ladies in one room." Acid laced Bruno's words. "This must be my lucky day."

"What the fuck are you doing here?" Victoria demanded. "We agreed to stay out of each other's business."

"And yet you still interfered with my business." Bruno sneered. "Give me the flash drive and we'll call it a day."

"What makes you think I have it?"

"Don't insult me. I was halfway to the hacker's apartment when I thought more about what she told me." He jerked his head toward Cristina. "Once I understood you'd been spying on her at work, I knew you must already know what's on that drive and paid the hacker a visit yourself."

An ache started in the back of Cristina's throat. *Devi* . . .

Victoria sniffed. "What do you want with it?"

"That's not your concern."

"Oh, but I think it is. I have my own plans, so if you want to make any kind of deal, I need to be sure our goals don't conflict."

Bruno side-eyed Cristina, then coolly diverted his gaze back to Victoria. "My objectives no longer match Zero Dark's. I want them forever out of my life, as, I suspect, do you. But no matter how carefully we watch our backs, they will find us and force us back into the fold. And guess what they'll use against us to ensure we don't betray them again?"

"Tabula Rasa," Cristina said. "They'll wipe your brains clean."

"Precisely." He snorted. "I have no desire to end up like the two of you. That's why I've taken precautions to protect myself."

"You made an antidote." Victoria jutted her chin. "Her detective boyfriend was right."

Bruno's lips stretched into a leer. "Like I said, that job you passed up in Salt Lake turned out to be a win for me. I have the only sample, enough for one dose, but I also have the one existing copy of the formula with Wakefield's modifications to make more safely hidden away. Give me the flash drive, and the antidote is yours. All your memories will be restored."

Victoria glanced at Cristina, who shook her head. Victoria had been programmed to be a killer. Bruno had chosen it. He couldn't be trusted.

"What will happen to me?" Victoria asked. "My memories? My identity?"

His grin faltered. "I couldn't say. It hasn't been tested on someone like you. Perhaps those memories will remain."

"Or they may disappear," said Victoria.

Bruno shrugged.

Victoria inclined her head toward Cristina. "What happens to her? There can't be two Cristina Silvas."

The corner of Bruno's mouth twitched. "I'll take care of her."

"Victoria," Cristina said, "you can't trust him. He—"

"Stop calling me that!" The woman's eyes blazed. "My name is Cristina."

Bruno smirked.

"She's right, though." Victoria turned to Bruno. "I can't trust you—not to deal with her, anyway. That's why you wanted me to stay away from her, right? Not because of Zero Dark's orders, but because you care for her."

Bruno's eye twitched. "It's . . . more complicated than that."

"Is it?" Victoria narrowed her gaze. "Then go ahead. Kill her."

Every muscle in Cristina's body tensed. Bruno met her gaze, lips smashed together, brow furrowed. He drew in a breath.

His eyes slowly drifted back toward the female assassin.

"You can't do it." Victoria scoffed. "You're so full of shit. No deal. I don't want your antidote. This bitch was right. I need to accept who I am, and I accept that I'm Dama Branca." She shifted her aim, targeting Cristina. "A killer."

CHAPTER EIGHTY-NINE

As she stared directly down the barrel of the gun in Victoria's hand, a bitter chill seeped into Cristina's bones. It wasn't being at gunpoint. It was the dead look in the woman's eyes, the same look she once saw in another patient before he'd killed an innocent man.

"Put the gun down," she said, shifting her aim to target Victoria. "Let's talk about this—"

"You can't save everyone." Victoria's voice was flat. "Goodbye, Cristina Silva."

Victoria swung the gun barrel toward Bruno.

Bruno fired two shots.

"No!" Cristina shouted.

Victoria jerked and fell to the ground.

Cristina whipped the Glock back toward Bruno. She fired twice.

He was already on the move. One bullet tore a swath through his leather jacket, sinking into his shoulder. He howled and dropped his rifle. The other bullet thudded into the wall behind him. He scurried past Victoria's body, scooped up Maria, chair and all, and carried her down a short hall.

Cristina's heart sank. *No.* She ran after him.

She rounded the corner to find Maria in the center of a small kitchen, still tied to the chair. She was groggy but awake. Sunlight shone through a window, casting an eerie glow over Bruno standing behind her. He pushed her face down to her chest. In the other hand, he held a syringe full of blood-red liquid. The tip of the long needle pressed against her cervical spine.

"Toss your gun over here." He gave her a firm look. "Now."

Cristina slid it across the floor and under the refrigerator.

He made an ugly face. "Cute. Now, go find the flash drive."

"I don't know where it is."

"Dama Branca always played things close to her chest. Search her dead body for it." The tip of the needle pierced Maria's skin. "Do it, or you won't be the only one with memory problems."

Cristina exchanged glances with Maria. Tears streamed down Maria's cheeks as she shook her head, biting against the gag.

"All right." Cristina held up an assuaging hand. "I'll go get it. Don't hurt her."

Cristina turned back, searching frantically for the gun he'd dropped or anything else she could use as a weapon. When she reached the living room, she froze.

Victoria was gone.

Cristina searched the room. All that remained was a blood splatter on the carpet where the body had been. Her heart sank. Victoria had fled and taken the flash drive with her.

She stumbled back to the kitchen. Bruno and Maria were still locked in the same twisted embrace.

"Well?" He looked her up and down. "Where is it?"

"Gone. Along with Victoria."

His brow furrowed. "*Que merda.*"

"She dodged your bullet." Pieces clicked into place. "She's better than you, isn't she? That's why you wanted her out of the way. So she wouldn't turn you into Zero Dark herself."

Cheeks turning crimson, he said, "You were always smart, Sabrina."

With panther-like speed, he shoved Maria aside and pounced on Cristina. She punched. He deflected her fist. His meaty hand wrapped around her wrist and wrenched her arm until she screamed.

"I don't want to kill you." He aimed the needle at her neck. "But I need to ensure you don't tell anyone where I am."

"Somerville PD!" Wilson appeared in the archway. He trained his pistol on Bruno. "Down on the ground and hands where I can see them!"

A low growl rumbled from Bruno's lips. He glanced over his shoulder. His lips stretched into a leer. "You're in no shape to do anything. The Tabula Rasa should have kicked in by now."

Cristina's heart shriveled as Bruno's words sank in. It couldn't be true. Not Wilson.

"I said down on the ground." Wilson continued to point the gun at Bruno, but his hands were shaking, his aim wavering. Sweat trickled down his cheeks. "Let her go."

Bruno's eyes met Cristina's. Her muscles stiffened.

"Wilson!" she shouted, but it was too late.

In one movement, Bruno turned, drew his pistol from his waistband, and charged at Wilson.

The detective's mouth dropped open. He took a step back and fired. His shot went wild and sank into the kitchen wall.

Bruno barreled into Wilson and knocked him against the wall.

Cristina sprang to her feet, grabbed a butcher's knife from a block on the kitchen counter, and started sawing away at the knots securing Maria to the chair.

A sickening crack echoed down the short hallway.

Cristina froze. She forced herself to go and investigate the other room.

Wilson was lying prone on the ground, facing away from her. She couldn't tell if he was breathing or not. Bruno stood over him, holding his pistol with the butt facing out. Casually, he flipped it around and directed the barrel at Cristina.

Bruno strolled toward her. The gun barrel seemed to swell in size, threatening to consume her as he approached. "He won't remember anything about this." He held up the syringe with his other hand. "And soon, neither will you."

CHAPTER NINETY

Each step he took as he crossed the room made Bruno loom larger over Cristina. She gripped the kitchen knife, knowing it was no match for his gun.

A flash of black reflected in the window.

In an instant, Victoria clung to Bruno's back, her feet digging into his sides. Her hands clamped around his throat. The gun and syringe tumbled from his hands.

"You should've made sure I was dead," Victoria hissed in his ear. "Big mistake."

Bruno staggered backward, clawing at her hands, but she held tight.

Cristina sliced through the ropes around Maria's ankles. "Wake up," she whispered, patting her sister's cheeks. "We have to get out of here."

Bruno grabbed Victoria's shoulders and bent forward, flipping her off his back. She crashed into the refrigerator and sank to her knees.

"None of you are going anywhere." He recovered his pistol and lumbered toward Cristina. "Zero Dark will use you to find me. I won't let that happen."

Cristina searched for the syringe. Where was it?

Victoria sprang forward and tackled Bruno. He rolled to escape.

She punched him in the face. He grabbed at her neck. She bit his hand. He howled and scrambled to his hands and knees.

Victoria leaped onto his back. He flopped onto his belly. She threw punch after punch at the back of his head.

He dragged himself forward, stretching a hand toward the refrigerator.

Cristina stopped untying Maria's bonds. The Glock. She needed to get there first.

A gasp escaped Bruno's lips. Cristina stopped in her tracks.

Victoria, still straddling Bruno, held the syringe with the needle deep inside his neck.

"Oh, Zero Dark will find you," she said. "But you won't be any use to them."

"Don't." Fear crept into his voice. "Please."

Victoria depressed the plunger. The red fluid drained into him.

"Too late," she said.

Bruno howled and bucked. She tossed the syringe aside and wrapped both hands around his head. With a ferocious twist, she smashed his head against the linoleum. His body went still, only the sound of his breathing confirming he was still alive.

As Victoria remained on Bruno's back, her chest rising and falling, Cristina braced herself for the other woman's next move. The assassin was still a threat. Cristina inched her way toward the refrigerator. If she could grab the Glock before Victoria could react . . .

Victoria aimed Bruno's pistol at her. "You'd never reach it in time."

The certainty in her voice made Cristina freeze in place. Hoping to appeal one last time to the woman who once inhabited that body, she said, "I'm not your enemy."

Victoria dug through Bruno's pockets. She withdrew a test tube filled with a yellow liquid and tossed it to Cristina, jerking her head toward Wilson's unconscious form. "Use that on your detective friend. He shouldn't have to suffer what we went through."

Cristina stared at her. "Why help me?"

"Because I get it. We're both victims. Zero Dark stole our lives. I still don't fully understand what they did to us, or why." Victoria withdrew the flash drive from her pocket and held it up. "But with this, maybe I can find out. For both of us."

Cristina shook her head. "I can't let you take that."

A mischievous grin stretched across Victoria's face. "Try and stop me."

She scrambled over the sink, opened the window, and climbed through it.

"No!" Cristina jumped up and raced to the window.

Victoria was gone.

Wilson groaned as he dragged himself into a sitting position.

Cristina ran over to him. He had a goose egg on his forehead but seemed otherwise unharmed. She threw her arms around him.

"You're okay," he said breathlessly.

"Yes." Cristina said, her eyes filling with tears.

He nudged her to pull back. His head tilted as he gazed into her eyes. Her skin grew cold. The way he was staring at her—was his memory already gone?

He blinked twice. Then he slid a hand over each of her cheeks and pressed his lips against hers.

Heat rushed through her body, chasing away the cold fear, as they embraced other for what felt like eternity. At last, Cristina understood. She'd feared being with Wilson would make her vulnerable. But with him, she was stronger than ever.

"Ahem."

Cristina and Wilson disengaged and turned their heads at the same time. Maria, still bound to the chair, was watching them, a smile playing at her lips.

"I don't want to interrupt, but could one of you untie me?"

Cristina helped Wilson stand. He pointed at Bruno's unconscious form. "What happened to him?"

"Victoria—the *real* Cristina Silva—took care of him. She escaped." Cristina tilted her head toward the window, the evening breeze cooling her cheeks, and then crouched in front of Maria to finish cutting away the ropes. "Bruno could wake up any minute."

Wilson nodded. "Backup should arrive soon."

Cristina frowned at Wilson. "You came alone?"

He wiped the sweat from his face. "Straight from Devi's."

"Is she okay?"

"Victoria did a number on her but she'll be fine."

Cristina exhaled in relief.

"I put a trace on your cell phone and it led me here," Wilson said. "When I heard the commotion inside, I knew I couldn't wait."

"That was incredibly reckless." A smile crossed Cristina's lips. "Thank you."

"You're welcome." As Cristina removed the last rope and Maria stood, rubbing her wrists, Wilson stared at Bruno's unconscious body. "Who's this guy?"

Fear crept into Cristina's chest. "That's Bruno Gomes."

"Who?"

Oh-no, oh-no, oh-no. This couldn't be happening. Wilson couldn't be this far gone. "He's Sack Man."

His eyes widened. "You caught Sack Man?" He fished in his pocket and knelt, pulling out a set of handcuffs and slapping them on Bruno's wrists. "Good work."

"Gary." Cristina placed her hand on his cheek. He turned toward her, but the sparkle was gone from his eyes. "What do you remember?"

"I was trying to catch this creep. He was experimenting on teens to create an antidote to a memory eraser drug and then killing them. And someone attacked Devi and stole a flash drive . . ." He rubbed his forehead. "But I can't remember why."

The words strangled in Cristina's throat. She held out the test tube of yellow fluid. "This is the antidote. We need to inject you with it right away."

He stared at it. "That'll restore my memories?"

"Yes."

"How much?"

"I don't know, but it should restore most, if not all of them."

"No." He swallowed. "I mean, how much is there?"

"Just this syringe."

"Is there enough for more than one person?"

"Bruno made it sound like he only had enough created for one dose."

Wilson shook his head. "Then you need to get it to Reggie Horne."

"Who?"

"The teen who risked his life to help us catch Sack Man. He has a future ahead of him. He deserves that chance."

Sirens approached from outside.

The room spun as Cristina struggled to meet his gaze. "You need to take the antidote. We can create more for this Reggie later."

"No, we can't." Wilson pursed his lips. "I heard a voice mail from Hawkins when I left Devi's. Allison Wakefield, the one who created the antidote, is dead."

"But Bruno said he has her formula. We can find it—"

"Reggie's almost gone." Wilson dug his nails into his cheek. "And it's my fault he's in this mess. I made a promise if we found a cure, he'd get it first. According to Wakefield's notes, if he doesn't take the antidote before the process is complete, it won't work." His eyes met Cristina's and caused her heart to thump. "Promise me you'll get it to him."

She shook her head. "No. Don't do this."

A nervous chuckle passed Wilson's lips. "You never give up, do you? That's one of the many things I love about you."

She stared at him. "What did you say?"

He slid his fingers along her jawline and behind her ear. His touch sent thrills down her spine. "I love you."

Her knees buckled. She wanted to laugh, cry, and shout at the same time. She'd gotten through to him. She seized him and pressed her lips against his. His musk intoxicated her as she drank him in. They held each other until she had to pull back to catch her breath. She met his gaze and said, "I love you too."

His face grew serious, and right at that moment, Cristina realized how wrong she was. His tone determined, he said, "But I have to do this."

"No!" Cristina wanted to shake him. This couldn't be happening. "Please, Gary, think about what you're saying. I need you."

"That's the thing. I have thought about it. And you're wrong. You're stronger than you think. You can handle anything. If there's another way to cure me, you're the one who's going to find it." He smiled a lopsided smile. "You don't need me. I need you."

Her throat constricted, clogged with tears.

"Promise me," Wilson said, and for a moment, Cristina saw the spark in his eyes she'd noticed when they'd first met.

She shook her head. "I can't."

"Promise."

Tears blurred her vision as she studied his face. The curve of his nose. The faint wrinkles around his cheeks. What if she told him what he wanted to hear, and then gave him the antidote anyway?

He'd never forgive you.

She bit her lip. *At least he'd still be him.*

But he'd hate you forever. Look, I betrayed my family. My friends. I lost all of them. Don't do that to him.

Cristina choked back a sob. It was too much.

You're strong. You can handle it. And you survived amnesia. You can help him. But only if he trusts you. Emotions—those are rooted deeper than memories. No toxin can destroy them.

Sabrina's voice faded into the background as Cristina stared into Wilson's eyes, her heart pounding out of her chest until it hammered like boots at the door.

"Somerville PD!" Detective Hawkins crowed. "Wilson—Detective Wilson, are you in there?"

"In here!" Wilson called back, his gaze never leaving Cristina's. "All clear."

He held his breath, waiting.

Waiting for her answer.

Waiting for her to decide his fate. Their fate.

The lump in her throat swelled with tears. She smiled sadly and nodded, tasting salt and fear.

CHAPTER NINETY-ONE

THREE WEEKS LATER

Grizabella mewled happily, playing with a ball of yarn in a corner of the living room. Morning sunbeams shone through the window, making Devi's crystal earrings sparkle. Cristina leaned forward on her couch, resting her elbows on her knees. Her voice was hoarse from speaking, but it felt both comforting and terrifying to say everything out loud. "That's it. That's the whole story."

Across from her, Devi slouched against the loveseat, eyes wide, face pale. She opened her mouth to say something, stopped, touched her lips, and then closed her eyes.

"I know, it's a lot. I'm sorry to unload on you."

Devi shook her head, drew in a deep breath, then opened her eyes. "Cristina, you know you can always tell me anything. I'm still in your debt."

"In *my* debt?" Cristina scoffed. "Thanks to me, Victoria gave you a concussion. Are you having any late effects, by the way?"

Rubbing her forehead, Devi said, "An occasional headache, and I'm having some trouble remembering things." She half-smiled. "I suppose you could help with that."

Cristina winced. "I don't know about that."

"You're still working at the Memory Center, aren't you?"

Cristina thought back to her conversation with Dr. Campbell the previous day. He'd been understanding about her need for time off. Maybe *too* understanding. Perhaps he hadn't been working with Sack Man, but Cristina wasn't entirely convinced he was innocent. He'd been surprised and disappointed when she told him Victoria wouldn't be returning, but he made another speech about commitment and loyalty. If he were working for Zero Dark, he should've recognized Victoria, right? And he had Dr. Kobayashi's files—he might've seen the photo of Sabrina with the other Renascimento researchers.

"I've accepted Dr. Campbell's offer to join his Mnemosyne project," said Cristina.

"That's his top-secret memory restoration study, right?"

She nodded. "I need to find out what he's really up to, and why. Worming my way into his brain trust is the best way to do that. And there's another reason."

"Wilson." Devi leaned forward and held Cristina's hand. "How is he?"

Cristina clenched her jaw, thinking back to her visit with him at the hospital earlier that morning. He hadn't recognized her. He could carry a conversation, but his own name was unfamiliar to him. The spark in his eyes was gone. She wondered if that was how she had appeared three years earlier when she'd awoken to find her entire life had been erased.

"He's stable enough that they plan to discharge him tomorrow," she said at last. "Now that Maria's back in Rio, he's going to stay here at first so I can help, at least until he's able to take care of himself. But he's on indefinite leave from the police force."

"I'm so sorry, Cristina." Devi squeezed Cristina's fingers. "If he'd stayed at the hospital instead of rushing to help me—"

"It wouldn't have mattered. Without the antidote, there's nothing the doctors could've done." Cristina managed a chuckle. "And if he hadn't gone to help you, he would've rushed to help me. That's Wilson. Always the hero."

Devi smiled faintly. "And you weren't able to use Dr. Wakefield's antidote on him?"

"I managed to save a few drops to analyze before delivering it to Reggie Horne's doctors, but I feared if I took too much it wouldn't work. Fortunately, it did. Reggie made a full recovery." Cristina smiled inwardly.

Detective Hawkins had told Captain Harris about the maltreatment Reggie received and, to everyone's surprise, the captain responded by starting a lunch series between officers and Black teens to find solutions. Wilson would've been proud—if he remembered who he was. "Even in prison, Bruno refused to reveal where he stashed Dr. Wakefield's formula right up until he forgot who he was. Detective Hawkins scoured the city and found nothing. So my only hope is now that Dr. Campbell knows the components of Tabula Rasa, if I share the antidote sample with him, he'll be able to recreate it."

"But if he has ulterior motives, won't that be playing into his hands?"

You can't save everyone.

Victoria's words hummed through Cristina's brain, but she couldn't be sure if they were a memory trace, or an echo by Sabrina or even herself. Seeing Wilson's vacant look tore her heart into shreds. Pushing him away when she and Sabrina dissociated from each other had been a critical error. Dealing with Victoria made her realize that to resolve her differences with her alter ego, she needed to be the best version of herself, and she was her best when she was with Wilson. Hell, she was practically two people and yet incomplete without him.

"No matter what it takes, I'll do what I have to do." She dug her nails into her palm. No, she couldn't save everyone, but she didn't need to. She just needed to save one. "Even if it means hunting down Zero Dark— and my father—and forcing them to help me undo what's been done."

Poised on her e-scooter, DB gazed up at the impostor's apartment. The flash drive revealed some surprising things about her employers—and about herself, like the secrets Quinn had erased her memories to protect. Now the question was how to use that information.

DB ran her palm over the silencer of Bruno's pistol. She'd been prepared to die, to end her torment, but at the last second, when Bruno had fired, her survival instinct kicked in. Or maybe it wasn't instinct. She reached into her pocket and wrapped her fingers around the toy robot. The fraud had been right. Accepting her dual identity had put a stop to the glitches. She was both Dama Branca and Cristina Silva, and she could live with that.

But even if she fled to a distant corner of the globe and created a new life for herself, Zero Dark would find her. They would always find her.

Unless she found them first.

She tucked away the pistol and kicked the scooter into drive. With a wicked grin, she sped off toward the horizon.

ACKNOWLEDGMENTS

Writing a sequel proved to be far more challenging than I'd anticipated, and if it weren't for the help of some incredible people, you might not be reading this book at all.

In this second book, Detective Wilson has a much larger role, and as I don't have a background in law enforcement, I wanted to ensure the policework was realistic. Both Police Detective Adam Richardson (host of the *Writer's Detective Bureau* podcast) and retired Police Sergeant Patrick O'Donnell (of the *Cops and Writers* podcast) were invaluable in dishing out detailed information about how police operate in real life, as were members of their respective Facebook groups who answered my many questions and offered their own personal insights. I also want to thank retired FBI Special Agent Jerri Williams (of the *FBI Retired Case File Review* podcast) for taking the time to answer my specific questions about how to make scenes at the Chelsea field office more realistic.

Even though I'm a doctor, it's not possible to know everything about every specialty. Neurologist Ann Lipton, MD, was a great help as an early beta reader of *Toxic Effects*, catching inconsistencies and inaccuracies in the neurologic premise underlying this story. Beta readers and fellow authors Christine Clemetson and Ralph Walker were also extremely helpful in resolving plot holes and finding ways to restructure the story to make it both more plausible and enjoyable.

Adverse Effects debuted shortly after the peak of the Black Lives Matter movement and a growing concern over institutional racism within law enforcement. Many authors began to rethink the concept of the White "hero cop" and how people of color are portrayed in fiction. I was left in a quandary with *Toxic Effects*. Wilson, a White detective, was already a major part of the story. I couldn't retcon him into a different race, and it wouldn't make sense for me, a White man, to try to write from a background that's not mine. I strongly believe there are many good cops out there, like Adam and Patrick. But just as in medicine, there are bad apples. So I began to think about how one of those good cops might react when faced head-on with racism and discrimination within his precinct. To help get Reggie's character right, I had help from fellow author Edward Farmer. I encourage you to read his book, *Pale*, and work by other Black authors.

I'd also like to thank the many authors I've met along this journey, through social media and in person, who've inspired me, helped promote my books, and shared their experience. There is no real competition between authors; we're all in this together.

Once again, I need to thank my agent, Lynnette Novak of the Seymour Agency, for all her help and support even as I was struggling to make this book work, and to my editor Dana Isaacson for suffering through my early drafts. Big thanks as well to the Blackstone team, editor Ember Hood, and cover designer Alenka Linschke. And, of course, my everlasting gratitude to my amazing wife, Geiza, for putting up with my hours of writing, rewriting, and complaining; giving me the keys I needed to overcome the major stumbling blocks and make this book work; and for being my number one supporter.

Finally, thank you so much for reading this book. If you'd like to leave a review, which can help in uncountable ways, please visit https://www.amazon.com/Toxic-Effects-Memory-Thieves/dp/1094022888/